SHADOWS

OF

FRENCHMEN

SHADOWS

OF

FRENCHMEN

A JONATHAN GRAY, M.D.
MYSTERY

MICHAEL RIGG

"…I think that I may say that an American has not seen the United States until he has seen Mardi-Gras in New Orleans."

—Samuel L. Clemens
(before he adopted the pen name Mark Twain) in a letter to his sister, Pamela A. Moffett
(March 1859)

Contents

Praise for Shadows of Frenchmen

"A chilling, razor-sharp mystery set against the explosive energy of Mardi Gras. This cat-and-mouse hunt fuses cryptic clues, relentless suspense and rising terror into a tale that gives us a horrifyingly intimate glimpse into a killer's mind. Dr. Jonathan Gray is a hero you won't forget—and the Mardi Gras Sweeper is a nightmare you won't escape."—**Kathleen Antrim**, bestselling author, President-Outliers Writing University

"Michael Rigg does it again, with another thrilling mystery that you won't be able to put down featuring New Orleans Coroner Jonathan Gray. *Shadows of Frenchmen* takes readers into the darkest corners of New Orleans' lush settings and spooky cemeteries as Gray and his colleagues hunt for a possible serial killer, all against the backdrop of raucous Mardi Gras celebrations. Rigg's love for this extraordinary city shines through on every page, even as danger lurks among the Spanish moss and above-ground tombs."—**Ellen Byron**, *USA Today* bestselling & Agatha Award-Winning author

"As a coroner, Dr. Jonathan Gray is the new Kay Scarpetta. In *Shadows of Frenchmen,* author Michael Rigg skillfully uses beads, beignets, bullets, bombs, and bodies to make New Orleans vivid and alive."—**John DeDakis**, former CNN editor, writing coach, and author of the Lark Chadwick mystery-suspense-thriller series, at johndedakis.com

"Great action from the get-go! Atmosphere, characters, and all the right ingredients. A great read by Michael Rigg!"—**Heather Graham**, *New York Times* bestselling author

"Featuring smart and complex characters, *Shadows of Frenchmen* pulses with energy, taking the reader on a breathless chase for a serial killer terrorizing the city in the days leading up to a city-wide Mardi Gras celebration. Fans of the intrepid New Orleans coroner Dr. Jonathan Gray will not be disappointed!"—**K.L. Murphy**, author of the Detective Callie Forde Mysteries, *The Great Forgotten,* and the award-nominated *Her Sister's Death*

"The second installment in Michael Rigg's Jonathan Gray, MD mystery series is a rollicking good time from start to finish. *Shadows of Frenchmen* has it all—taunting coded notes from a serial killer, seemingly resurrected from the dead, bodies with mysterious carvings stacking up all over New Orleans, and a race-against-time urgency as pulse-pounding as an episode of *24.* Set amidst the raucous energy of Carnival, Jonathan Gray must piece together the clues. Can he solve the mystery before the Mardi Gras Sweeper strikes again? You'll be turning pages faster than beads fly at Mardi Gras to find out."—**Christi Keating Sumich**, author of the Old New Orleans Bookshop Mysteries

"With Book 2 in his addictive Jonathan Gray, M.D. series, Michael Rigg ups the ante for fans of New Orleans-based mystery. A propulsive thriller set against the backdrop of Mardi Gras season, *Shadows of Frenchmen* takes the reader on an unrelentingly tense exploration of the sinister underbelly of the Crescent City's carefree façade. Rich with atmosphere and populated with memorable characters, including an enigmatic serial killer who taunts the police with riddles and cyphers, *Shadows of Frenchmen* will leave readers thirsting for the next installment in this arresting series."—**Norman Woolworth**, author of *The Lafitte Affair* and *The Bolden Cylinder*, books 1 and 2 in the Bruneau Abellard Novel series

A Note from the Author

Once you visit New Orleans (and if you haven't, I hope you will very soon), you discover many unique aspects of the city and its residents. Some—like architecture, cuisine, weather, and "aroma"—are easy enough to for a writer to describe. But one of the most difficult aspects of New Orleans to bring to life in a novel is the various dialects spoken in the city, including pronunciation of individual names, street names, neighborhoods, and such. If you'd like to lean more about the dialects, such as "Yat," "Cajun French," and "Cajun English," check out the article on Babbel.com, The United States Of Accents: New Orleans And Cajun English.

For most names, you can rely on your high school French. But beware. Here are some examples from *Shadows of Frenchmen* of words with unique pronunciations:

New Orleans: Pronounce the "Orleans" part almost any way except "Or-leans." "Nawlins" is acceptable, but frowned on by many locals. Try "New Orlins" or "Norlins" instead. BUT, if you're referring to the parish (county) where New Orleans is located, it's "Or-leans" Parish.

Burgundy Street: Don't pronounce it like you're at a bar ordering red wine. Rather, it's pronounced, with an emphasis on "gun," as "BurGUNdee."

Carondelet Street: Pronounce the final "t." It's Caron-da-let, not Caron-da-lay.

Chartres Street: In New Orleans it's pronounced "Charters" Street.

Tchoupitoulas Street: The first "t" is silent. It's pronounced "CHOP-uh-too-las." Locals often call it "Chop." But the pronunciation isn't the real challenge. I've been told that if you're stopped for suspicion of driving under the influence, police don't ask you to say the alphabet backward. Rather, they ask you to spell "Tchoupitoulas." A word to the wise.

<u>Canal Street</u>: Canal is pronounced just like it's spelled. You know, like the Suez Canal or the Panama Canal or the Erie Canal. But one thing you'll note on your visit to New Orleans is that the streets in the French Quarter change names when they cross Canal Street. For example, in the French Quarter, it's Bourbon Street. Once you cross Canal Street, it's Carondelet Street; Royal Street becomes St. Charles Avenue and so forth. The reason? Canal Street was the dividing line, geographically and culturally, between the primarily French-speaking French Quarter and the new English-speaking "American" sector after the Louisiana Purchase.

I'm sure there are other unique pronunciations. But these are the primary ones in *Shadows of Frenchmen*.

My best advice for your next (or first) visit to The Big Easy is to enjoy yourself and listen. You'll find the residents of New Orleans are generally helpful, understanding, and "100% American." Another word of wisdom, however. If a kindly gentleman in the French Quarter (or anywhere else for that matter) offers, for a small donation, to tell you "Where you got your shoes," the answer is "I got my shoes on my feet."

Michael Rigg

Virginia Beach, Virginia

Chapter One: Alpha and Omega

Sunday, February 1, 2015 – 1:47 a.m.

Twenty-plus years with the Orleans Parish Coroner's Office taught Jonathan Gray to expect the unexpected. But Washington Square Park had always been a tranquil haven on the fringe of the French Quarter. So crime-scene tape draping the square's wrought-iron fence presented the visual equivalent of fingernails on a chalkboard. Moonlight filtering through stately live oaks cast eerie—almost funereal—shadows, adding to the dissonance.

Fluttering in the nippy midwinter breeze, the neon-yellow ribbon communicated a mute warning. On this side, normalcy. On the other, insanity. Stepping into the dysfunction never got easier. Regardless, turning back wasn't an option. As if speaking the incantation aloud would immunize him against the unfolding drama, he repeated his trite pre-crime scene mantra: "Abandon all hope, ye who enter here." His breath lingered in the frosty air before evaporating.

After checking in with the uniformed officer monitoring access, Jonathan angled toward floodlights illuminating a temporary canopy above the city's AIDS memorial. More tape—red as opposed to yellow—identified the innermost "Do Not Cross" perimeter. Crime scene technicians in white Tyvek protective suits busied themselves measuring and photographing what must be the reason he'd been summoned. A male corpse sitting upright on the ground—its arms and legs twisted at seemingly impossible angles—

leaned against the memorial's circular cut-glass and steel panels surrounded by a pool of thick, dark crimson liquid.

A curved, nearly rectangular piece of wood with brass edges—most likely a knife handle—protruded from under the right side of the dead man's rib cage. A portion of his intestines spilled out of the wound. A second knife—its handle and part of its blade visible—had been thrust downward into the soft tissue between the left collarbone and neck.

Cause of death seemed too obvious to require someone of Jonathan's seniority. A first-year med student could have made the call. But markings carved into the dead man's forehead and chest hinted at something more sinister. No wonder Mitch Broussard from NOPD had called him in the middle of the night.

The man's heavy flannel shirt lay open, exposing his chest and a series of capital letters etched into his skin. The letters—G I D I A I D I V—made no sense, at least not in English. A folded piece of paper with similar letters and other symbols, not quite readable from that distance, lay under the man's left hand. Lack of blood covering the letters in the chest signaled they had been added *postmortem*. Jonathan focused on two marks in the man's forehead. An uppercase "A" and what looked like an upside-down horseshoe—the Greek letter Omega—apparently cut while the victim was still alive.

It couldn't have been two years already. But there it was. Alpha and Omega. Jonathan bit his lip and cursed under his breath. Then, a silent prayer. Looked like the nightmare was about to begin—again.

One of the CSTs stood and raised her clear face shield. "Hey, Doc. Welcome to Funsville."

"Good to see you, too, Shelly." Jonathan looked toward the dead man's body. "But I'd bet not everyone shares your enthusiasm."

"Sorry." Her face reddened. "Guess I'm kind of jaded."

"Happens to the best of us." Gallows humor. An understandable way to deal with a constant diet of tragedy and gore. Lord knows how many times Jonathan had used it as a defense mechanism, too. No use reaming out a dedicated CST—or anyone else—for it. Just change the tone. Move forward.

"Estimated time of death?"

"Not yet." She shook her head. "But he's still warm. Strong copper odor from the blood. No rigor. Must have occurred recently. Best guess? Within the last hour. Two at most."

"Roger that." Jonathan again regarded the body. "Two knives. Looks like someone wanted to make sure the job was done."

"Maybe. But I just process the evidence." She canted her head to her right, directing Jonathan to a man and a woman talking to one another about twenty feet away. "Putting all the pieces together? That's for you and the other…hotshots."

"Hmmm…Cass Melançon's here…that mean what I think it does?"

"It does."

"Female?"

"Affirmative. She was already on the way to the emergency room by the time I got here."

"Injuries?"

"To the female? Don't think so…nothing physical, anyway. But Detective Broussard can update you on that."

"Thanks, Shelly. Guess I should go chat with the experts."

"Got it, Doc. Back to work for both of us."

Jonathan hastened toward the pair he'd just mentioned, Dr. Cassandra "Cass" Melançon and Detective Sergeant Mitchell "Mitch" Broussard.

"What's the bottom line, Cass?" Jonathan asked. "CSTs say there was a female involved."

Cass, Deputy Coroner for Physical Examination Services—a euphemism used to describe the emotionally draining task of investigating sexual assaults—looked up from her notepad. She always seemed so poised, regardless of the circumstances. Her athletic build, raven-black hair, and sharp facial features emphasized her professional demeanor.

"Morning, boss. It's after midnight. That makes it morning, right? Sorry you had to come out so late—or…I mean…so early."

"You got it," Jonathan said. "Morning. Sunday morning. Comes with the territory, Sonny Rabideau being out-of-commission and all. Besides, Mitch said there was something I needed to see, regardless. So what about the female—"

"Wouldn't have asked if it wasn't important." Detective Broussard extended his hand toward Jonathan.

Mitch could pass for a professional wrestler—tall and muscular, with a nose that looked as if it had been broken at least a half-dozen times. But appearances could be deceiving. Barely out of his twenties, he enjoyed a reputation as a skilled detective—dogged and tenacious. Chomping on a small cigar—a cheroot cut in half—whenever he was involved in a case had become his trademark. A cliché, perhaps, but it fit.

"Understood." Jonathan accepted the handshake. "But we're really behind the curve as it is."

"Seems like things have been moving quick since you took over for Dr. O'Malley." Mitch spit out several small pieces of tobacco. "Reckon you're still getting your sea legs."

Regardless of how tempting it might be, Jonathan couldn't reveal how daunting the six weeks since his former boss and mentor died unexpectedly of a stroke had been. Forced into the limelight as chief medical examiner for a city perpetually in the running as "Murder Capital of the USA." Self-doubts about whether, at fifty-four, he was past his prime and not up to the challenge. How he'd nearly broken under the strain and submitted his resignation. Besides, they had an apparent murder and a possible sexual assault to investigate. So he acted as if it were just another day at the office. "Robby was a great teacher."

Jonathan coughed. Partly to clear his throat, but mostly to break the awkward silence. "But I guess we have to get on with it." Now wasn't the time for small talk. "Thoughts about our friend over there? Is it the Sweep—"

"Maybe." Mitch cleared his throat. "Regardless, looks like we've got a strange one. Dr. M has her work cut out for her."

"Right." Cass yawned. "Sorry…I'm here long enough to make sure you're up to speed, then I'm off to Tulane ER."

"Figured as much," Jonathan said. "Highlights?"

"Trying to identify the dead guy," Mitch said. "Our conclusion going in is that he's homeless. Maybe just passing through…a vagrant…a drifter."

"Well, he's somebody's son…or father…or husband…or…" Jonathan's words trailed off. "I guess that, for now, his name is John Doe…John Doe Number-Whatever-the-Hell number we're up to this month."

"One," Cass said. "First day of the month, so he's John Doe Number One. Technically, Twenty-Fifteen dash Zero-Two dash Zero-One…but John Doe Number One's close enough."

"And here we are, standing around with our thumbs up our…" Jonathan breathed deeply and then exhaled, to prevent himself from completing the sentence. "Estimated age, Mitch?"

"Not sure," Mitch replied. "Anywhere between thirty and sixty. Life on the street can be merciless."

"True that, Mitch." Jonathan turned to Dr. Melançon. "Any idea what happened, Cass? I mean…beyond the obvious?"

"Not yet. NOPD received a 9-1-1 call. Noises…no real details…coming from the park. Patrol car nearby on Elysian Fields got here in less than three minutes. They found the guy on the blocks, already dead. And the female—"

"The one taken to the ER?"

"That's right," Cass said.

Three minutes. So damn close. Just a few seconds earlier, and maybe they could have prevented what happened. Jonathan struggled to avoid saying something he might later regret about why the police hadn't responded faster than they did. He stepped closer to the dead man on the AIDS memorial. "And Mitch, I assume the body art and note are why I'm here."

"Right." Mitch shifted his position so he was next to Jonathan, then held out his phone. "Didn't want to get too close while the CSTs work, but I took some photos."

Jonathan squinted at Mitch's phone. The same letters he had just seen on the dead man's chest and forehead. "And the note?"

Mitch changed the image. "Looks like standard printer paper. White background. Capital letters and symbols. More like full sentences, maybe. A statement of some sort. We'll know more once we examine it."

"Interesting." Dread from seeing the Alpha and Omega marks earlier returned. "A manifesto, maybe?"

"Could be," Mitch said.

"So." Jonathan swallowed hard. "Sounds more and more like—"

"Yeah." Mitch closed his eyes. "The Mardi Gras Sweeper."

"Some called him the Two-by-Four Killer," Cass said. "You know. Every two years, four murders."

"At least the news media dubbed him that," Mitch said. "Never caught on with NOPD."

"God help us." Jonathan grimaced. "Regardless what we call this... miscreant."

"Unfortunately, the Two-by-Four thing fits." Mitch aimed his eyes toward the body. "Some unknown homeless...or whatever...guy killed while apparently committing a crime. Coded communications. All happening during alternate Mardi Gras seasons."

"And Fat Tuesday's less than three weeks away." Cass counted silently as she moved her thumb from one finger to another. "Seventeen days, to be precise."

"Jesus," Jonathan said. "Any suspects? Witnesses...except for the female?"

"Just the female," Cass said. "The reason I'm off to the ER."

"Details?" Jonathan asked.

"Maybe eighteen...nineteen," Cass said. "Curled up in a fetal position, nude from the waist down, covered in blood. Still had patches of duct tape stuck to her wrists." She exhaled noticeably. "When the officer touched her, she came to—or woke up—and started crying like a baby."

"Double Jesus." Jonathan winced. There was something about this case that nagged at him—got under his skin. "Must have been brutal. Hell, I'd be blubbering, too, if I'd been through what probably happened here." He swallowed as if to clear a bitter taste from his mouth. "College student?"

"We think so," Mitch said. "She was wearing an Ole Miss sweatshirt."

"ID?" Jonathan asked.

"Driver's license," Mitch said. "Not much else. Discarded clothes. No credit cards. Some throws from tonight's parades scattered around."

"Krewe du Vieux and krewedelusion, right?" Cass said.

"Yeah," Mitch said. "And a cell phone we can't open without the password."

"Turned twenty-one day before yesterday, right?" Jonathan said.

"Close," Mitch said. "Twenty-one today. Or, well, yesterday by this time. From Tupelo."

Mitch removed what was left of his stogie—about an inch-and-a-half nub of well-worn tobacco—and flicked it into the darkness, well away from the AIDS memorial. His eyes widened when the spent cigar landed at the base of a nearby live oak. "What the...?" He directed a flashlight beam toward what appeared to be a bicycle wheel partially hidden by the tree.

The trio walked, almost in tandem, toward the mysterious object.

"Shit," Mitch said. "A bike."

"One of the NOLA-Blue Bicycles," Cass said. "City's experimenting with a free rental program...grab a free ride and help clear up traffic congestion."

Jonathan pointed to the baskets on each side of the rear wheel. "Or carry your duct tape and other rape kit supplies...then escape afterward...courtesy of the City of New Orleans."

"Looks like we're dealing with a real sick bastard," Mitch said. "Maybe he got what he deserved."

"Mitch," Jonathan said, "what's the name on the driver's license?"

"Crawford. Joan Crawford." Mitch peered at Jonathan, as if looking over a pair of reading glasses.

"Hmmm. Joan Crawford," Jonathan said. "Not exactly an everyday name."

"Most likely fake," Mitch said, "but we sent an inquiry to the Mississippi State Patrol just the same. And we're canvassing establishments up and down Frenchmen. Someone must have seen them. Maybe they're on surveillance footage."

"I suppose." Jonathan's mind wandered to his kids—the triplets. A son and two daughters, away in Europe as part of their sophomore-year college study abroad programs. About the same age as the girl. If *they* were partying where law enforcement couldn't protect them, there wasn't much he and Emma could do from across the ocean. What a helpless feeling. A child, or children, in danger and not a damn thing you could do about it.

Surely the parents of the girl in the Ole Miss sweatshirt worried about their daughter, away from home, away from their protective gaze. But, no doubt, they'd be comforted in their reasonable belief that she was at a safe place—the University of Mississippi—under the watchful eyes of her sorority sisters and campus police. How despondent they'd likely become once they learned that she wasn't at school. Wasn't protected. And had just been involved in a brutal attack and violent homicide.

No wonder this crime scene got under his skin. "Cass, I take it you're off to the hospital to supervise the sexual assault examination."

"Right."

"Good. After we bag the cadaver and send it to the morgue, I'll drop by to talk."

Chapter Two: Tulane ER

Sunday, February 1, 2015 – 4:30 a.m.

Jonathan yawned as he walked into the Tulane Hospital Emergency Room. Four-thirty. Too much burning the candle at both ends since Robby's death. Balancing both his duties as Chief Deputy, along with the administrative headaches that came along with being elevated to Coroner. And on top of everything, picking up the slack while Sonny was laid up. All-nighters might have been manageable in medical school, but those days were long past.

What an odd situation. They had identified two witnesses to what happened in the dark expanse of Washington Square Park. First, there was John Doe Number One—the dead man resting against the AIDS memorial. And the other was the female, found lying nearby, covered in blood, that Jonathan was coming to see. Soon, at least, they might have half of the story—unless someone else, as yet unidentified, had been there.

"Morning," he said to the triage nurse, a stocky woman in a brown cardigan.

"Same to you, Dr. Gray. You looking for Dr. Melançon?"

"I am."

"Number Six. Been there a bit over an hour, I think."

"Got it. Thanks, Giselle."

Jonathan struggled to recall the hospital's numbering scheme. Was it even on the left or the other way around? That was it, even on the right, odd on the left.

"So that's Number One on the left," Jonathan mumbled, not realizing he was talking out loud, and not certain he'd made the right choice. But he plunged ahead, counting even numbers on his right as he passed the examination areas, each enclosed by heavy, light green privacy curtains.

Two, four, six. Jonathan slid the curtain back. "Hey, Cass." Oh. Not Cass. A nurse taking blood pressure. "Excuse me…Sorry…I'm looking for Number Six."

"Over there." The nurse looked to her left. "This is Five."

Jonathan's face warmed as he pulled the curtain closed. He really needed to get more sleep. Why did the hospital have to make something so easy so hard? Knock on wood, he had it right this time.

"Dr. Melançon." He reached for the cloth barrier, then stopped. "You in there? It's Jonathan Gray."

The curtain shifted. Cass appeared in the open space. In the background, a young woman lay on a hospital bed. A female NOPD officer stood guard in the corner. A third figure, most likely a nurse, hovered nearby.

"Jonathan, hello. Give me a minute."

"Okay." Jonathan stepped back as the curtain closed. Curious. Was the NOPD officer there because the female in the bed was a murder suspect? Or—

His phone vibrated. "P. Bondurant" displayed on the Caller ID. Only one way to find out why the Superintendent of Police would be calling him, especially at this hour. Jonathan pressed the speakerphone button.

"Superintendent Bondurant…Polly…good morning."

"Morning, Doctor, sorry to disturb."

"You're up before the crack of dawn. And on a Sunday morning." Jonathan yawned. "Must be important."

"Can we meet?" Bondurant's voice sounded officious but tentative.

"Sure. Want me to drop by your office?"

"That'd be great."

"Something come up?"

"Well…yes…I suspect you can guess what."

"The Sweeper?"

"Very good, Doctor." Bondurant cleared her throat. "And I'd just as soon discuss it face-to-face."

"Got it. I'm at the Tulane ER. I can be at your office in just over an hour."

"Outstanding. I'll make sure to have a fresh pot of joe ready."

Jonathan hit the End Call button. What could be so hush-hush that Polly Bondurant needed to tell him in person? Whispers grew louder from the other side of the curtain. Metal hooks holding the cloth barrier in place scraped along their track in the ceiling as the curtain moved.

"Sorry for seeming so mysterious." Dr. Melançon's face reflected something odd. She looked both confident and fearful.

"Don't give it another thought, Cass. What's going on?"

"We can't get her to talk. She just stares into space. Won't even tell us her name."

"Conducted a physical?"

"She didn't speak," Cass said. "But she followed instructions. Nonverbal responses...head nods and so forth. We obtained sufficient consent to take samples and swabs for the rape kit."

"Good enough to stand up in court if challenged?"

"I think so. And we got her prints so we can run an ID check."

"Good thought."

"Thanks. But I suspect it won't get us anywhere. She looks so young. Bet she's never given prints or had her DNA swabbed."

"Maybe," Jonathan said. "It might take some time, but we'll get to the truth of who she is and what happened."

"And that's another thing. I don't think she was raped. There's no evidence of penetration. It was a sexual assault for sure, and probably with intent. But no penetration."

"Looks like she took care of the attacker before he could consummate the act," Jonathan said.

"Maybe. But I don't have the impression that this girl's strong enough to do what appears to have been done. I'm not even sure that she knows exactly what happened."

"Adrenaline," Jonathan said. "Under the circumstances, I can imagine she had the strength to do whatever was necessary."

"Perhaps. But that doesn't explain the facial and chest carving, or the note."

"True. Have you told her she may have killed her attacker?"

"Not yet. Not quite sure how to do that. Or even if we should at this point."

"Interesting. I wonder what would happen if she knew. She's the only suspect in the stabbing death of the man who tried to rape her. Sounds like she has a good claim for self-defense. Maybe if she knew the guy was no longer a threat at this point, she'd talk."

"Look, I don't have a crystal ball," Cass said. "And interrogation's more of an art than a science. Maybe we should tell her. For now, I say no."

"Got it. You're the expert. But when do you think we should tell her?"

An unfamiliar voice spoke from behind Cass. "Tam. What happened to…"

As Cass peeled the curtains back further, there she was. The woman identified on the Mississippi driver's license as Joan Crawford. Despite the age indicated on the license, she couldn't have been more than eighteen. Slightly younger than his daughters, Abby and Marjorie. Jonathan's gut turned somersaults.

"Hello, dear," Dr. Melançon said. "Sorry about your tam. But we didn't find a hat or cap. Can you tell us about it?"

The girl in the bed stared ahead—a thousand-yard stare—looking at nothing and at everything. Though her eyes focused outward, the real gaze seemed inward.

"Good morning, Miss Crawford. I'm Jonathan Gray. I'm Coroner of Orleans Parish. Dr. Melançon works in my office."

As if jolted with a cattle prod, the girl sat up in the hospital bed and looked straight at Jonathan. "Coroner?" Her voice reflected fear and anger. "I know what that is. Why are you here?"

Jonathan held up his hands, palms open toward the girl, as if in surrender. "It's not what you think." He moved closer, making certain to respect her personal space. "In Louisiana, the Coroner doesn't just perform autopsies.

The Coroner also conducts examinations in, well, intimate personal attacks."

"You mean rape?"

"Well, yes, Miss Crawford," Jonathan said. "That's part of it. We're here to find out what happened to you."

"Why did you call me that name?"

Cass must not have told her. Oh, well, the cat was out of the bag. Maybe it was time to tell her what the investigation had revealed, despite what Cass recommended.

"Oh, I'm sorry," Jonathan said. "That was the name on your driver's license. Crawford. Joan Crawford." Jonathan looked at Cass Melançon, as if to apologize, and then back at the girl. "Can you tell us what happened to you, Joan? May I call you Joan?"

The girl returned to her thousand-yard stare. She rolled onto her left side—facing away from Jonathan—and curled up in a fetal position.

"That's okay, dear." Cass closed her eyes, inhaled, and held her breath. She exhaled slowly. "You need your rest. We can come back later."

Warmth spread across Jonathan's face. Rather embarrassing for someone in his position. Their conversation hadn't gone as expected. Oh well, it wasn't the first time he had ham-handed a sexual assault interview. His bedside manner needed some fine-tuning. He should leave the talking to experts like Cass.

Regardless, it had been a long night and looked like it was going to be a long day as well. But if the Mardi Gras Sweeper—the so-called Two-by-Four Killer—had returned, they didn't have a minute to waste. They needed to figure things out and be ready in time for Friday's parades. Seemed like plenty of time. But they were starting at square one and probably tracking an elusive serial killer. Someone operating under his own agenda and schedule.

Chapter Three: Polly Bondurant

Sunday, February 1, 2015 – 6:19 a.m.

Jonathan sipped coffee as he studied several photographs spread out on the conference table in NOPD Superintendent Joyce Pauline "Polly" Bondurant's office. Several of the photos reflected the scene at Washington Square Park. Apparently, someone—probably Mitch Broussard—had already briefed Bondurant. Must be something big if the Superintendent of Police was involved this early in the investigation.

Other photos depicted two green Pearly Thomas streetcars from the St. Charles line. Both cars had been tagged with graffiti—stylized images of the Greek letters Alpha and Omega, a broom, and other letters similar to those carved into the body from the park.

No doubt, the Greek letters and broom served as a reminder of the so-called Mardi Gras Sweeper. The symbols had appeared in the Sweeper's previous visits during Carnival, two and four years ago. Jonathan focused on the letters 'D V F I I A I E I V F I V,' painted with almost no space between them. There must be a message in the letters. But what?

Polly, seemingly deep in thought, faced an office window overlooking the city.

Jonathan struggled to keep himself calm. "Had the streetcar photos very long?"

Polly turned toward Jonathan. Faint rays from the pre-dawn sun and the eerie glow of the street lamps outside highlighted her sharp facial features.

She eased her muscular, five-feet-seven-inch frame into a chair across from Jonathan. "Yes and no."

"Which means?"

"Photos are about three weeks old."

"Hell, Polly. Why wait so long? Looks like the Sweeper's had almost a month's head start."

She looked away. "The photos came into the Gang Unit around January sixth. So, the department's had them. That's the 'Yes' part of the answer."

"Okay. And the 'No'?"

"Nobody made the connection." Polly looked directly at Jonathan. "The streetcars were scheduled for the Krewe of Phantastic Phirst Phellows."

"For their party-on-the-rails along the St. Charles line on the Twelfth Night?"

"Affirmative. January sixth. The department's initial take was that it was just one of the local gangs making a statement, marking their territory. So, they took the photos and let them paint over the markings."

"Doesn't look like any gang tags I've ever seen."

Polly again looked away. Her eyes glazed over, as if her mind were somewhere else. "My thoughts, too."

"I suppose last night's festivities in Washington Square Park changed somebody's mind."

Polly pushed a file folder across the table. "And we're examining video footage from the Streetcar Barn off Willow Street."

Jonathan opened the folder, revealing a single sheet of white printer paper with various capital letters and other symbols. "The note from the victim's left hand?"

"Affirmative. We're working to figure out what the code means. They tell me it's different from the ones from before."

"Right. You weren't here during the Sweeper's previous visits. You were—"

"Punching my chief-wannabe ticket. You know how these things go."

"Sure. Was it St. Louis or—"

"First time, I was Deputy Chief in St. Louis. Then Chief in Baltimore. Now, I'm back home. This'll be my second Carnival season as Superintendent."

"But you're first dealing with the Sweeper."

"And I'm getting a crash course in what I missed."

"So, I assume NOPD. will be all over this now."

Polly didn't answer immediately. "Well, about that." Her eyes wandered, as if searching for the right words. "The administration feels—"

"By administration, you mean Max Jamerson?"

"Right. Mayor Jamerson and I discussed the matter at some length."

"Let me guess," Jonathan said. "Max is worried about what'll happen if it gets out that there's a serial killer on the loose during Mardi Gras."

"He wants us to investigate, but keep it low-key. He's hoping to keep this out of the news and social media."

"I see."

"He feels that the Sweeper targets—"

"Dirtbags and lowlifes?"

"Not in so many words—"

"Or is it too plain to say that the Sweeper doesn't bother people who ride in the parades or tourists who pay the freight while they're here, so who cares?"

"A bit harsh, don't you think, Doctor?"

"Right. The rich get rich, and the poor get murdered." Jonathan snickered. "Okay, Polly. I'll bite. How can the Coroner's Office help?"

"I knew you'd understand." Polly's facial expression changed—appeared more relaxed—as if she had just been relieved of an impossible burden. "Your office has many resources at its disposal. I mean, along with autopsies, your office has investigators for sexual assaults, mental health matters, and even works alongside NOPD in a lot of death cases."

"Yes, we have resources. But we're not the police. And with Sonny Rabideau out, I don't know how we'll be able to make it work."

"I know how dedicated you are. I'm sure you'll find a way."

"Okay. I'll do what I can, but I'll need your support."

"Of course." Polly flashed a quick smile, her voice now more upbeat. "NOPD will provide support where it can. But it can't be high viz. You know that."

"Well, for starters." Jonathan grinned. "You've got one of the best investigators I know on ice."

Polly closed her eyes. "No way. We can't—"

"Give me Betsy Sprance to work as my Lead Death Investigator."

"Are you crazy?" Polly's eyes, now open, seemed ready to pop. "For God's sake, Betsy accused the Mayor of New Orleans of being a pimp and running an international prostitution ring."

"Well, the Feds thought there was enough evidence for an indictment."

"Right. Scuttlebutt is that Max pulled strings in D.C. and got the indictment withdrawn." Bondurant's jaw tightened as if Jonathan had just saddled her with a problem she'd hoped to avoid. "Indictment or not, the U.S. Attorney isn't the one who has Max Jamerson breathing up her effing backside. Hell, Betsy—"

"Worked the previous Sweeper cases. Two years ago, she almost caught the son of a—"

"That might be. But right now, she's toxic. Jesus, I've got Betsy on paid admin leave to keep her out of the line of fire. I mean…If I…I mean…Max Jamerson will absolutely—"

"Listen, Polly, we all have our challenges. I'm sure you can handle Max. And if you want me to help you, you need to help me." Jonathan suppressed a smile. "I know how dedicated you are. I'm sure you'll find a way."

Polly's eyes reflected both anger and fear. Anger, no doubt, at having her own words used against her as he made the request. And fear of failing to bring a serial killer to justice if she declined. Jonathan had her boxed in. She probably didn't want to say "yes," but couldn't say "no."

She swallowed, as if clearing her palate of the bitterness. "Fine…I suppose you'll need—"

"No need." Jonathan stood. "I know exactly where to find Betsy. Headed there now. You can email me the transfer paperwork."

Chapter Four: Skywatch

Sunday, February 1, 2015 – 7:25 a.m.

"You said *that* to Polly Bondurant?" Detective Lieutenant Mary Elizabeth "Betsy" Sprance—dressed in the dark gray slacks, white polo shirt, and blue blazer worn by members of the Asset Protection team at Harrah's casino on Canal Street—shook her head and grinned. "Ms. 'I'm the Goddamn Superintendent of the New Orleans Police Department, so shut the hell up.' That Polly Bondurant?"

"Well." Jonathan leaned forward in his chair at the small conference table in the casino's camera room. "That's the gist of it."

Betsy chuckled, but her eyes didn't show much joy. "After these past weeks, you made my day." She reached for a cup of coffee from Hot Benny's, a shop across South Peters Street from the casino. "And I don't mean by showing up with fat pills and java."

"Understood. It's been a bumpy ride."

"An understatement, but part-time work at Harrah's has helped. Keeps my mind off things." Betsy managed something close to a smile. "You know. Eye-in-the-sky. Learning new ways to cheat at blackjack."

"Well, at least NOPD suspended you with pay."

"Right. Maybe Polly's not as much of a bit…um…not as much of a bureaucrat as she seems."

This probably wasn't the best timing, but he had little choice. "So, any word on Ranger?"

Betsy bit into a beignet. She shook her head, her eyes drifting downward toward the floor as she chewed. A chime sounded from a bank of computer screens showing various locations in and around the casino. She turned her attention to the monitors. Any lingering happiness from hearing about his conversation with Polly Bondurant had faded.

"Sorry." Jonathan's lowered voice matched Betsy's somber countenance. "I shouldn't have said anything. It's just—"

"You need to make sure I have the time and energy to do what you're about to ask me to do." Betsy spoke into a walkie-talkie. "Blue Team. This is Skywatch. Check out Table Nineteen. New dealer. Looks like a Code Purple. Player in third position." She looked at Jonathan. "Sorry. We get a lot of new dealers during Carnival season. College kids, retirees following the circuit—sort of like migrant farm workers going where the work is. Lot of 'em have motorhomes. Tow cars for transport around town."

"I see."

"The Walmart on Tchoupitoulas has the same thing with its seasonal help. Lots of transients."

"Got it."

"So," Betsy said, "you're worried I can't cut the mustard after what's happened?"

"In a word, yes."

"I mean, all I did was shoot my husband to keep him from killing you and Sonny."

"But you couldn't know it was Ranger. He was wearing a ski mask."

"Then he was kidnapped from the hospital by guys in black suits."

"Well—"

"And now Ranger's dropped off the grid. That's what got you worried?"

Jonathan's face warmed in embarrassment. "Listen, I'm sorry."

"Don't be." Betsy sipped her coffee. "I'd do the same thing if I were in your shoes."

Jonathan slid a file folder toward Betsy.

"What's this?"

"Printout of photos from the scene. And some that Polly Bondurant showed me."

Betsy spread the photographs out in a grid pattern. The last three photos showed the dead man's body against the AIDS Memorial and a close-up of the symbols carved into his forehead and chest.

Betsy closed her eyes and massaged her temples. She opened her eyes and pointed at the symbols. "Different from the last time."

"Apparently."

"Manifesto?"

Jonathan placed a piece of paper on the table, covering up some of the photos. "Here's a copy of the note police found in the dead man's left hand."

"Mostly matches the chest and forehead." Betsy shook her head. "But there are a few different symbols in the note." She crossed her arms, then placed her right hand over her mouth as if trying to stifle a negative comment. "This can't be the Sweeper."

"Why? Just because the code's different?"

"Cipher."

"Come again?"

"A code usually involves numbers or symbols substituting for words or phrases…a cipher involves switches for individual letters."

"I see," Jonathan said. "So, just because the *cipher's* different?"

"There's that." Betsy tapped her finger on the note as if making a point. "No way he could have survived the fall from the Crescent City Connection."

"Well—"

"A hundred-fifty feet off a bridge into the Mississippi? Give me a break. Besides, I know I hit the bastard with at least one shot, maybe two." Betsy shook her head. "I know they never found a body, but still…"

"Regardless, I could really use your help on this one. Max Jamerson wants to keep it on the down-low. Doesn't want to panic Mardi Gras crowds."

Betsy shook her head, actually more of a quiver as if being tugged by an internal debate about what to do. "Look, Doc, I hate to let you down. But I've got so much other stuff going on right now. And Brandon—"

"Damn. I forgot about Brandon. How's he holding up?"

"Not much he can do sitting around thinking about his dad. He graduated early. Finished his freshman orientation at Auburn a couple of weeks ago. Spring practice starts soon. You know, best to keep busy. Idle hands and all that."

"I understand. But I really could use your expertise."

"I got it, Doc. It's just…I mean…I just can't right now."

Chapter Five: Ships Passing

Sunday, February 1, 2015 – 8:37 a.m.

Jonathan sat on a brick retaining wall in the casino's drop-off entrance near the foot of Canal Street. What a difference daylight made. Under forty degrees when he arrived at Washington Square Park. Now, nearly sixty. By mid-afternoon, it would likely be close to seventy. Typical roller coaster New Orleans winter weather.

The last few hours had been especially challenging. Dragged out of a sound sleep at home with his wife, Emma, by Mitch's phone call. Dealing with the bloody mess at the park. His disastrous interview of the young female at the Tulane ER. And now Betsy. He was exhausted and knew it. But he couldn't stop—not yet.

Passers-by gave him a wide berth, glancing his way and then walking in the opposite direction. He stroked his cheeks and chin. Stubble. So, he needed a shave. And a hot shower would be great. But that shouldn't be enough to make people steer clear. Not even if he appeared like he was just another casino patron after a night of chasing their losses and failing to turn their bad luck around. Maybe he was giving off negative vibes from Betsy's understandable but disappointing decision not to get involved. Whatever.

Along with maintaining his professional reputation and ego, so much depended on finding the person who killed the guy in Washington Square Park. At the very least, providing closure to the young woman who'd been attacked. And for the sake of society, bringing a murderer to justice. Of even greater urgency, preventing any more deaths if it turned out they were, indeed, dealing with a serial killer—whether or not it was the Mardi Gras Sweeper. With or without Betsy on the team, failure was not an option.

But first things first. He needed to let Emma know he was still alive after disappearing in the middle of the night. So, he thumbed a text:

Won't make Mass. Big case. Details later.

The reply came within seconds:

8:39 am: Figured as much. Got your note on the fridge. Love, F

He smiled. "F." Short for Fen. His pet name for Emma since their first date at a Red Sox game when they were in college. Before he could respond, another message appeared:

8:40 am: Visit Beatrice?

His face warmed as he typed the response:

No. Can't today. Maybe later this week.

He stared at his phone and waited. The dreaded three- dots and annotation "Writing a reply" appeared, then disappeared, twice. They went to the mausoleum together almost every Sunday after Mass. Beatrice. How could he not find the time to visit with their daughter, their first child—dead these twelve years, killed in a school shooting when she was just nine?

Fen must be giving her reply a lot of thought. After what seemed like an eternity, her answer popped onto his screen:

8:42 am: Must be serious. I'll give B your love. Off to Mass now.

Thank God. Fen didn't seem angry. Relieved, he responded:

Thanks. Regards to Dan R. XO, Gray

Monsignor Dan Rossignol, Rector of St. Louis Cathedral, had always accepted Jonathan—an Episcopalian—as part of the congregation when he accompanied Emma to Mass. Though forbidden—as a non-Catholic—to take part in Holy Communion, being at services with Emma brought them closer together. She drew strength from the liturgy and rituals. Her faith had sustained her through the hardships they'd faced during their thirty years of marriage.

And over the years, he and Dan had become friends—at least as much as you can be friends with a priest. Lord knows Jonathan would need all the help he could get in dealing with the Mardi Gras Sweeper—or whoever the killer turned out to be. A prayer or two from Dan couldn't hurt. In the meantime, he'd have to settle for a walk along the riverfront to wake himself up and get his brain in gear.

He crossed Canal Street, navigating its maze of intersecting streetcar and railroad tracks, and headed toward the river. The area outside Audubon Aquarium would be a great place to think. A circular bench surrounding a stone planter containing a small willow oak—its branches almost devoid of leaves—beckoned to him. He removed the briefcase slung over his shoulder and placed it on the bench. Gulls floated overhead. He sat. His riverfront stroll could wait.

Two petroleum tankers passed each other, traveling in opposite directions. Both rode low in the water, filled with cargo. The northbound vessel—a Panamanian-flagged tanker—likely carried crude oil on its way to one of the refineries upriver. The southbound vessel—flying the distinctive flag of the Marshall Islands—likely carried gasoline, perhaps from the same refinery. What a testament to this *laissez-faire* city on the Mississippi. Ships from around the world. So many transient sailors, representing God knows how many different cultures, each adding spice and diversity to New Orleans, day in and day out.

Despite the restful scene, he couldn't relax. They'd already accomplished a lot in the short time available. But there was so much to do. Susan Miller would probably finish the autopsy on the dead guy soon. He'd asked her to give it priority. And with any luck, NOPD might crack the code—the cipher—in the Sweeper's manifesto. If that's what it was—a manifesto. And the skin carving. Part of the Sweeper's declaration to the world? Or just another way to torture his victim?

The letters and symbols passed before his eyes. Alpha and Omega. No secret meaning there. The Sweeper had used them before. His hallmark. His way of announcing his biennial return. He was the beginning and the end. But the tag from the streetcar and the chest carving almost certainly had special significance.

Jonathan pulled two photos of the symbols from the file Polly Bondurant had given him and held them side-by-side. On the left was the graffiti from the streetcar, D V F I I A I E I V F I V, painted sometime on the sixth of January. The photo on the right—the chest etchings from the Washington Square Park victim—were similar: G I D I A I D I V. The Sweeper was telling them something. But what?

The longer he stared at the photos, the less sense the symbols made. Soon, everything blurred together. Lowering the photos to the bench, he cradled them on his left side between his body and the wrought-iron armrest. He closed his eyes, placed his head in his hands, and rubbed his face. Despite screeching mews of the gulls, his mind wandered.

Just over six weeks since Robby O'Malley—his friend and mentor for nearly forty years—had died of a stroke. He'd experienced almost constant tumult since being thrust, without warning, into the limelight as Coroner.

Then came images of Emma and their children. The triplets away at college. And Beatrice. So tragic, her death. Such a precocious little one. Their pride and joy. Gifted in every way—language, music, mathematics. Math. A skill she must have inherited from her architect mother. And her mom's love of solving puzzles, too. Sunday mornings, drinking coffee. Watching Emma tear through the *New York Times* crossword, then conquering the cryptogram. Coffee. His mouth watered, and his nostrils flared at memories of the taste and smell. What he wouldn't give for a cup of freshly ground Sumatra Dark or an Ethiopian mountain blend right now. And Sunday afternoons watching the Saints or visiting—

A sharp metal-on-metal scraping sound dragged Jonathan back to reality. His eyes jolted open, blinded by the brightness. As he blinked to adjust his eyes to the light, his right hand reached for the holster clipped to his belt. Empty. Damn. Who—

"Looking for this?"

Jonathan focused on the handle of a Glock 19, probably his, with the barrel facing away from him, chamber open. The lump in his throat tightened. His face and arms tingled as if he were breaking out in goosebumps. "Betsy? What the hell?"

"Nice nap?" Betsy handed him the pistol and magazine.

"Where did you come from?" Jonathan inserted the magazine into the pistol and holstered the weapon. Warmth spread across his face, no doubt signaling his embarrassment. "And what time is it?"

"Almost eleven." Betsy pointed to Jonathan's holster. "You really need to keep one in the chamber. Surely the Navy taught you that. Never understood why they trusted doctors with firearms. 'First do no harm,' my ass."

"Right." Jesus. Had he been there for almost two hours? And how long had he slept? Thank God it was only Betsy.

"And staying awake's always advisable."

"Semper Fi, Marine." Not much else he could say under the circumstances. "Just resting my eyes."

"Don't try to Semper Fi your way out of this one. This. Is. Serious. What if a kid or—"

"What brings you here?" Best to change the subject before he dug himself in any deeper. "How'd you find me?"

"Detective's instinct. You can run, but you can't hide."

"Fair enough…but why?"

"Maybe it's the old leatherneck in me saying not to back down in the face of adversity." Betsy frowned. "And I might live to regret it, but I came to help. I have a couple of shifts at Harrah's I need to work this week. And I've still got issues at home…but I'll do what I can."

"Outstanding. I'll take your help. Whatever conditions you set."

"One more thing." Betsy almost smiled. "Promise me you won't 'rest your eyes' anymore if you're packing."

Jonathan's phone vibrated. "Gray, here." His voice reflected his exhaustion. "Got it. We'll be there in fifteen minutes."

"What was that all about?"

"You jumped on board just in time. That was Susan Miller. She's finished the autopsy. Let's head for the morgue." He removed his Glock from the holster. "And I promise. A round in the chamber and eyes wide open."

Chapter Six: Knives Out

The RideShare carrying Jonathan and Betsy traveled along a mostly light-industrial section of Earhart Boulevard. Despite thunderclouds forming north of Lake Pontchartrain, the late morning sky shone brightly. Purple, green, and gold spotlights illuminated the Superdome in the distance. Must be to emphasize the ongoing Mardi Gras season.

"You can drop us off up there." Jonathan pointed toward an unremarkable plaster and faux-brick building ahead on the right, identified by an equally unremarkable sign stating in large block letters: New Orleans Coroner. The building had opened about six months ago, over nine years after Katrina forced the Coroner's office to bounce from temporary facility to temporary facility. But the new morgue proved to be too small to house the entire organization, requiring Jonathan to maintain their previous administrative offices in City Hall.

Susan Miller, an emergency-room physician at Tulane Medical Center who sometimes worked in the morgue, greeted Jonathan and Betsy at the front entrance. Susan's raven-black hair, tied in a bun, stood out in contrast to her white lab coat.

"That was quick," Susan said. "Detective Sprance, I thought—"

"Betsy's on loan from NOPD," Jonathan said.

"Welcome, aboard." Susan smiled. "The more the merrier."

"Thanks. Happy to be here." Betsy rolled her eyes. "I guess it's better than watching gamblers throw away their money…even if I have to put up with a cadaver or two."

"That's the spirit," Jonathan said. "Okay, Susan. Show us what you've got."

Dr. Miller escorted the pair into the morgue's inner sanctum—its autopsy room. Two stainless steel examination tables occupied the center of the room, spaced approximately fifteen feet apart. One table was unoccupied. On the other, the outline of a human body lay stiff and lifeless under the standard white cloth sheet often used to protect post-autopsy cadavers. The ventilation system provided steady background noise as frigid air rushed through the ducting. A sharp metallic odor from the blood released during the autopsy mixed with fumes from the bleach used to clean up afterward. Overall, the morgue's pungent atmosphere underscored the facility's grizzly, though necessary, purpose.

"*Soc au' lait.*" Betsy shuddered. "It's always like a glacier in here."

"Occupational hazard." Susan peeled back the cadaver sheet, folding the excess slowly as she went along—much like one might fold the Stars-and-Stripes—as if honoring the deceased. "I guess we're used to it."

"Maybe." Betsy grimaced. "But I could never get used to looking at something as gruesome as that."

"Not a pretty picture," Jonathan said. "Another occupational hazard… Susan, take us through the basics. We can look at your full report for the finer points later."

"Cause of death's obvious." Susan pointed to the cadaver's torso. "Deep slashing wound to the lower abdomen leading to exsanguination and—"

"Gutted like a fish, then bled out," Betsy said.

"Always right to the point." Jonathan smiled. "The Betsy Sprance we all know and love."

Betsy rolled her eyes. "So, the second knife wound, the one near the collarbone—"

"Window dressing," Susan said. "In a manner of speaking."

"Seems like overkill," Betsy said. "I mean, it's like the killer was making a statement. Showing the world that he meant business."

"Almost," Jonathan said, "like it was—"

"Personal," Betsy said. "Emotional. Angry. Like a revenge killing. Not to mention the intimacy of the body art."

"And," Susan said, "there had to be a lot of force applied to cut through the layers of skin, fat, and muscle to expose the intestines."

"Exactly." Jonathan looked at Susan. "Anything you can tell us about the body carving?"

"Confirmed what you thought," Susan replied. "The Alpha and Omega on the forehead were done while the victim was still alive. The chest marks, *postmortem.*"

"I see," Jonathan said.

Susan looked first at Betsy, then Jonathan. "But there's something else."

"Hang on." Jonathan lifted his buzzing cell phone to his ear. "This is Gray."

"When?" He looked at Betsy. "Where?…Okay, Got it. I'll let her know."

Jonathan hit the End Call button. "That was Mitch Broussard." He yawned. "Sorry…they located the pair that tagged the streetcars."

"Holding them?" Betsy asked.

"Sixth District Headquarters. Mitch is waiting for you there. Has your badge and gun."

"Got it. I'll grab a RideShare."

"Why don't you check out a car from the motor pool?" Jonathan said. "We'll add you to the RideShare use agreement once we get the paperwork straightened out."

"Great," Betsy said. "Motor pool it is. Talk to you soon."

Jonathan turned to Susan as Betsy departed. "So, what's your other thing?"

"Notice anything about his right knee?"

"Damn." Jonathan shook his head. "Distortion's pretty obvious once you point it out. Got any snapshots?"

"Took a couple." Susan pointed toward a keyboard on the counter underneath a large computer monitor mounted on the wall. "You mind bringing them up on the screen?"

"No assistant?"

"Called out sick. Tried to get Jimmy Caplan to come in, but he's already scheduled for the eight o'clock shift tonight."

Jonathan tapped on the keyboard. "Jimmy's probably hungover, anyway." Two digital X-ray images appeared on the monitor. "Said he was going to check out Frenchmen Street and the parades last night."

"His gain. My loss." Susan pointed to the screen. "You can see the damage for yourself."

"Hmmm. Clear Comminuted fracture of the patella." He squinted at the images. "Shattered into…what would you say…at least half a dozen pieces?"

"Looks about right," Susan said. "And the fragments don't line up like they should. Must be what makes the distortion on the external exam so noticeable."

"What would account for the damage?"

"Not sure. Could have happened if he banged into the metal and glass orbs on the AIDS memorial."

"Do we know if the knee injury happened before—"

"Before he was gutted?" Susan winced. "Not sure about that either."

"What about the weapons?"

Susan directed Jonathan to a nearby table with two knives on it. One had a wooden handle with brass highlights, a stainless-steel blade, and a logo with two crossed anchors interlaced with the initials IMWU. The other knife had a composite material handle and a dark, probably steel, blade. Each knife lay adjacent to calibrating strips used to show relative size for photographs.

"Cleaned them after the autopsy, of course. But there they are."

Jonathan picked up the knife with the slightly curved wooden handle. "Sturdy, but still not that heavy…What would you say, about four ounces?"

"Just over."

"Straight blade, blunt end. Meant for cutting, not stabbing."

"Right. Called a sailor's rigging knife."

"I'm aware," Jonathan said. "Patched up more than one sliced hand during my Navy days."

"Understandable, I suppose. But how—"

"Primary purpose is working with rope—splicing mooring lines and such."

Jonathan turned the blade over several times, studying both sides. "And there are different designs. Foldable blades. Curved blades. Even ones with a marlin spike."

"A marlin spike?"

"Helps in fixing cut ropes…not important here…and hands sometimes slip…but nothing like what we found in the park."

"I'd hope not," Susan said.

"Blade's about one inch wide, just over three inches long, wouldn't you say?"

"Almost four inches. Seems like a perfect weapon for the damage inflicted."

"This is the one I saw covered by the guy's intestines?"

"It is."

"Thoughts on how he used it?"

"The wound started on the left side, mid-abdomen. And got wider and deeper as it moved toward the right."

With the blade facing him, Jonathan made a slashing motion from left to right. "Like this?"

"Mostly. And look at how the wound comes almost straight-up on the right side."

"Nearly a ninety-degree turn. Intentional. Probably what led to the disembowelment. Almost like someone committing hara-kiri."

"Maybe," Susan said. "Except this was clearly murder. Not self-inflicted. Not ritual suicide."

"Agreed. And it appears that the Sweeper…or whoever…must have attacked from behind and cut across the guy's front torso, digging in as he went."

"That's how I reconstructed it as well."

Jonathan returned the sailor's rigging knife to the table.

Susan picked up the second knife. "This one's called an Out-the-Front—OTF. Some call it an automatic knife. Even more sinister."

"How so?"

"First of all, size—about eight-and-a-quarter inches long. Not quite as heavy as the other one…but watch."

Susan placed her thumb on a switch on the top of the knife and shifted it toward the rear. With a noticeable click, the blade retreated into the handle. She moved the switch forward, and the sharp-tipped blade shot outward, returning the weapon to its full eight-and-a-quarter-inch length.

"Jesus," Jonathan said.

"Right. From a five-inch harmless rectangle of composite material to an eight-inch weapon of death in an instant. Has a serrated cutting edge as well. A victim wouldn't know what was coming until too late."

"And the tip would make a great flesh carving tool."

"Exactly." Susan returned the knife to the table.

"We're dealing with a sick one. Bringing two knives—"

"Don't be so sure."

"Because?"

"The OTF would have been quite deadly on its own. But this guy used the sailor's rigging knife to disembowel his victim. Why not just use the OTF to cut his throat and then carve the figures?"

"Hmmm." Jonathan nodded. "Good observation. You think the Sweeper brought the sailor's rigging knife and found the other one there?"

"Maybe. What did the girl say?"

"Good question. Looks like the next stop's Tulane ER. I'll message Betsy to join me there when she's done at the Sixth District."

Chapter Seven: The Claiborne Boys

Sunday, February 1, 2015 – 12:07 p.m.

Betsy approached NOPD's Sixth District Headquarters—a two-story cinderblock structure—with a combination of apprehension and satisfaction. This was the first time she'd been there since her suspension-with-pay approximately three weeks before. The building had a brick façade, apparently an attempt to add a touch of class to the otherwise drab exterior. Nothing fancy. No waste of taxpayer dollars here. Nonetheless, the police station seemed right at home in the working-class neighborhood surrounding the intersection of Martin Luther King Boulevard and South Rampart.

"Upstairs, in Observation Room 'A.'" The Desk Sergeant leaned back in his chair. "Detective Broussard's waiting for you."

"Thanks, Sarge."

"Oh, and welcome home."

Betsy smiled as she angled toward the stairs. "Roger that. Feels good."

It did feel good. Maybe not a hundred percent vindication. But Polly Bondurant must be shooting angry lightning bolts out of her backside. Agreeing to Betsy's return, even on special assignment to work with the Coroner, couldn't have been easy on Polly. No doubt, Mayor Jamerson wouldn't be pleased, either. It would likely be a long time before Betsy regained her former position as Chief of Detectives for the district. She couldn't worry about that now. There was a job to do.

Mitch Broussard leaned back in his seat in front of two computer monitors as Betsy entered the observation room. "Nice uniform." He chewed on his trademark half-stogie.

"Haven't had a chance to change."

Broussard chuckled. "The citizens of New Orleans appreciate your personal sacrifice." He pointed to a gun and an NOPD badge on the table. "Might as well make yourself official."

"All right, wise guy, ease up." Betsy smiled. First, Polly Bondurant's lightning bolts about bringing her back. Now, her badge and gun returned. Sweet. "What's the scoop?"

Broussard pitched the remains of his cigar into a nearby trash can. "Surveillance cameras from the Car Barn and a couple of local businesses helped us identify the two kids who tagged the streetcars."

"Kids?"

"Affirmative. Both juveniles."

"That them on the monitors?"

"Affirmative. Marcus Dumaine and Jefferson Thibodeaux. Both sixteen." Mitch pointed toward the monitors. "Got 'em in separate rooms. That's Marcus on the left and Jefferson on the right."

"Gang involvement?"

"Claiborne Boys."

"Both?"

"Affirmative."

"Priors?"

"Nothing yet. But we need to check the sealed juvenile records. Should take a couple of hours to get permission."

"Got it. Talked to them?"

"Both clammed up. Asked for lawyers. So I got them each a cold drink out of the vending machine. Told them someone would be around soon."

"They're well trained—ask for an attorney and shut the hell up. You think they were involved beyond the graffiti?"

"Could be wrong." Mitch removed a new cigar from his shirt pocket. "Gut feeling says 'no.' Seem to be wiseasses, but not killers. At least not yet."

"Well, we need to find out why they tagged the streetcars."

"You know the rules. Once they lawyer up. We stop."

"By the book, right?"

"Goddamn federal consent decree," Mitch said. "Department of Justice'll put us *under* the jail if we—"

"*If* they find out." Betsy grabbed the doorknob. "We've got bigger fish to fry. There's a serial killer on the loose."

The door closed, then opened again. Betsy leaned into the room. "And it'd be a shame if the video recorder malfunctioned." She smiled. "Wouldn't it?"

Marcus Dumaine sat up straight as Betsy entered the interrogation room. He placed his hands on the small table in front of him, as if to show he didn't have a weapon. An unopened can of Mountain Dew sat on the table near his hands. The kid might be sixteen, but looked younger. Skinny. Hardly old enough to shave. Wearing a black hoodie must be to add to a tough appearance. Perhaps it covered the telltale gang tat of the Claiborne Boys—a Mardi Gras joker's head over crossed knives—on his upper left arm. They could check later, if they decided to book him.

"You my attorney?" His voice sounded deeper than his slight build and youthful appearance suggested. No doubt another part of his tough-man act.

Betsy displayed her badge. "Detective Lieutenant Sprance, New Orleans—"

"Told the other cop I wanted a lawyer." Marcus snickered. "Can't do nothing to me until he gets here."

"I'm not a normal cop." Betsy returned her badge to her jacket pocket. "I'm on special assignment to the Coroner's Office. Same rules don't apply."

"Coroner? What the—"

"Investigating a murder."

Marcus appeared more serious, worry in his eyes. "Murder? Don't know nothing about a murder. What the fu—"

"We got camera shots of you and your pal tagging streetcars with some funky-looking symbols. Found the same type of symbols on a dead body off Frenchmen Street."

The teen's eyes bulged as if ready to pop. "Don't know nothin' about no killing." His voice no longer reflected a false machismo. "You ain't going to stick me with that."

"That's not what Jefferson told us."

"What the hell he tell you?" Back to the angry gang-member tone. "Rat bastard…and where my mouthpiece?"

"Wouldn't worry about that if I was you." Betsy sat down across the table from Marcus. "Why did you tag the streetcars? Didn't realize that was something the Claibornes were into."

"They don't know nothing about it." Marcus again looked surprised, his voice more docile than before. "You ain't going to say nothin' to nobody, are you?"

"I'm sure it won't come to that." Betsy leaned forward. "If you're straight with me."

The can of Mountain Dew clicked and hissed as Marcus opened it. After taking a sip, he returned the can to the table. "Got a message on the Hide-It app—"

Betsy shifted position, no longer leaning forward. "The secure program?"

"Yeah."

"From?"

"Don't know. Someone called 'WannaEarnMoney?'" Marcus sipped more of his cold drink.

"And what did 'Mr. WannaEarnMoney?' want you to do?"

"Asked me to mark the cars. Had a description of what the tags should be."

"Payment?"

"Said I'd find a Benjamin in an envelope at a playground off Pine Street."

"St. Rita's school?"

"Yeah." Another sip of the Mountain Dew.

"You did this for a hundred bucks?"

"Down payment. Once I finished, there'd be another nine hundred in the same place."

"And was there?"

"Yeah."

"You never saw the guy?"

"No."

"Didn't speak to him?"

"No."

"Any clue who it was?"

"No."

Betsy stroked her chin. "Still got the message on your phone?"

"Yeah."

"Let me see."

Betsy examined the secure texts and took several photographs of the contents. She handed the phone back to Marcus.

He drank the rest of the Mountain Dew and returned the can to the table. "We done?"

"Maybe. Maybe not. I need to consult with my colleague."

"What about my lawyer?"

"I'm sure he'll be here soon. In the meantime, I suggest you don't mention this to anyone else. I'd hate to see what happens once Terrence finds out you been working a side hustle without telling management." Betsy used air quotes when she said "management."

"You know Terrence?" Marcus licked his lips, then shook the can, apparently hoping there was some more Mountain Dew left.

"Let's say that we're acquainted and leave it at that."

"You ain't going to tell him, are you?"

"Like I said. You be straight with me. I'll be straight with you. But if your story doesn't check out, I promise that Terrence will be the first to know."

Marcus's eyes moistened. "Yes, ma'am." The wiseass gang member from before seemed more like a scared puppy.

Betsy stood. "Sit tight. Let me see if I can locate your lawyer."

"Bravo." Mitch feigned applause as Betsy reentered the observation room. "Thought he was going to wet his pants when you threatened to rat him out to his gang leader."

"Wouldn't be the first time." Betsy smiled as she sat down next to Mitch.

"And what's that stuff about different rules?"

"Well, a cop's gotta do what a cop's gotta do." Betsy frowned. "No time to play nice guy…not with the Sweeper out there somewhere."

"But you know, nothing will stick to this guy if we deny his right to a lawyer."

"Didn't deny it." Betsy chuckled. "Delayed it a little, maybe, but—"

"Still, Bondurant won't like it."

"Not on her Christmas Card list, anyway. And Marcus?…*Un 'tit couyon.*" Betsy shook her head. "You can talk with the other one—Jefferson, right?"

"Sure. You think he's a little dumb ass, too?"

"I'm betting Jefferson was the lookout. If he confirms what Marcus says, cut 'em loose. Threaten to tell Terrence if they say anything. We'll be fine."

"Sounds like a plan."

"In the meantime, Doc Gray texted me earlier. I need to meet him at Tulane Hospital. Maybe I can change clothes on the way." Betsy stood and grabbed the doorknob. "And thanks for the help. I know Polly's not exactly happy right now. Hope nothing blows back on you."

"No worries. Got it covered. Now get your tail out of here. You got a killer to catch."

Chapter Eight: Caesars and Pigpens

Sunday, February 1, 2015 – 2:39 p.m.

In just over twelve hours since police found the dead male and a live, half-nude female in Washington Square Park, Jonathan must have consumed a gallon of coffee. He'd certainly been to the head—the bathroom—enough times to prove it. Still buzzed by caffeine and greatly in need of meaningful sleep, he sat in a small doctor-patient consultation room at Tulane Hospital with the door propped open.

Over the years, Betsy Sprance often reminded him of the old saw about the critical first forty-eight hours after a murder. Not finding the killer in that time period increased the chances of the perpetrator escaping and the investigation being lost in the nether regions of the cold-case file room.

If the saying were true, they still had thirty-six hours—a day and a half. Much had been accomplished. And there were many investigative irons in the proverbial fire. But each lead had resulted in multiple loose ends. Perhaps there'd be a break in the case that would connect the dots. DNA on the weapons. A witness hidden in the bushes with a video camera. The girl confessing to killing her attacker. Likely, though, it would come down to a combination of legwork and luck.

Key among the remaining "things to do" was figuring out the letters and symbols carved into the dead man's forehead and chest, those printed on the note, and the tags marking the streetcars. Jonathan placed the photographs of the graffiti and the body etchings on the small conference table, alongside the single sheet of letters and symbols he had referred to as the Sweeper's Manifesto. Yes, NOPD had promised to put their resident experts to work on solving the puzzle. But what if they didn't do it in time?

"Knock. Knock." A familiar voice came from the open door.

"Betsy?" Jonathan's voice reflected both surprise and pleasure. "Didn't expect to see you so soon. Finish both interviews already?"

"Only had to do one."

"How's that? Get a confession? Nab our killer? Sit and tell me about it."

"No confession." Betsy eased herself into a chair on the opposite side of the table from Jonathan. "Both suspects belong to the Claiborne Boys."

"Gangbangers?"

"Juvenile street punks is more like it."

"So, what'd you learn?"

"Punk One claimed he was contacted by an anonymous source using an encrypted app. Offered him a thousand bucks to tag the streetcars. But he doesn't know anything about the murder."

"You believe him?"

"For now. Mitch is going to interview Punk Two. If their stories match, he'll check a couple of details and cut 'em loose. We can always drag 'em back in if something comes up."

"Another loose end, I guess."

"Maybe," Betsy said. "At least we know two things. First, there's a connection between the streetcar graffiti and the symbols at the scene. Second—"

"Someone's pulling the strings. Someone who wants to send us a message."

"Winner, winner, chicken dinner."

"Now if we can just figure out who's pulling the strings and what the message is."

"Right." Betsy pointed to the photos and document on the table. "Looks like you're working on figuring out the message."

"Cass Melançon called…running late…should be here by a little after three so we can interview the victim again. So, thought I'd keep busy. Maybe something will pop out at me before the tech guys figure it out."

"Any luck?"

Jonathan shook his head. "I think the Alpha and Omega are simple enough."

"Sweeper's calling card."

"And the words on the streetcars and the guy's chest seem to be using the same basic code as the note."

"Cipher."

"Right. Cipher." Jonathan rolled his eyes. "The cipher on the note adds some letters and symbols not on the other messages."

Jonathan turned the photos of the chest etchings and streetcar symbols and the note so Betsy could see them. He pointed to the letters on the streetcars: D V F I I A I E I V F I V, then the letters on the chest: G I D I A I D I V. "No symbols. Just letters."

"Right," Betsy said.

"But look at the first line of the document:
A I F I I I E I I I A I A I D I I A I G I I [+] D I I D I V G V E I I I C I D I F I I I [♪]"

"Same basic letters," Betsy said, "but with some symbols added."

"And the rest of the document has additional symbols—diamonds, hearts, clubs, and spades."

"Suites from a deck of cards."

"Exactly," Jonathan said. "How does it compare to the previous ones?"

"First time around, the Sweeper used what's called a Caesar Cipher."

"Okay. In English, that means…?"

"It works on shifting the starting point in the A-to-Z alphabet."

"Okay?"

"If you determine the starting point is 'E,' your A-to-Z alphabet starts there."

"So 'E' becomes 'A,' 'F' becomes 'B' and so on?"

"Another chicken dinner, Doc." Betsy smiled. "Then you just need to make the substitutions. Easy peasy."

"But no lemon squeezy with the current one?"

"Right," Betsy said. "I'm no expert, but the current one doesn't look anything like the original Caesar Cipher. Not all the letters of the A-to-Z alphabet are there."

"But even though we figured out his code, we couldn't catch him first time out."

"Cipher."

"Right," Jonathan said. "Cipher."

"He switched gears the second time—two years ago."

"More complex?"

"But still pretty basic."

"How so?"

"It was called a Pigpen Cipher."

Jonathan's forehead wrinkled. "Pigpen?"

"Some call it the Freemason's Cipher."

"That clarifies it."

"Come on, Doc. I bet you've seen a Pigpen Cipher before. Even if you didn't realize what it was."

"Oh?"

"It's a substitution cipher, like the Caesar. Each letter in the A-to-Z alphabet is represented by a symbol. The symbols are based on how the letters line up in a grid that looks like a combination of a tic-tac-toe board and the letter "X." Each letter is represented by lines, 'v' shapes, and dots, depending on the letter's location."

"Sounds complicated."

"Looks complicated, but it's relatively simple once you recognize the patterns."

"But this time around, the Sweeper's not using a Pigpen Cipher."

"Bingo. And my knowledge isn't very deep, so I can't really say what this one is."

"Got it. Looks like the Sweeper's trying to keep us on our toes."

"Sure looks that way," Betsy said. "He wants us to work for it. But I'd lay money down that the tech geeks will crack the code relatively easy, once they analyze it."

"Cipher." Jonathan grinned.

"Right." Betsy rolled her eyes. "Cipher." She smiled. "You're a quick study."

"Let's hope our geeks are just as quick. And once Cass Melançon gets here, we can interview our victim. Maybe that'll move things off dead center."

Betsy pointed toward the door. "Speak of the devil."

"Sorry for crashing your party." Cass stood just outside the room. "Ready to talk to our star witness?"

Chapter Nine: The Sweeper's Challenge

Stryker's nostrils flared at the pungent, yet sweet, odor of melting solder. Wearing two KN-95 face masks had proven insufficient to block the noxious fumes. Time to shift the fan to blow everything out a window from the small indoor space to the chilly weather outside. The noise and exhaust might rouse the neighbors' curiosity. But it was a necessary risk under the circumstances.

Construction of the smaller devices had been aided by a combination of YouTube videos and internet searches. Knock on wood, the searches had been concealed sufficiently to avoid discovery by the FBI and its web-sniffing bots. Goddamn federal authorities and their fishing expeditions to crush citizens' First Amendment rights. But that was a complaint for another day and a different venue. Besides, the mission would probably be completed well before the feds caught on to who was behind the inquiries.

Stryker removed the masks. The fan had worked, the fumes dissipated. And no one was banging on the door to gripe, at least not yet. Time to clean up and prepare for tonight's activities.

Success depended on the public fearing that the Mardi Gras Sweeper had returned. But they wouldn't know to worry unless someone told them about it. There should have been a mention in the newspaper by now, at least the early-morning online editions. Not about something minor like graffiti on streetcars in the maintenance facility on Willow Street, of course. That might never be reported. Tagging public facilities had become so common, few ever gave it a second notice. A pity how much civilization had been slipping lately. Yet another grievance for another day.

Given the Sweeper's history, though, graffiti on two of the city's prized Pearly Thomas streetcars—wherever located—should have jogged someone's memory, raised an alarm. Especially the Alpha and Omega. How soon people forget. But a body—complete with the offending weapons and exquisite skin carvings—adorning the City's AIDS memorial? *That* certainly deserved a headline. A small one, perhaps, given the number of murders in the city, but *something*.

Nothing about the Challenge document, either. No doubt the police were keeping a lid on things. They probably hadn't figured out the latest cipher yet. It might be too hard for them. The previous ones were easier, but would be of no help in solving this one. Careful study and analysis guaranteed that. So, it would probably take them longer. Or, maybe they had figured it out and were just playing dumb, in hopes of forcing an error.

Another possibility came to mind. What if the copy sent to the *Times-Picayune* hadn't arrived yet? Those lazy bastards at the U.S. Postal Service had no incentive to work hard. Taxpayer-subsidized slugs like them would be good targets. Government overreach. Government bureaucracy. Cut the deadwood. Thinning the herd would force efficiencies. Or maybe it wasn't their fault at all. Perhaps the document hadn't made it out of the newspaper's mail room, or lay unopened on the reporter's desk. Seemed like the New Orleans media covered bead-throwing Carnival participants in painstaking detail, but didn't give a damn about real news. So much for the public's right to know.

The other cities knew the Sweeper by different names. But they had been more interested, or at least acted like it. Front page news for a few weeks as bodies piled up. Then, reporters and cops scratching their heads when the killings stopped for no reason, as mysteriously as they had begun. Police must have scared the killer off, the papers would speculate. Or maybe the killer was dead, a suicide made to look like a murder. And it would be that way until the next time, months or even years later, like in New Orleans.

What a convenient target the Big Easy offered. Hit one year of Mardi Gras, skip the next year. Lull them into a sense of complacency and then strike again. This would be the Sweeper's third dance with the NOPD. And call it fate or kismet or just plain luck, the stars had aligned. The Sweeper's cover would allow this year's visit to be the best, certainly the most memorable. The proverbial shot heard 'round the world.

Killing someone in combat situations had become an automatic reflex after years of training and experience. Second nature. A necessary part of defending against all enemies, foreign and domestic. And there was always collateral damage. But targeting non-combatants, civilians, intentionally was another matter. The first step along a slippery slope to barbarity. A Rubicon not to be crossed—except in exceptional circumstances.

Exceptional circumstances, indeed. However unappealing it might be, killing someone not directly involved—not the bastard who had caused the pain in the first place—had been easier than imagined. Maybe the key lay in killing only those who had forfeited their humanity, their right to live in a civilized society. An enemy not identified by a military uniform, but an enemy nonetheless. A rapist prevented—permanently—from inflicting horror on an innocent young woman just seemed the right thing to do. If it served to further the overall plan, all the better.

And the rush proved infectious, invigorating. Almost too invigorating. Mission accomplishment depended on discipline. The rapist's knife was there, easy to grab and thrust into the dead man as an emotional reaction in the moment. Unnecessary because the man—if he deserved to be called a man—had already been sent to Hell. But a satisfying release of the pain coiled inside. The pain that led to following the Sweeper's path.

Yet sleep, deep and restful, came quickly. Maybe bearing one's soul to a priest made the difference. Regardless, exhaustion and emotions couldn't get in the way. Keep eyes on the prize. Stay focused.

So, if the streetcar art and Washington Square Park handiwork hadn't captured the public's attention, it was time to ratchet up the pressure. Add to the chaos. Maybe that would force NOPD to react faster and make the *Times-Picayune* more responsive. Maybe all it would take was adding one of the newly completed devices to the mix. The design worked for the other, larger ones, already fully vetted. It should work for this much smaller version. Tonight would be the first real test. If it worked, that would keep everyone, especially the police, off balance, guessing.

Everything was in order, ready for the next event. But that was hours away. Now, there were more pressing matters. Being a vigilante warrior cleaning up the streets might be meaningful self-employment, but it didn't pay well at all. This month's retirement check wouldn't post for another twelve days. And the budget didn't have any wiggle room. Time to get dressed and head for work. It was only part-time employment, but could be the difference between eating off the dollar menu at McDonald's or enjoying a memorable repast at Muriel's on Jackson Square. Even a vigilante warrior deserved the finer things New Orleans had to offer.

Work first. Hunting later. Justice always.

Chapter Ten: One Team. One Fight.

Sunday, February 1, 2015 – 3:17 p.m.

Jonathan winced. Sexual assault examinations. Probably the most emotionally draining of the tasks assigned to Coroners in Louisiana. Death investigations—especially murders and suicides—and mental health commitments could be tough to deal with. But the rigors of the physical examination and verbal interrogation required by the legal system seemed cruel and unusual punishment for a victim—usually female. Someone who had likely already been violated in a most intimate and personal manner.

Yet, society and law required them to be thorough. Ensuring that a perpetrator was brought to justice required proof beyond a reasonable doubt. Despite the horror of the alleged crime, due process rights of the accused must be respected. A fine balance. Sometimes they got it right. Sometimes they didn't.

Cass Melançon completed the physical examination—the most unsavory aspect of the process—last night. They hadn't learned much. The driver's license they found identified her as Joan Crawford, a twenty-one-year-old from Tupelo, Mississippi. But the actual assault remained a mystery. Their exam pointed toward a simple sexual assault. Simple? Nothing simple about an attack on personal security and sanctity. Perhaps there hadn't been penetration, but the emotional toll that likely resulted from the events in Washington Square Park was significant, deserving of all they could do to investigate and find the truth.

Thank goodness for Cass Melançon, for her supreme skills and training in such matters. And today, they had Betsy Sprance, another well-respected veteran of handling investigations in a sensitive and humane, yet decisive, manner. Complicating matters, they faced two victims—the young woman and the man leaning, lifeless, against the city's AIDS memorial. Perhaps the man had brought it on himself by attacking her. Perhaps it was something less apparent. Regardless, they had to find the truth of what happened. Justice would follow truth. Without truth, there could be no justice.

"Afternoon, Lieutenant." A uniformed NOPD officer outside the victim's room stood as the trio approached. "Good to see you again."

"Good to see you, too, Officer Friedrich," Betsy said. "Unfortunate circumstances."

"True dat," Friedrich said.

"Things calm here?" Betsy asked.

"Just the expected flow of medical staff," Friedrich said. "Nothing out of the ordinary."

"The doctors and I need to chat with the witness. So if you want to grab some coffee…or whatever…we'll watch things until you get back."

"Roger that, Lieutenant. See you in a few."

At least the room the hospital had moved the young woman to would provide a private venue. As yet identified only by the name on a most likely fake Mississippi driver's license, she lay on a hospital bed with her head turned away from the door, toward a window. An intravenous tube led from a needle in her right hand to a bag of clear liquid on a pole attached to the bed. A television in a metal wall-mount in the corner, almost at ceiling level, sat dark. The woman turned her head toward the door as the trio entered.

"Good afternoon, Miss…Crawford." Cass smiled. "Not sure if you'll remember—"

"Dr. Melançon." The young woman seemed more aware of her circumstances, her eyes focused. "From the Coroner's Office, right?"

"That's right," Cass said. "And this—"

"I remember what you did." The young woman's eyes narrowed. "You touched me…down there."

"Yes, of course, it was part of the examination."

"I didn't do anything wrong."

"Yes, of course." Cass hesitated as if searching for the right words. "Unfortunately, Ms. Crawford, the law requires—"

"Harrison."

"Beg pardon?" Cass angled her head slightly. "You're not Joan Crawford?"

"It's Harrison. Not Crawford. Harrison. Janelle Harrison."

"I see." Cass blushed.

Janelle pointed to Jonathan. "And I remember him, too."

"Jonathan Gray. I'm—"

"Coroner."

"That's right," Jonathan said.

"And who is she?"

Betsy displayed her badge. "Detective Lieutenant Sprance, NOPD."

"Finally. The cops. You going to do anything?"

"Well, Ms. Harrison." Betsy put her badge back in her jacket pocket. "That's why I'm here."

"Tam…" Janelle rolled onto her left side, toward the window. "Have you found—"

"Well," Betsy said, "about your hat—"

"Not my hat." Janelle squinted as she turned and looked directly at Betsy. "My sorority sister Tamara."

"Well," Cass said, "you never told us—"

"What's Tamara's last name?" Betsy peered at Cass and shook her head slightly, but enough to signal that *Betsy* would be asking the questions.

Jonathan looked toward Cass and shook his head slightly as well. Ms. Harrison—Janelle—had already formed a negative opinion of Cass. No use adding to a victim's trauma with questions from multiple people.

"Espy," Janelle said. "Tamara Espy."

"But you call her Tam?" Betsy said.

"Yes." Janelle's eyes reflected both affection and fear. "Tam."

Jonathan shifted to a position behind Betsy and Cass, then sat in a chair in the corner. He pulled out a notepad. He could be the scribe. Let Betsy concentrate on the interview.

"Why don't you tell us about last night?" Cass asked.

Janelle's face turned pale, and she turned her head toward the window.

After another stern look from Betsy, Cass moved closer to Jonathan. Her jaw tightened.

"That's okay, Ms. Harrison," Betsy said. "Let's not worry about that right yet."

Janelle turned back toward Betsy.

"Which sorority?" Betsy asked.

"Alpha Delta Gamma."

"At Ole Miss?"

"Yes."

Jonathan removed his iPhone from his pocket and examined the screen. "Excuse me. I just received a text." He motioned to Cass. "Dr. Melançon, can you step outside a moment? There's been a development."

"Sure." Cass appeared puzzled. "What's this—"

"Betsy." Jonathan got up from his chair. "I'll be back shortly."

Officer Friedrich hadn't yet returned. Jonathan and Cass stood in the hallway, still able to see Betsy and Janelle through a window in the door. They were talking, but it didn't look like a formal interrogation.

"What's this about?" Cass asked. "What's the development?"

"Look," Jonathan said. "I didn't get a text."

"Oh? Then why—"

"We need to clear the air."

"Clear the air?"

"Maybe I'm misreading the room, but you don't seem pleased to have Betsy Sprance involved."

Cass blushed as if she were a kid caught with her hand in the cookie jar. "Well…I've never…how could you possibly think such a thing?"

Not a denial. More of a deflection. His instincts must have been correct. "You know that we're hanging out there. Mayor Jamerson wants to avoid publicity."

"I understand you promised Superintendent Bondurant and the mayor—"

"That we'd do what we could."

"That *you* would do what *you* could."

Interesting. This was Jonathan's show now. So much for a team approach.

"I didn't agree to put my professional reputation on the line." Cass pursed her lips. "And if I can't take full advantage of my skills—"

"Got it. I only agreed to help out if we got support from the police behind the scenes."

"So they gave you a suspended police detective? What kind of bargain is that?"

"We need Betsy's help. She's one hell of an asset, suspended or not."

"Okay. Tell me what you want me to do."

"I need a full-court press from everyone in the office. We're doing this for the good of the city and the people. Maybe you can check on the test results. Contact Mitch Broussard to see what he's learned."

Cass remained silent. Her eyes reflected obedience, but not enthusiasm.

"One team, one fight...right, Cass?"

"Of course." I'll head for the admin office in City Hall. I'll check in later."

Jonathan exhaled slowly as Cass proceeded past the Nurses' Station and turned the corner leading to the elevators. *His* promise to the Superintendent? Knock on wood, he hadn't burned bridges with Cass. She was a critical asset, like Betsy. But they needed to avoid competing egos and personal histrionics. Not much he could do at this point. He reached for the door handle. Time to get back to Betsy and Janelle.

Chapter Eleven: Twins from Tupelo

Sunday, February 1, 2015 – 3:37 p.m.

"Sorry," Jonathan said. "What did I miss?"

"Not much," Betsy said. "Just some small talk about sororities."

"I see. Well, don't mind me. I'll have a seat and go back to taking notes."

"Is Dr. Melançon coming back?"

"Cass had some work to catch up on. Thought it best if she returned to the morgue."

"Got it," Betsy said. "So, Janelle, what brought you and Ms. Espy to New Orleans?"

"Frenchmen Street." Janelle spoke softly. "And parades."

"Why Frenchmen?"

"Tam's been talking about it for weeks." Janelle's voice seemed more confident, but remained barely above a whisper. "Tam said it's where New Orleans locals go to avoid the tackiness and high prices of Bourbon Street."

"I see."

"And there were a couple of parades—"

"Krewe du Vieux and krewedelusion?"

"I think so. But our faculty adviser told us to stay in the French Quarter."

"Your faculty advisor?"

"Professor Faulkner. She told us that the police could protect us better in the French Quarter."

"But Ms. Espy didn't agree?"

"Tam knew better. Frenchmen Street was the place to go."

"When did you come to New Orleans?"

"We left school Saturday morning. Got here in the early afternoon."

"And then?"

"We checked into our room. By the time we got settled, it was getting darker. So we went looking for a bar and to watch the parades."

"Which hotel?"

"The Marigny House."

Betsy looked toward Jonathan. He held up his notepad. She turned back toward Janelle.

"Where did you go?"

"We walked around for a while. It was great. I mean, there was one bar. The Spotted Cat, I think. There was a saxophone that seemed to be having a duet with a cornet from a club across the street. Weird name…d.b.a., maybe? And there were no cops hassling anyone. Just people out for a good time. There was a scraggly guy sitting next to a blue bicycle and holding a sign asking for money. No one bothered him, either. It was freedom. It seemed like *real* New Orleans."

"Did you go to the Spotted Cat?"

"No. First place we went was…I can't remember the name. But it had a laundromat in the back."

"The Bunker, maybe? Painted up like it was in Berlin during the Cold War?"

"That's it. The Bunker."

"What happened there?"

"We did shots…tequila."

"Did you see anyone there…talk to anyone?"

"There was one guy." Janelle's eyes seemed brighter, her voice louder, but still calm.

"Tell me about him."

"I went to the bathroom. He was playing video games. Real cute guy in a flannel shirt and baseball cap. And a down vest."

"I see," Betsy said.

Jonathan smiled, more like a silent snicker. Flannel shirt. Baseball cap. Down vest. That narrowed the list to maybe two-thirds of young men bar-hopping in New Orleans on a chilly Saturday night.

"He asked me if I was here for Mardi Gras. Called it Carnival. Like in Rio, only better. Said he's in a parade next week. Has a *Star Wars* theme."

"Chewbacchus?" Betsy asked.

"Sounds right. And he seemed nice enough. Told me he was pre-med. Even warned me about using the bathroom. Said it was filthy." Janelle's eyes brightened. "Said he hoped I would come back next week."

Pre-med. Wearing a flannel shirt and a down vest. Betsy and Jonathan exchanged glances.

"Told him I would think about the parade. And he's right. The bathroom *was* filthy."

"So, what happened?" Betsy asked.

"We…me and Tam…left. She didn't like the bar. Sticky floors." Janelle's eyes had lost their sparkle. "Smelled musty. And she didn't like me talking to the guy in the flannel shirt. Didn't believe he was pre-med. Said he looked creepy. Afraid he might follow us."

"I see. And after you left?"

"We watched the parades for a while. Bought drinks from a food truck. After the parades passed, wound up at the Spotted Cat."

"Great place."

"But didn't serve food. After all the alcohol and being out in the cold for the parades, we needed something to eat."

"And?"

"We walked around for a while. Maybe about ten minutes. Tam spotted another club, Jazz Harbor Bistro & Brews." Janelle returned to her unfocused stare. Her eyes closed, and her breathing slowed.

"Ms. Harrison?" Betsy said.

Janelle's eyes opened. "Sorry…And then she saw him."

"Him?"

"Tam froze. Said she saw the guy from the bar. The guy in the flannel shirt. In an alley between two buildings."

"The guy from the Bunker?"

Janelle again stared into the distance. "She said he was watching us."

"Did you see him?"

"No. But Tam was so convinced…I told her we should get inside the restaurant."

"Jazz Harbor?"

Janelle nodded.

"And?"

"It was great. Warm. A real welcome-home vibe. You could smell the cayenne and filé gumbo from the kitchen. It seemed safe."

"I see."

"Ian asked us if we wanted to eat in the restaurant or bar. And told us he could still get us into the jazz club session starting at ten-thirty."

"Ian?"

"The guy at the front desk."

"The maître d'?"

"I guess that's what you'd call him."

"What did you decide?"

"The bar. Ian told us they had the best small plates in New Orleans."

"You guys were lucky," Betsy said. "I'd think Jazz Harbor—or any other establishment on Frenchmen—would be too crowded on a parade night."

"Well…Tam and Ian…I mean they—"

"Seemed to have a connection…something special?" Betsy asked.

"Tam had that look." Janelle sighed. "She always moved too fast. And Ian…"

"I think I understand."

"I've seen that look in a guy's eyes before. There's something about Tam and men. She seems to have some magic power. I mean, I can't even talk to a guy without her criticism. But when Tam zeroes in? Nothing, and no one, had better stand in her way."

"Any other issues?

"Everything seemed fine. We ate. We drank. I had a Pimm's Cup. I'd never had one. The Alpha Delta sisters told me…" Janelle hesitated, her face flushed as if she were embarrassed. "Sorry…And Ian hovered around our table—or at least Tam—a lot. But I could see the front door and the street. No guy in the flannel shirt."

"Fake IDs?

Janelle's eyes darted to the left, as if the answer was hidden near the window.

"Don't worry. We're not here about that."

"Tam had them made."

"What name did she have on hers?"

"Bette Davis." Janelle shook her head. "They both had the same birthday."

Jonathan worked hard to avoid rolling his eyes and chuckling out loud. Joan Crawford. Bette Davis. Same birthday. The guy forging the fake IDs must have a perverse sense of humor.

"Ian didn't ask any questions?" Betsy said.

"Mumbled something about 'twins from Tupelo.' Then he winked. Said 'Happy birthday.' I think he was too interested in Tam to say anything else."

"What happened to Ms. Davis…I mean Ms. Espy?"

"We fought."

"About Ian?"

"Tam said Ian was hot. She wanted him something fierce. I asked what her mother and father might say if they found out. She went crazy. Told me to worry about what my parents might say about me."

Janelle turned her head toward the window. What was so sensitive that their parents shouldn't find out about it? Something worth exploring. Best not to press about that right now.

"Where did they go?" Betsy asked.

"To the John. Not the bathroom, though."

"The bar up on Burgundy?"

"But they didn't go together. Tam said she would think about it and might join him later…after we finished our drinks."

Janelle closed her eyes. "Why didn't we just go to the French Quarter?" Her voice was barely audible, as if she were thinking, without realizing she was saying it aloud. She opened her eyes.

"Beg pardon?" Betsy leaned toward Janelle.

"I tried to talk her out of it. She hardly knew the guy. It was nearly midnight. Professor Faulkner had warned us about the nuts who—"

"The nuts who…what?"

"Who come out after midnight." Janelle's eyes darted back and forth, as if she were having an internal dialogue, arguing with herself or with someone else. "Tam told me that she came here to have fun…told me she was going to meet Ian." Her eyes moistened. "Demanded to know if I was coming along or not."

"You didn't go?"

Janelle shook her head. "Told Tam I was going back to the room. Tried to get her to at least let me call a RideShare. But she left anyway…just like that…headed up Frenchmen, past the park across the street."

"And then?"

Janelle shuddered as if she had been hit with an electric shock. "And then I saw him."

"Who?"

"The street lighting…it was just a flash…movement in my peripheral vision…turning the corner…behind Tam."

"Could you see who—"

"The guy from The Bunker…flannel shirt…down vest…baseball hat."

"Could you see his face?"

"No. But it was him. I'm sure of it."

"What did you do?"

"Called out to Tam and then ran after her. But I couldn't run very fast. The tequila and Pimm's Cups. And the food. I lost sight of Tam. I stopped to catch my breath. And to keep from throwing up."

"Okay."

"Then I heard a muffled noise from the park. I walked across Frenchmen Street. It was dark. The streetlights didn't add much…light…just shadows through the trees. The sign said the park was closed. But the chain on the gate was broken."

"So you went into the park?"

"I had to. If Tam was in trouble…she would have done it for me."

Jonathan bit his lip to keep from commenting. Doubtful. Tam, the friend who had left her at the restaurant to meet a guy she hardly knew at a bar? No way would she have risked herself by going into a park after midnight, especially not knowing what was inside.

"And?"

"I didn't see it coming. I heard a noise. Leaves rustling. Or a twig breaking. Something, or someone, hit me on the side of my head, and things turned black. I woke up, and this guy was over me."

"Was it the man in the flannel shirt?" Betsy asked.

"I don't know…" Janelle closed her eyes. "I was crying. I couldn't see clearly…" A single tear plowed a rivulet down her cheek. "I didn't have on any pants or underwear…he had a knife…" Janelle wept openly, as if an emotional dam had burst. Her lips and cheeks quivered, and her breath came in short bursts.

"That's okay." Betsy handed her a box of tissues from the bedside stand. "We can stop."

"No." Janelle wiped her cheeks, then blew her nose. "I need to get through this." Her voice modulated, sounding fearful but determined. "He put the knife down and started to…" She struggled to breathe through mucus-filled nostrils, then blew her nose again. "He got on his knees and touched my legs." Janelle inhaled, held her breath for a couple of beats, then exhaled a cleansing breath. "Everything seemed to happen at once and in slow motion at the same time…I pushed him away and grabbed for the blade…then warm wetness…smelled salty, like sea water…and metallic…was all over me. And then it's like he was a puppet on a string and someone yanked him away. He flailed around, in a blur…like one of those Hindu gods with multiple arms and two heads. He staggered back from me."

Betsy's eyes moistened—an uncharacteristic reaction from a normally dispassionate investigator. "Holy—"

"The knife…everything happened so fast…I fainted. I don't know how…I must have…the knife."

Betsy put her hand on Janelle's right arm. "That's okay, Ms. Harrison…Janelle…you've given us a lot of useful information. You should rest. Officer Friedrich will be just outside to make sure you're safe."

A single tear dribbled down Janelle's cheek. "Tam…please find Tam…my Tam…" Her words trailed off as she turned her head toward the window.

Chapter Twelve: French Truck

Sunday, February 1, 2015 – 4:27 p.m.

"That was…intense." Jonathan placed a disposable coffee cup on the small table in front of Betsy. Seemed odd that they were the only two patrons in Tulane Hospital's cafeteria on a Sunday afternoon. "What Ms. Harrison went through is—"

"Thanks for the joe. French Truck's becoming one of my favorites. Surprised they offer it here." Betsy picked up her cup and blew on the steaming contents. "And intense sure as hell is an accurate description."

"What, the coffee?"

"No. The interview."

"Right…the interview." Jonathan yawned.

"So, where do we go from here?" Betsy asked.

"There's so much to do. Not sure where to start."

"How about the autopsy?" Betsy sipped her coffee. "Did you learn anything new after I left to chat with the Claiborne Boys?"

"A couple of things come to mind." Jonathan sipped his coffee. "Man, that's good."

"And other than the coffee being good?"

"Right. Sorry." Jonathan yawned. "Guess my mind's wandering…about the weapons."

"What about them?"

Jonathan described the knives and his discussions with Susan Miller about their probable connections and uses—as instruments of death and body carving.

"Soup to nuts," Betsy said. "Never ceases to amaze me how creative our citizens can be…but I don't recall anyone ever using a rigging knife like that."

"And in a town so involved with commercial shipping, you'd think there'd be more, wouldn't you?"

"Maybe there's a clue in the emblem on the handles," Betsy said. "I'll see if Mitch can check with the local maritime unions…under the radar."

"Good thought," Jonathan said. "But, back to the autopsy, the other thing that stood out was the guy's right knee."

"Oh?"

"Medical term's comminuted fracture of the patella. Looks like someone took a hammer to a fine piece of china."

"Ms. Crawford…Harrison…Janelle…talked about a struggle. You know, the two-headed Hindu god thing. Could that explain how his knee got smashed?"

"Maybe," Jonathan said. "Susan Miller thought it could have happened if he had banged into the metal and glass orbs on the AIDS memorial."

"But she wasn't entirely convinced?"

"Right. And neither am I. Not much else about this case has a simple explanation, so why should the kneecap be different?"

"Then there's the mysterious Tam," Betsy said. "And her Bette Davis eyes."

"Listen." Jonathan turned his head toward Betsy. "I wonder if we can have Mitch track down Tamara…and Ian."

"Damn. I should have thought of that first thing when Janelle mentioned them. Guess I'm starting to get overloaded."

"I know the feeling."

"Sorry, Doc, but did I detect a hint of recognition when Ms. Harrison talked about the pre-med guy in the flannel shirt?"

"You mean did I think about Jimmy Caplan?"

"Well, the description fits. You know Jimmy's penchant for flannel shirts."

"Therapy from his days as a Navy Corpsman." Jonathan shook his head.

"Something about making up for his days in battle dress utilities. Sure, I thought about him."

"Probably nothing," Betsy said. "Flannel shirt and ball cap. Could be gazillions of guys in this neck of the woods, especially this time of year."

"Still, seems an odd coincidence. He said he was going to check out last night's parades. Maybe I'll talk to the on-duty pathologist. Jimmy's scheduled for the eight o'clock shift tonight. Seems like he'd remember talking to someone like Janelle."

"Sounds like a plan. Can't hurt to check. And I'll see where Mitch is with locating any surveillance footage. We seem to be chasing a lot of loose ends."

"And speaking of loose ends." Jonathan removed two copies of the message found under the dead man's left hand. He slid one copy across the table to Betsy and kept one. He held up his copy. "There's this."

"This is the same one you showed me in the conference room—before Dr. Melançon showed up, right?"

"Affirmative. Figured you might like a closer look."

Betsy studied the document. "Still might as well be Greek, Doc, this makes absolutely no sense."

"Just like the chest carving and graffiti on the streetcars."

"Actually, looks more like Russian to me." Betsy placed her pointer finger on the document and read the first part of the cipher aloud. "A, I, F, I, I, I, E, I, I, I, A, I, A, D, I, I, A, I, G, I, I." She angled her head to the left and then to the right as if reading the cipher from a different point of view might make a difference. "And those symbols…plus-signs, hearts, diamonds, spades, and clubs…I wonder—"

"Don't forget the musical notes."

"Right. The musical notes."

"I guess that's why they call it a cipher."

"Don't go there, Doc. I've been having flashbacks about the Sweeper's last two visits…and his previous ciphers. And the lack of sleep hasn't helped."

"Fair enough," Jonathan said. "But there's got to be some good info in it…if only we could…any word from Mitch on a translation?"

"Just that the NOPD tech support person assigned to this type of thing is out on paternity leave. And he won't be back until—"

"Jesus. There's only one person in the entire NOPD who can figure it out?"

"I've gained some expertise," Betsy said. "But this one's like nothing I've seen."

"How did you solve the last one?"

"Both times before, we used Dr. Miller's husband. Teaches in the Economics Department at Tulane. And he's some kind of cryptology wiz."

"Boris?" Jonathan's forehead wrinkled. "Interesting."

"Why do you call him that? His name is—"

"Boris Spassky. Chess Master. Susan's husband always beats me at chess, so I call him Boris."

Betsy rolled her eyes. "Got it."

"Why don't we try him this time?"

"Didn't you say that Mayor Jamerson wanted to keep this one close to the vest?"

"I did," Jonathan said. "But this is a special situation."

"Maybe it's time to pay a visit to His Honor the Mayor. Get him on board. He's got to get past that indictment thing sooner than later."

"Good idea...but not today." Jonathan yawned. "We'll talk about it tomorrow." He yawned again. "Sorry...I have a quick stop, then I'm headed home. I need some sleep."

"Lucky you." Betsy inhaled, puffed out her cheeks, and exhaled slowly. "Remember those additional shifts at Harrah's I told you about?"

"I do."

Betsy closed her eyes. "Well, tonight's one of them."

Chapter Thirteen: Maison Gris

Sunday, February 1, 2015 – 7:32 p.m.

Even on the best of days, navigating the Quarter's maze of one-way avenues and streets—often blocked to create pedestrian malls—presented a challenge. And over the past few months, detours around repairs to the antiquated water and sewer system transformed each trip via car into an adventure. Worse, the GPS satellite must be taking a vacation day, because Google Maps didn't track some of the detours. Regardless, by memory of the traffic patterns, some guesswork, and a bit of luck, Jonathan wound up on Bienville, headed away from the river. The move put him on his final approach to *Maison Gris*, his nickname for their home, which occupied two floors above the street-level shops below.

Jonathan turned into the internal courtyard of their building, pushed a button in his car, and lowered the metal door covering the entryway. He stepped out of his vehicle and proceeded up the stairway leading from the courtyard and entered their foyer. Noise from the family room signaled that Emma must be watching TV.

"Hey." Jonathan entered the family room, greeted by televised images of the Budweiser Clydesdales pulling a wagon filled with beer barrels. He cursed under his breath. "Is that the—"

"Must be something really big going on for you to forget about the Super Bowl." Emma frowned.

"Jesus, Fen." Jonathan rolled his eyes. "Got so busy. I forgot all about—"

"And missing a visit with Beatrice? Thought maybe you'd been sucked into a giant wormhole."

"Nothing so dramatic." Jonathan yawned. "But I finally had a chance to drop by and see Beatrice. Talked Arthur into letting me slide in as he was about to close up."

"Arthur's such a sweet man."

"And he asked me to give you a big smile."

Emma smiled. Any lingering ill feelings over his tardiness or not being along on her visit to Beatrice at the mausoleum seemed to have dissipated. "What else is going on?"

"It looks like the Mardi Gras Sweeper has returned."

"But I thought…didn't Betsy Sprance kill the Sweeper two years ago?"

"That's what she thought, too."

"How could the Sweeper survive a fall from the Crescent City Connection? I mean, that's over one hundred and fifty feet…and the river must have been freezing."

"Beats me." Jonathan yawned. "Betsy was beside herself in disbelief."

"Maybe it's not the Sweeper."

"Doubtful. Too many similarities at this point."

"Alpha and Omega?"

"Apparently carved while the guy was still alive."

"Jesus, Mary, and Joseph."

Jonathan removed a folder from his briefcase. "Close hold at this point." He handed the folder to Emma. "He apparently left us a manifesto in a scrambled message."

Emma looked at the cipher, then returned the folder to Jonathan. "So what are you doing here? Shouldn't you be investigating?"

"Right now, we think he won't strike until this weekend's parades. So we have a couple of days. And I need to sleep. I'm exhausted."

"I'll bet. You want something to eat before?"

"Not that hungry. Although…some mirliton pie might hit the spot. Don't suppose we have any leftovers?"

"Let me see what I can do."

"Thanks." Jonathan sat on the couch and placed his folder with the cipher on the adjacent end table. Then, he removed his sidearm and put it in the table's single drawer.

"Oh, I almost forgot. Monsignor Rossignol pays his respects. Wants to know if you'll be by for confession. Said he'd be available same time, same place as before." She cleared her throat. "There something you're not telling me?"

"Inside joke. Dan and I…" Jonathan yawned "…listen I'll tell you while I eat. In the meantime, I'll just rest my eyes and listen to the game until you get back."

Chapter Fourteen: St. Louis Number One

Monday, February 2, 2015 – 2:17 a.m.

New Orleans Police Department cruiser Four-One-Two traveled along South Rampart Street toward Canal. Corporal Grace Jividen—riding shotgun—stared out the window, thankful to be inside, warm and toasty, on yet another miserable mid-winter night. She turned to the driver—her partner, rookie officer Silas Michaud. A pale green patchwork of light cast by the cruiser's electronic displays illuminated his face. Combined with his high-and-tight haircut, he looked like a cartoon Martian. Or maybe he was more like one of those scaly, absinthe-hued anti-heroes in an *Avengers* comic book. Whatever.

"Kinda boring tonight, isn't it, Corporal?" Michaud said.

"Thank your lucky stars for that," Jividen said. "Boring's good."

"And it beats the hell out of being on parade duty."

"What, you don't like standing around, freezing your ass off, and watching drunks catch beads?" Jividen smiled. "Isn't that why you joined the force?"

"A hundred percent." Michaud chuckled. "That and for the aroma of body odor, vomit, wet hair, and ganja wafting from the crowd."

"Perks of the job." At least Michaud had a sense of humor. "Doesn't get better than—"

The radio crackled. Jividen cursed under her breath. "So much for boring."

"Report of screams coming from St. Louis Cemetery Number One. Probable assault. Nearest unit, respond and investigate. Code One."

Jividen picked up the handset. "Unit Four-One-Two, Dispatch. Just crossed Canal on North Rampart, approaching Iberville. ETA on scene…one minute."

Jividen shook her head. "What the hell is it about this city and cemeteries after dark?" She replaced the handset. "All right, rookie. You know what to do."

"Affirmative," Michaud said, his tone officious and precise. "Police Regulation Three-One-Six Point Two. Code One. Routine response. Proceed directly to the scene, obeying all traffic laws. Lights. No siren."

Jividen shook her head and grinned. "Straight As at the academy. Right?"

"Mostly."

"Left on Bienville, then right on Basin." Jividen activated the flashing blue lights mounted on the roof and in the grille. "Main gate's on Basin."

The cruiser sped forward, past Bienville Street.

"What the hell, Michaud?"

"Basin has a neutral ground separating one-way travel lanes. Can't get to the gate directly. We need to go up to St. Louis and double back."

"Jesus, Michaud, can't you just this once—"

"Got to obey all traffic rules."

Jividen gritted her teeth. Goddamn police academy. Goddamn regulations. Goddamn rookie police officers from Mars. Someone's life might be at stake.

The cemetery's dusty-white walls came into view across the broad neutral ground and the other travel lanes as the cruiser sped along North Rampart toward St. Louis Street. Sparse street lighting cast oddly shaped shadows on the cemetery. Eerie. Damn eerie.

Jividen grabbed the handle on the door frame when Michaud turned onto St. Louis, increased speed, and almost immediately fishtailed left onto Basin Street. Butterflies tickled her stomach. The sensation increased as the cruiser completed its turn and sped up. "Slow down, Michaud, you trying to kill us?"

"Just trying to get there as fast as…what's that?"

A figure emerged from the cemetery, running toward the cruiser. A woman—hair disheveled, face bloodied—waved her arms as she ran. Jividen jumped slightly at a loud thud when something—or someone—collided with the car's right-rear quarter-panel.

"Shit." Michaud slammed on the brakes. The cruiser screeched to a stop.

"What the hell, Michaud?" Jividen opened her door. "Let's go…and remember to switch on your body-worn camera this time."

The woman appeared dazed, but able to stand. Blood dripped onto her blouse, which lay open, exposing her bare breasts.

"Officer Jividen, NOPD, Miss." Jividen handed the woman a blue bandana. "Here. Press this against your mouth and nose. Can you tell me what—"

"He's killing him." The woman's breath came in short bursts, apparently hampered by blood draining into her mouth. "He's got…a knife."

"Who?" Jividen moved closer to the woman. "Where?"

The woman's arm and hand shook as she pointed toward the cemetery.

Jividen spoke into the radio handset clipped to her tactical vest. "Ongoing assault in St. Louis Cemetery Number One. Officers in pursuit. Send backup. Witness with visible injuries to the face. Losing blood. Require immediate EMT presence." She turned to the woman. "Can you show us?"

The woman angled toward the open cemetery gate. Jividen and Michaud followed.

The woman stopped just inside the gate. "Down that row." She pointed to her left. "I'm not going any further."

"Understood," Jividen said. "Will you be all right if we leave you here? Ambulance is on the way."

The woman nodded. Tears flowed down her cheeks. But the bleeding appeared to have stopped.

"Okay, Michaud," Jividen said. "Let's go. You take the first row. I'll go one up and take that one."

"Shouldn't someone stay with her?"

"Goddammit, Michaud, don't argue."

"Got it." Michaud unholstered his sidearm.

"Good," Jividen said. "I'll give you a nod when I'm in place."

Gravel crunched underneath Jividen's shoes as she proceeded along a narrow path between two rows of mausoleums and above-ground crypts. A small flashlight sent light beams into the shadows. Her nose crinkled at the musty odor, no doubt from mildew and decay surrounding her.

"Corporal." Michaud's voice cracked with nervous energy. "Over here."

Jividen squeezed between crypts, moving toward Michaud's voice. Damn, what a scene. Michaud stood over a male body lying face down on the ground, a pool of blood under his midsection. The man's pants had fallen about midway down his thighs, exposing his buttocks. Michaud placed his hands on his knees, bent over, and breathed rapidly as if he were about to hyperventilate.

"First bloody crime scene?"

Michaud stood, inhaled deeply, and exhaled a cleansing breath. "First fresh one, anyway."

"Well, it doesn't get better," Jividen said. "No matter how many you see. You just need to—"

"What in God's name?" Michaud pointed toward the cemetery wall to their left.

A figure clad in black, face covered by a ski mask, crouched on top of the wall—silhouetted against the glow of a distant street lamp. The figure dropped something—perhaps a duffel bag—over the wall, made a gesture with their middle finger, and jumped into the darkness.

"That's on the Basin Street side." Jividen holstered her weapon. "Stay here. I'll go after him." She backed away toward the wall, still facing Michaud, then stopped. "Check to see if this guy's still alive."

"Got it." Michaud knelt next to the body.

Jividen turned, moved two more steps, then swiveled back toward Michaud. "But whatever you do, don't flip him—"

A bright flash and loud bang occurred so close together that it was hard to distinguish which happened first.

Jividen raised her arms and hands, palms outward, and covered her face. More from the surprise and suddenness of the motion than from the strength of the explosion, Jividen lost her balance. She staggered back and tripped on a chiseled headstone. As she fell, her head scraped against the corner of a marble mausoleum. She lay on the ground and touched her face and scalp. Thick liquid oozed onto her fingers. Probably blood. But not much. Good. Just a scratch.

She rose on her left elbow and looked toward where she'd last seen Michaud. Nothing but darkness. Her eyes and temples throbbed. Must have been blinded by the flash. Hopefully, only temporary. She rolled back onto the ground. Her ears rang. Sounds echoed. Could those noises be sirens? Coming closer now. Thank God.

"Michaud." Jividen's lungs ached as she spoke. The air smelled burned as if lightning had struck one of the graves. "Michaud, you okay?" Jividen coughed, then moistened her lips with her tongue. "Hold on…Michaud… hold on…cavalry's almost here."

Chapter Fifteen: In the Darkness

Monday, February 2, 2015 – 2:47 a.m.

Hidden from view by a dense thicket of bushes, Stryker slithered out of a black bodysuit and placed it in a plastic trash bag. Wearing an extra layer of clothing—uncomfortable but necessary when engaged in…well…such messy activities. Stryker dropped a pair of blood-covered latex gloves into the bag, closed it, and laid the bag on the ground. Disposal would be easy enough, but that would come later.

Stryker crouched lower as emergency vehicles, their sirens wailing and warning lights flashing, converged on St. Louis Cemetery Number One. The cops must have radioed for assistance before the device detonated. Otherwise, it would have taken them much longer to respond. Just seconds earlier and, no doubt, the police and EMTs would have seen a figure dressed in black, running along Rampart Street away from the cemetery. A close call, but worth the risk. Maybe they'd take the Sweeper's return more seriously now.

Operational objectives accomplished—mostly. The smaller device had performed well. Necessity truly was the mother of invention. Unfortunately, that panicky bitch running out of the cemetery into the arms of the cops meant that there was only time enough to leave the next challenge message, carve Alpha and Omega into the dirtbag's forehead, and set the booby trap. No warning etched in the chest. Maybe that wasn't critical. Perfect can't be the enemy of the good.

Best to remain hidden, observe events from this vantage point—at least for the time being. No doubt, police would pounce on anyone wandering the streets this time of the morning. No use giving them an excuse for a stop-and-frisk. As the saying goes, "Time to fight and run away. Live to fight another day." Hunker down, wait it out, then head home undetected.

Undetected. So many years associated with special forces—so-called snake-eaters—had served their purpose. Survival, evasion, resistance, escape—techniques burned into a soldier's psyche through training and experience. Blending into the surroundings proved especially helpful. Absent a lucky break or misstep on Stryker's part, NOPD wouldn't know they were being surveilled from just a few yards away.

Tonight turned out to be an unplanned quiz. An opportunity to improvise, adapt, overcome. The real test would come soon enough. For now, sit quietly and absorb everything. Learn more about how NOPD responds and investigates. Think about the successes and the setbacks. Confirm that the explosion hadn't caused any serious injuries. Few things would tarnish the righteousness of the ultimate mission more than being tagged as a cop killer.

Stryker stifled a yawn. A few hours' sleep, and maybe another trip to chat with the priest, then back at it. Final justice was just around the corner. Time was running out—for the prey.

Chapter Sixteen: Hurricane Max

Monday, February 2, 2015 – 5:37 a.m.

Claudine Guiteau, Mayor Max Jamerson's Executive Assistant, had a way about her. Always calm in the midst of chaos. No doubt, she'd been roused in the middle of the night by a phone call demanding that she get dressed, rush to the office, and coordinate this zero-dark-thirty Come-to-Jesus session with Max. Most people would be disheveled, harried, and confused. Not Claudine. There she was. Nattily dressed. Makeup applied perfectly. Not a hair out of place. Max didn't deserve someone of Claudine's efficiency and elegance.

She jolted ever so slightly when the phone console on her desk buzzed. She picked up the handset. "Yes, sir." She looked toward Jonathan, who sat in a straight-backed chair—obviously not designed for comfort—located between Betsy Sprance and Polly Bondurant.

What a sad trio they were, especially in comparison to Claudine. Polly Bondurant's bloodshot eyes hinted at a severe lack of sleep and more than one post-midnight shot of bourbon. Fortunately, she must have had her uniform pressed and laid out—ready to go for the next day—when Claudine contacted her. So, at least she could put on a professional appearance. And poor Betsy, dressed in her work attire from Harrah's, nodded off occasionally. No rest for the weary.

Thank goodness Jonathan had grabbed a few hours of shuteye, albeit on the living room couch at *Maison Gris*. A quick shower, a change of clothes, then a note to Emma—dozing in an armchair next to the couch—and he was out the door. Still exhausted and in need of caffeine, but at least feeling clean, semi-human.

Claudine returned the phone receiver to its cradle. "Mayor Jamerson will see you now."

The trio stood.

"Excuse me, Detective Sprance." Claudine cleared her throat. "Mayor Jamerson asked for Dr. Gray and Superintendent Bondurant."

"But," Jonathan said, "Lieutenant Sprance is a critical part of the team."

"Yes, Doctor...I understand." Claudine looked down at her desk, then back toward Jonathan. "Mayor Jamerson was quite specific. You and the Superintendent only."

"Polly," Jonathan said, "this is—"

"Not a battle I want to fight right now." Polly turned toward Betsy. "Lieutenant Sprance. Have a seat. We'll debrief you once we're done."

Betsy sat down. She leaned toward a coffee table and picked up a copy of Arthur Hardy's *2015 Mardi Gras Guide*. "No worries." She smiled. "I need to catch up on my reading, anyway. You two have fun."

Polly Bondurant's eyes narrowed. "Detective—"

"Not a battle you want to fight right now, Polly. Let's just get this over with." He cleared his throat. "All right, Claudine, lead us to the lion's den."

"Yes, of course." She raised her arm and gestured toward a door adjacent to a brass plaque announcing:

T. Maximillian Jamerson

Mayor

"This way."

The best description for the time leading up to a potential confrontation with the city's mercurial chief executive was "the calm before the storm." Hackneyed, but true. Fortunately, the storied Hurricane Max couldn't inflict any physical damage. Laws against assault and battery—and his political survival—wouldn't allow it. But emotional impact? Max could be anywhere from a light breeze to a Category Five. When faced with an actual hurricane, one could flee or batten down the hatches. But there was no place to hide in a face-to-face with Max Jamerson.

Claudine opened the door to the mayor's office, stood aside, and allowed Jonathan, followed closely by Polly Bondurant, to enter. Max sat behind a massive mahogany desk. His eyes shifted from some papers on his desk toward his visitors as if they were unwelcome intruders. Except for his eyes, Max remained as stationary as a statue.

"Dr. Gray and Superintendent Bondurant are here, Mr. Mayor…would you like me to transcribe your meeting?"

Polly Bondurant's stoic countenance revealed no hint of fear. But she had to be feeling the pressure. Little progress in the Sweeper investigation. Forced to bring Betsy Sprance out of purgatory to assist. And now another murder, this one accompanied by an explosive device that wounded two police officers. So, Polly was in the hot seat. Perhaps more accurately, she was on the front burner of a gas stove with Max about to turn up the flame.

To be sure, Jonathan would share the pain, despite having volunteered to help deal with tracking down the Sweeper. No doubt, Max would see to it that no good deed went unpunished.

Max looked up from the documents on his desk. "Thank you, Claudine." He shook his head and smiled. "That won't be necessary." His body appeared more animated, no longer immobile. "Please close the door as you leave."

As if the closing door had toggled an off-switch, Max's face shifted from friendly to hostile. His smile disappeared, and his jaw tightened noticeably. He closed his eyes, thrummed the desk with the fingers of his right hand, and balled his left hand into a fist. Max took several deep breaths—as if trying to control his internal emotions—then opened his eyes. Both hands relaxed.

"Good morning, Mr. Mayor," Polly said. "You wanted to see—?"

"You know." Jamerson held up his right hand, palm outward.

Polly stopped talking and pursed her lips.

"I'm doing my best to…" He looked to his left as if searching for something, then returned his gaze to Jonathan and Polly. "To hold my tongue…to keep from saying something…unkind or hurtful. You know, count to ten and all that." He shook his head, and his lips quivered. "Well, I've counted to ten a dozen times. And I'm still ready to cuss a blue streak, no matter whose feelings it hurts."

"Mr. Mayor." Polly's voice quivered. "I'm not sure what—"

"Put a sock in it, Polly."

Jonathan sat down in one of the two chairs facing Jamerson's desk.

Jamerson's jaw tightened. "I didn't say you could sit down."

"I didn't ask permission, Max," Jonathan said. "Simple courtesy dictates that you should have offered…I figured you must have forgotten."

"I'm the duly elected Mayor of the City of New Orleans." Jamerson's face flushed. "How dare you—"

"And I'm the duly elected Coroner of Orleans Parish." Jonathan's heart pounded. Where the hell did that come from? Had he just accused the mayor—to his face—of being a jerk for not inviting them to sit? No backing down, though. Only one way to deal with a bully, even a duly elected one. "Superintendent Bondurant might work for you, but I don't."

Jamerson leaned back and crossed his arms. "Well, I never—"

"So, are you going to offer the Superintendent a seat?"

Jamerson's jaw clenched as he stared at Polly. He shifted his eyes toward the second chair in front of his desk, a couple of feet away from Jonathan.

Polly didn't say anything. She occupied the chair, but sat ramrod straight, almost at attention.

"So, Mr. Mayor," Jonathan said. "How can Superintendent Bondurant and I be of service?"

"First, you can tell me why I shouldn't fire both of you right here on the spot." Jamerson leaned forward, his arms no longer crossed. "Your investigation seems—"

"You mean the investigation that I agreed to work in tandem with NOPD at your request?"

"Well—"

"The investigation into the potential return of the Mardi Gras Sweeper—"

"I don't think—"

"The investigation you don't want to risk the public learning about because they might panic?"

"What's your point, doctor?"

"The point is that Polly—the Superintendent—and I are moving Heaven and Earth to bring this miscreant to justice under the restrictive conditions you've set."

"So, how do you explain this latest development?"

"You mean another murder by a serial killer, Max?" Jonathan asked.

"Right," Max said. "Someone else butchered with the same type of knife used at Washington Square Park…with Alpha and Omega cut into their forehead." Max looked toward Polly and then back at Jonathan. "That, and a hand grenade rigged to go off when the body got moved."

"A non-lethal flash-bang, to be more accurate." Polly seemed tenuous. "Designed to disorient but not kill." Her eyes darted back and forth as if she had just realized that maybe she should have remained silent. "I mean…we use them all the time for breaching entries and crowd control."

"Really, Polly? A non-lethal hand grenade?" Jamerson glared at her. "You think the *Times-Pic* will make that distinction?"

"We need to be accurate."

"Accurate? Jesus Polly, whose side are you on?"

"Come on, Max," Jonathan said. "Be reasonable. You know we're dealing with someone operating on a different level of evil. You can't expect—"

"Expect what, doctor? That the two of you pull your thumbs out of your backsides and do something?"

"Max, I've thrown the assets of the Coroner's office behind this investigation. That's something I'm not required—"

"You're not required to what? Figure out who's murdering the inhabitants of this city because you're only a volunteer? Well, doctor, in for a penny in for a pound. Don't try to back out now. The voters won't forget."

"There's another three years left in Robby's term, Max. I'm not concerned about an election campaign."

"Yes, of course not, doctor," Jamerson said. "You always left that to others. Running for office. That was Robby O'Malley's worry, not yours."

"So, Mr. Mayor." Polly sounded more confident, but still not assertive. "Is there something specific you'd like us to do?"

"Something. Anything. How about the so-called manifesto the Sweeper left you?"

"About that," Polly said. "Our cryptologist is on paternity leave. So, we haven't—"

"Paternity leave?" Max looked at Jonathan, then turned again to Polly. "Paternity leave? What the hell's this city coming to? And I don't give a flying leap about your excuses."

"Well." Jonathan cleared his throat. "We'd like to use an expert at Tulane."

"No. Effing. Way." Max shook his head. "I told Polly that this needs to stay in the family. Under no circumstances will I allow you to involve others."

"Okay," Jonathan said. "But if we can't break the cipher, we probably can't—"

"Doctor." Max closed his eyes as he inhaled, then exhaled a deep breath. He opened his eyes and turned his head toward Jonathan. "My suggestion is that you…the Superintendent…and that so-called detective you have waiting in the anteroom…hire a brass band and second-line your asses to wherever the hell the analyst is changing diapers and watching his wife breastfeed. Then, stay there until you have a goddamn solution." He shook his head and exhaled loudly. "Paternity leave."

"You know, Max," Jonathan said. "I'm not sure—"

"And *now* would be a good time to start."

Chapter Seventeen: Breakfast with Daisy

Monday, February 2, 2015 – 7:17 a.m.

"Too bad Polly didn't want to join us." Betsy wiped egg yolk off her cheek. "Nothing better than one of Daisy's Benedicts."

"There's something magic about Daisy Dukes, that's for sure." Jonathan sipped coffee. "But Polly's probably mainlining antacids after our tete-a-tete with Max."

"Sounded like you two were having fun with His Honor." Betsy rolled her eyes.

"You could hear?"

"Not everything." Betsy sipped coffee. "But Max seemed *very* animated."

"Animated's one word."

"What's with the brass band?" Betsy ate another forkful of her Crabcake Benedict.

"I don't want to say too much, here." Jonathan leaned toward Betsy and lowered his voice almost to a whisper. "But Max didn't seem pleased to learn that we haven't broken the cipher yet."

"Yeah, well—"

"And he couldn't understand…" Jonathan stopped talking as the metallic screeching and electric hum-and-pop of a streetcar traveling along St. Charles Avenue made it impossible to whisper. He lifted his fork, which held a piece of his half-eaten alligator sausage omelet, stared at it, then returned the morsel to his plate, uneaten. Maybe Polly had the right idea.

Some antacid would hit the spot right now. The noise outside subsided. "He really couldn't understand why we didn't anticipate last night's attack in St. Louis Number One."

"I suppose Max had a crystal ball and knew all about it in advance."

"Something like that. But I reminded him that we're dealing with someone who's unpredictable and working according to his own plan and schedule."

"Right on, Doc," Betsy said. "Thanks for standing up for us. I wonder why Max is being such a peckerwood. Is it just because of me being there?"

"I'm sure your involvement in the indictment was part of it. And I'm not sure Max cares much for me, either."

"Soup to nuts, Doc. We've got a serial killer to track down, and Max still holds a grudge?"

"Yeah, well…" Best not to re-litigate the accusations about Max from weeks ago that led to his indictment. Fair or foul, the indictment had gone away, evaporated somewhere between the local U.S. Attorney's office and the politicos in Washington. Whether Max was angry at Betsy or Jonathan or life in general didn't matter. Catching the Sweeper needed to take precedence. "At least Max didn't seem to know about the witness."

"The woman who ran away from the scene?"

"Affirmative."

"Probably a hooker who didn't want to be caught up in a murder," Betsy said. "Another unpredictable event…I'll bet there's something on the officers' body-worn cameras…maybe we can locate her before Max finds out."

"But still." Jonathan stared at his plate, then looked at Betsy. "I think we… or at least I…became complacent. I assumed we had a few more days…at least until the next parades on Friday…to figure something out." He stroked his cheek. "Maybe if I hadn't gone home—"

"Don't do that to yourself," Betsy said. "You needed to sleep, and I needed to work my shift at Harrah's. Stuff happens."

"Maybe, but still…"

Betsy pointed toward a bowl on Jonathan's breakfast plate. "Doc, you going to eat your grits?"

Jonathan placed the bowl on the table and slid it toward Betsy.

"Thanks." Betsy smiled. "No use letting food go to waste."

"I guess I'm not very hungry right now."

"Understandable." Betsy scooped a spoonful of grits. "But you need to keep up your strength. I suspect we'll be going pretty hard at it from here on out...until we catch this guy."

"Good advice." Jonathan sipped his coffee. "Maybe I'll grab a po' boy later."

Betsy scooped another spoonful of grits. "So, where do we go from here?"

The only other patrons in the restaurant, a pair of young women dressed in matching red t-shirts with a Dr. Seuss-themed rip-off, discussed their bill with the server. "Drunk One" signed a credit card slip. "Drunk Two" smiled and twirled her fingers through her purple hair. Probably tourists. They stood and walked past Jonathan and Betsy toward the door.

Jonathan leaned forward and kept his voice low. "I told Dr. Melançon that we needed a full court press because—"

"Because she was being a pain in the ass at Janelle's interview?"

"That's a bit harsh, don't you think?" Jonathan looked up to his right as if trying to pick the correct words out of the air. "She just felt that we were duplicating our efforts."

"No use having two people asking questions, right?"

"Something like that." No use telling Betsy that he'd asked Cass to leave and find something to do. "There were other things she could have been doing to help the cause."

"We *are* stretched pretty thin with the restrictions Polly and the mayor have put on us."

"Right."

"So, next steps?" Betsy sipped her coffee.

"Long pole in the tent seems to be the cipher. The Sweeper's telling us something, but what?"

"Especially after last night's *soirée* and a new note."

"Another twist," Jonathan said. "No chest carving. Only one murder weapon—another sailor's rigging knife. Same crossed emblem as on the first one. I wonder how our friend etched the Alpha and Omega in the forehead." He crossed his arms, then stroked his chin and cheek with his left hand. "And use of an explosive device ratchets up the stakes…we can't wait for Friday, either. Clock's ticking."

"Thank God no one sustained permanent injuries." Betsy yawned. "You want me to check with Dr. Miller's husband about the cipher?"

"No." Jonathan shook his head. "I'll drop by the morgue later and check in with Cass Melançon. She was supposed to run some test results to ground…not sure if Susan Miller's working autopsies or not today. But I'll contact her and see if Boris is available to look at the cipher."

"Makes sense." Betsy yawned.

"And who knows. Maybe the Sweeper did us a favor last night."

"How's that?"

"No way to hide that someone boobytrapped a dead body."

"Won't be long before the buzz is out among the patrol officers… someone's targeting police."

"Exactly." Jonathan sipped coffee. "So, we can put out the word that anyone coming across a corpse needs to contact us before turning the body over. We can leverage additional police assets without mentioning the Sweeper."

"Sounds like a plan." Betsy stifled a yawn. "And your friend the mayor will be happy that we're keeping his little secret."

"No doubt," Jonathan said. "As for you…it's your turn for some shuteye."

"Look, Doc, I'll be fine. I'm used to it."

"Wrong answer." Jonathan shook his head. "A respected source told me that we'll probably be hitting it pretty hard from here on out." He grinned. "So we need you well rested." He pointed at her blue blazer. "And not dressed like a casino's house detective."

"Well." Betsy's face reddened. "You got me there."

"Maybe after you grab some Zs—and change clothes—you can review the previous Sweeper files. Go over the similarities…and differences…again. See if other jurisdictions have reported killings using a rigging knife. That kind of thing."

"Roger that. I'll give you a call this afternoon to let you know what I've learned."

"Great."

"So." Betsy yawned. "Sorry…you off to the morgue now?"

"No. St. Louis Cathedral."

"Oh?"

"Time to find out if confession really is good for the soul."

Chapter Eighteen: Forgive You Father…

Monday, February 2, 2015 – 8:34 a.m.

Jonathan hastened along Chartres Street toward Jackson Square and his destination—the triple-spired Cathedral-Basilica of St. Louis, King of France. He turned up the collar of his jacket against a brisk breeze coming off the river. Clouds moving up from the Gulf signaled that precipitation would likely arrive in the early afternoon. After the past couple of weeks—drier than usual for this time of year—the city would welcome a few rain showers.

St. Louis Cathedral, in one form or another, had existed in almost the same location since the earliest days of the tiny settlement that grew into the City of New Orleans. More meaningful to the residents than perhaps Mardi Gras, or jazz, or unequaled culinary delights, the storied Cathedral *was* New Orleans, an indivisible part of the whole.

No matter how many times he'd visited St. Louis—usually accompanying Emma—he stared in awe at the magnificent nave, with its vaulted arches and richly adorned ceilings. But he questioned the grandeur. How much did it cost to maintain the facade and interior? Surely the money would be better spent to support the poor and homeless. Yet the Church did so much good work. Maybe he was too harsh in his criticism.

He sat in a rear pew as the eight o'clock Mass—the first of the two cele-brated each weekday—neared its end. Weekday Masses were usually much quicker than the more elaborate services on Sunday or other significant occasions. No choir or organ music or other such niceties, Monday through Friday. A more cynical observer might comment about the businesslike efficiency. Stop by for a sip of wine, a magic wafer, and a prayer or two, then off to work, your holy obligations satisfied.

Jonathan looked over his right shoulder. Near the rear exit sat a mahogany structure, slightly larger than the combined size of two porta-potties—though more elegant and much less malodorous. The confessional. Two artificial Mexican fan palm trees and several potted ferns served to isolate it from the main part of the nave as if to emphasize the secrecy involved.

Satisfied that no one paid attention to his arrival, Jonathan slipped away and headed toward the far side of the wooden edifice, where he could remain hidden from the rest of the congregation. He peered around the corner. The congregants faced away from him, seemingly intent on the prayer being offered by a young priest.

Jonathan moved to the front, three doors facing him. The center door, marked "Priest," had another door on either side, marked "Penitent." He pulled the door handle of the leftmost "Penitent" door. It didn't budge. Damn. The confessional was never locked. Perhaps it was simply stuck—expanding wood in an often-humid environment. With a stronger pull, the door opened with a noticeable groan and pop. He froze and held his breath. His eyes darted about, watching for any sign of movement in the congregation. Thank goodness. No one seemed to have noticed.

He entered the booth and closed the door slowly to avoid making more noise. He sat in the solitary, straight-backed chair occupying the space and waited as the service finished. Normal confession time during the week was between 7:30 and 8:00 a.m.—the thirty minutes leading up to Mass. But for special situations, the confessional was available "by appointment." Sounds of the faithful exiting the church faded, soon replaced by a single set of footsteps echoing off the terra cotta floor.

Promptly at eight forty-five, the door to the priest's booth opened and closed. A slight scent of cigar and coffee wafted through the latticework screen separating the Priest and Penitent areas. The coffee? Understandable. But it must have been one hell of a morning if Dan had already been smoking.

Jonathan smiled as the screen lowered. "Forgive you, Father, for you have sinned."

"Spoken like a true Protestant, my Son." Monsignor Dan Rossignol, Auxiliary Archbishop of New Orleans and Rector of St. Louis, extended his hand through the opening where the lattice had been. "And good morning to you, my friend."

Jonathan accepted the handshake. "How have you been since our last visit?"

"I was about to ask you the same thing."

"Well, Dan, I'm not the one who had a Cohiba for breakfast."

"Red Dot, not Cuban." Dan chuckled. "But you've got me there. It *is* kind of early."

"Stress?"

"Didn't sleep well."

"Another nightmare?"

Dan remained silent.

"I know it's only been a few weeks," Jonathan said. "But I thought the bad dreams had been easing up."

"Of course." Dan inhaled a deep breath, then let it out slowly. "Had been."

"Something trigger it?"

"On Saturday night, I ministered…gave last rites…to a stabbing victim at University Hospital." Dan closed his eyes. "The fatal wound was in the same location as—"

"Look, Dan, you couldn't know someone would take the crucifix you gave him during confession and stab his lawyer in the neck."

Dan's eyes, now opened, moistened. "Of course, I wasn't around when the victim at University Hospital got stabbed either…but something about the location of the wound got to me."

"And what were you doing at University Hospital? Don't you have junior priests for that sort of thing?"

"Of course…" Dan shrugged. "Archbishop Fontenot thought—"

"It would be good therapy for you?"

"You know, best to get back on the horse…face your worst fears."

"I see."

"He reminded me that confession's good for the soul. Even if it's not *your* confession."

"Like a Catholic version of cognitive-behavioral therapy?"

"Maybe."

"Learn to control your reactions…your emotions."

"Something like that."

"Well, I'm sure the Archbishop means well. He strikes me as very sincere."

"Of course."

"I know you blame yourself," Jonathan said. "But there was no way you could know someone would take the crucifix you gave him and use it as a weapon."

"I guess."

"Dan, what really concerns you about what happened?"

"You're right. I couldn't know, back then. But I had suspicions. Something seemed off. I don't usually deal with penitents in jail cells." His head shook—more like a quiver—as if he were trying to decide whether to say what he was thinking. "I didn't have to give him my crucifix. I could have said something to the police about my suspicions."

"But you know you couldn't. What's said in confession goes no further."

"Right. The Archbishop would have buried my excommunicated body under the Cathedral."

"You know, Dan, I'm not sure that explains what's going on."

"Well, there *is* something else."

"Oh?"

"Yesterday, I heard a confession." He hesitated as if deciding whether to say anything else. "The penitent sat in the same seat—the one you're in." He cleared his throat. "Claimed to have killed someone…using a knife…just like the victim at University Hospital."

Jonathan squirmed at the thought of occupying a killer's chair. But he dared not show any emotion for his friend's sake. "And almost like someone using your crucifix to stab someone?"

"True," Dan said. "I guess the memories…"

"Must be tough."

"Gets worse." Dan inhaled deeply then exhaled slowly. "The person from yesterday's confession was thinking of killing again."

"So, you want to say something."

"But can't." Dan's head dropped toward his chest. "It's in the Lord's hands now."

"I think I understand why you're having nightmares again." Not much Jonathan could say to guide Dan through the philosophical morass he faced. Platitudes and opinions wouldn't work. Best just to listen and be there for his friend. "So, what will you do?"

"Pray." Dan placed his hands together, palms inward, and brought them to his chin. "And worry." He smiled—or at least made an effort at something approximating a smile. "Maybe have another Cohiba to calm my nerves."

"Well, I don't envy the position you're in. And there's not much—" Jonathan's phone buzzed. "Sorry."

Jonathan glanced at his phone and clicked through to an incoming text. He fought back the urge to curse as he read the message. He typed a reply, then hit send:

Okay. Got it. Twenty minutes.

"Bad news?" Dan asked.

"Don't know. But it's something that…look…I'm sorry…but I'll need to cut our meeting short. Will you be okay if I—"

"Of course," Dan said. "I've appreciated your visits. You know this… the doubts these past few weeks…this newest dilemma…I mean…it's not something I can discuss as freely with the other priests or the Archbishop."

"I understand. Maybe we can talk again on Wednesday. Same time and place?"

"I'd like that." Dan's face seemed less tense—almost relaxed, at peace. "In the meantime, Godspeed, my friend."

Chapter Nineteen: The Bench

Monday, February 2, 2015 – 9:35 a.m.

Jonathan smiled to himself as the streetcar passed Daisy Dukes Café on St. Charles Avenue. What a morning it had been. Roused from a sound sleep, and having his ass handed to him by the mayor. Breakfast with Betsy at Daisy's. Dan Rossignol's revelations about a confession. And now, full circle back to the Central Business District for a meeting with reporter Bryan Whitcomb from the *Times-Picayune*. And it wasn't even ten o'clock yet.

Could Dan have met—and offered penance to—the Sweeper? Jesus. The possibilities. Should he have mentioned his investigation to Dan? That wouldn't do anything except add to Dan's stress. Make him feel even more guilt about not being able to say anything to authorities. He couldn't—*he wouldn't*—do that to his friend. But still…

If the Sweeper were, indeed, a practicing Catholic, he'd need to absolve himself of last night's murder in St. Louis Number One. Absolution for executing someone in cold blood. What a thought. Perhaps the Church could cleanse the Sweeper's soul. But that wouldn't save him from the death chamber at the State Prison in Angola. And by the time the Sweeper exhausted all his appeals, challenges to using a lethal injection would likely be resolved.

But first they had to catch the bastard. Maybe Betsy could surveil the cathedral. Keep tabs on who came and went. Christ. No. That wouldn't do.

Jonathan would never take advantage of something Dan said in a private conversation as he sought guidance from a friend—a voice from someone outside the church hierarchy. Jonathan wasn't *that* desperate. Yet.

The streetcar passed Lafayette Square. Time to pull the cord running along the length of the passenger area, just above the windows. A buzzer signaled the driver that she should stop at the upcoming intersection with Girod Street. He stood and made his way to the rear door as the driver engaged the brake. The metal wheels screeched, and the streetcar rumbled to a stop.

Jonathan exited, waited for the streetcar to move forward, then crossed St. Charles. He angled toward the temporary parade viewing stand erected adjacent to Lafayette Square, across the street from Gallier Hall—the former City Hall and current ceremonial event venue. As he drew closer, a tall, lanky man in his early thirties with beaded hair braids stood near the top of the reviewing stand. He turned toward Jonathan and waved. Bryan Whitcomb. Jonathan quickened his pace.

"Morning, Doc." Whitcomb sat on the aluminum bench. "Thanks for coming."

Jonathan offered a handshake. "Morning." Whitcomb had lost weight since the last time they'd been together. He was never fat, but his then-and-now appearance—pretty damn stark. His face reflected worry and pain. Coming within inches of being blown to bits in a car bombing would likely do that to anyone. "Your message said you had information I needed to hear. I knew it must be important."

Whitcomb grimaced as he extended his right arm to accept the handshake. "Sorry, didn't mean to—"

"No problem," Whitcomb said. "Just a little residual pain when I move in certain directions."

"I understand." Jonathan pointed toward a cane resting on top of a small briefcase on the bench. "Didn't realize you were using a cane."

"It's nothing. I'm making good progress. But the doctors wanted me to bring it along in case I get dizzy from the concussion…or if the punctured lung causes breathing issues and I need support."

"I'd have been happy to come to your office."

"Thanks, Doc. But I've been cooped up so much. I needed to get out. Consider this part of my rehab."

"Fair enough. So, what's important enough to drag you out here?"

"First." Whitcomb removed a single piece of printer paper from his briefcase and handed it to Jonathan. "You may want to sit down before you read it."

"A press release from the mayor's office?" Jonathan sat.

"Came across the wire just before I contacted you."

Jonathan's face warmed. He cursed under his breath.

"Sorry, Doc, didn't catch that."

Jonathan handed the press release back to Whitcomb. "No comment."

"You weren't aware?"

Jonathan shook his head. "No."

"Thought you were supposed to finish out Robby O'Malley's term in office. No election for another three years."

"Apparently, Max Jamerson thinks otherwise."

"Release says candidates need to register by February 16th and there'll be—"

"A special election on March 17th. I can read."

"Seems strange." Whitcomb returned the press release to his briefcase. "The timing, I mean. Registration day before Fat Tuesday. Election on St. Patrick's Day."

"Strange is one word. And I can think of a couple of others."

"Sorry to be the bearer of bad news."

"Listen, I appreciate it. Probably wouldn't have learned about it until I read it in the *Times-Pic*."

"Sure."

"Earlier, you said this was the first thing. Any other good words to impart?"

Whitcomb handed a business-size manila envelope to Jonathan.

Jonathan retrieved a single document from the envelope. "Where did you get this?"

"Arrived in the mail room a few days ago. They put it in my inbox unopened. I've been in and out so much with medical stuff…didn't see it until late yesterday."

"I see."

"A coded message during Mardi Gras?"

"Hmmm."

Whitcomb frowned. "You've been here long enough to remember the Mardi Gras Sweeper, right?"

"Right."

"Well, you don't seem very surprised."

"I really don't know what to say."

"Don't suppose there's a relationship between the mayor calling for a special election and the return of the Mardi Gras Sweeper, is there?"

The standard "neither confirm nor deny" answer almost always caused more questions, more digging by the press. Best not to say anything. Find out what Whitcomb knew. Figure out what to reveal and what to keep secret. "What makes you think that?"

"Reporter's hunch as much as anything." Whitcomb's face flushed. "I mean…I can't find any suspicious deaths in the crime reports. There's always a strange murder. Something." He pointed to the manifesto. "Then there's this. A coded *billet-doux* from an apparent maniac. Normally, I can find someone willing to talk. This time, zip. It's like NOPD's covering up something. Like they've put everyone under a gag order."

"So, why not go public with your conclusions?"

"*Times-Pic's* not a tabloid. We don't print hunches. We need solid leads."

"And you think I might be one?"

"Look, Doc." Whitcomb held his cane up, then returned it to the bench. "You owe me."

"How do you figure that?"

"I missed getting vaporized by inches. And I know you presented my research to the U.S. Attorney. Apparently, that was the final nail in the Mayor's coffin."

"Sounds like you have a beef with the U.S. Attorney's Office. My recollection is that you asked me to turn over your research if something happened to you. And it seemed to me that a car bomb was enough of a something."

"Well." Whitcomb seemed calmer now, his voice less strident. "That may be technically true. But Max Jamerson blames you—at least in part. Jesus, he's had a boner for you ever since…well, anyway, I don't see why you'd protect his sorry ass."

"Okay." Whitcomb was right. Jonathan *did* owe him. He'd provided the icing on the cake against the mayor weeks ago. But that was then. The charges had been dismissed after pressure from "higher-ups." Regardless, he needed help if he wanted to nail the Sweeper. "I see your point."

"All right, what can you tell me about the killer?"

"Off the record?"

"Not off the record, Doc."

No turning back now. "What I'm about to tell you is sensitive. I need to count on your discretion." His gut churned, but he didn't have much choice. He needed to keep Whitcomb on his side.

"Let me hear what you have, then maybe we can work something out."

"You're right. Looks like the Mardi Gras Sweeper's back."

"Hot damn. I knew it."

"But Max Jamerson believes that if the public finds out, it'll wreck Mardi Gras."

"How many?" Whitcomb asked.

"Two so far. One early Sunday morning. Another Sunday around midnight."

"Two more to go, if it really is the Sweeper."

"That's our assumption, too. But…"

"But what?"

"There are some oddities. Some small differences between the previous visits and this current one."

"I'm listening."

Jonathan outlined as much of the investigation and evidence he felt comfortable revealing—the body carving, graffiti tags on the streetcars, the weapons, the ciphers, and so forth. But he didn't mention his early morning meeting with the mayor or his discussion with Dan Rossignol.

"So," Whitcomb said, "translated the code yet?"

"Technically, it's a cipher," Jonathan said. "But no. NOPD's working on it."

"I see."

"Can I count on your discretion?"

"Well, so far, no one else at the *Times-Pic* knows about this. I wanted to talk with you first."

"What's your plan?"

"At this point," Whitcomb said, "I don't have anything solid. But I'll continue to dig. *Times-Pic* didn't get anything from last night's killing—as far as I know—assuming the Sweeper sent one to the paper. But I'm not sure how long I can keep it from my editors."

"Guess we're both groping our way." No use telling Whitcomb that the Sweeper left another manifesto with the St. Louis Cemetery Number One victim. Not yet anyway. Best to wait and see if the *Times-Pic* received a copy from the Sweeper. "So, can I count on your discretion?"

"I can probably give you a couple of days. It'll take me that long to get a translation and track down some corroboration. After that, no guarantees."

"Deal."

Chapter Twenty: Legwork

Monday, February 2, 2015 – 9:38 a.m.

Betsy Sprance hit the Enter key on yet another internet search, then yawned. She'd taken enough of a break to shower, change clothes, and grab a twenty-minute power nap. That would have to be enough to satisfy Dr. Gray insisting that it was her turn for some shuteye. She was used to pushing herself—especially when investigating a murder. Sleep was overrated anyway.

As Betsy leaned back in her chair, her phone vibrated. Another call from area code 808. Why would anyone be calling her from Hawaii? She cursed under her breath. Effing robocalls. Just let it roll over to voicemail, like the others. If it were something critical, they could leave a message.

"Special temporary duty" assigned to the Coroner's office wasn't exactly real police work—even if they allowed her to use the detectives' spaces at the Sixth District Headquarters. But it beat the hell out of lying around the house worrying about Ranger. Or the boredom of her part-time job watching over boozy gamblers at Harrah's.

She lifted her coffee mug, stared at the contents, and winced at her first sip. Cold. How could people drink iced coffee? She'd been sitting on her butt staring at a computer monitor far too long. Time for a refresh, get the blood flowing. She stood, stretched her arms above her head, and ambled toward the telltale aroma of coffee that's been on the burner too long.

The district's break room—stereotypical—like something out of a television crime drama. Bank of vending machines along one wall. Several tables and chairs. Microwave on the counter. A sink—as if most of the officers, the guys anyway—would actually wash dishes. And, of course, the communal coffee pot, source of the offending odor. Why couldn't they have a coffee vending machine instead of the do-it-yourself version? Sure, it'd be more expensive. But there wouldn't be any containers of dark liquid slowly becoming the consistency of molasses. Lazy-assed cops.

Mitch Broussard, the only other person in the room, sat at one of the tables. He looked up from his laptop computer. "Morning, Betsy. How's it hanging?" He clicked on the keyboard and closed the lid.

Betsy turned off the burner, removed the coffee pot, and poured the remaining sludge into the sink. "Going cross-eyed and starting to nod off looking at the computer screen." She rinsed out the pot. "Needed a jolt to keep me going." She finished prepping the coffee, put the carafe on the burner, and hit the "Quick Brew" button. "But it's better inside, clicking keys, than outside, knocking on doors on a day like this."

"Right. I guess we needed a little rain."

"Little being the operative word. Hope it's a quick one." Betsy rinsed her cup. "What're you reading, Mitch?"

"Not reading. Watching."

"Cartoons again?"

"Ease up. One time. It was once. And how many years ago?"

"Well, it *was* Woody Woodpecker." Betsy grinned. "So, if it's not cartoons, what has your attention these days?"

"If you must know, I'm reviewing video footage from Frenchmen Street."

"Saturday night?"

"Affirmative. Started with footage from Jazz Harbor."

"Anything good?'

Mitch opened his laptop. "Smells like coffee's done. Pour a cup and have a seat."

Jazz Harbor's video surveillance was state-of-the-art. But they only had one camera installed—fortunately, one with a wide-angle lens—that showed the outside of the facility. The exterior unit provided a partial view of

Frenchmen Street—about a block in either direction—and a small portion of one side of the building. Not optimal, but it would have to do until Mitch could parse through the remaining videos they'd collected from other locations.

Available footage included several views of two young women, one wearing an Ole Miss sweatshirt, strolling along Frenchmen Street—blocked off from car traffic for the night because of the parades. Almost certainly Janelle and Tam. The images supported Janelle's version of events. And the timeline fit. The pair arrived on Frenchmen, first walking—along with a large number of revelers—toward the starting point of the Krewe du Vieux parade. Several members of the crowd wore baseball caps, flannel shirts, and down vests.

Janelle and Tam returned after almost an hour, walked in front of Jazz Harbor, then disappeared in the direction of The Bunker. A few minutes before ten-thirty—after the parades had passed Frenchmen Street—the pair appeared again, headed toward the Spotted Cat. After a couple of minutes, they came back into the frame and stood in the middle of Frenchmen for at least thirty seconds. They appeared to be talking, perhaps arguing. Then they hastened toward Jazz Harbor, opened the door, and disappeared inside.

"Must be when they saw the guy in the flannel shirt lurking in the alley," Betsy said.

"Probably." Mitch paused the video. "It's grainy, but see the figure in the background? In the space adjacent to Jazz Harbor."

"Could be the guy."

"You said that the girls were in Jazz Harbor until about midnight?"

"Just after."

Mitch forwarded the video until 11:44 p.m. "Watch the front door to the restaurant."

"It's a lot less crowded." Betsy's eyes narrowed. "Is that Ian?"

"Looks like him—from the description you provided." Mitch paused the recording.

"And two other guys. Janelle told us Ian left after his shift and went to The John with a couple of his co-workers."

"Okay." Mitch pointed to the screen. "Look at the figure in almost the same place as he was before—in the alley."

"I see him. Barely in the frame, but there."

"Now let's move to 11:59—almost midnight. Watch the figure coming from the left."

"Ballcap, flannel shirt, and down vest." Betsy looked at Mitch. "The guy with the backpack? Is that Jimmy Caplan?"

"Could be. Watch how Jimmy—or whoever—hesitates in front of Jazz Harbor, then moves out of the picture on the other side of Frenchmen."

"Got it. Interesting."

"Next, we have Janelle and Tam come out of Jazz Harbor."

"Much clearer image. Can you make it any larger?"

"Not right now." Mitch shook his head. "You need to see the entire scene."

"Got it. Looks like they're arguing. And there goes Tam up Frenchmen toward Burgundy." Betsy leaned closer to the monitor. "Where's the guy from the alley?"

"Wait for it." Mitch pointed toward the computer screen. "Watch as Tam crosses Royal."

"She's moving pretty fast. Must be in a hurry. So what—"

"Give it a few more seconds," Mitch said. "Five...four...three...two—"

"Shit...Holy Shit. The guy in the flannel shirt. Coming around the corner on Royal."

"A guy in a flannel shirt, ballcap, and down vest. Could be almost anyone."

"Come on, Mitch. That's *got* to be him."

"Probably. Watch Janelle."

"She's looking at her phone. Must be checking on the RideShare."

"My guess, too."

"Then Janelle looks up, hesitates, and takes off up Frenchmen." Betsy leaned back from the monitor. "Any footage past Royal?"

"Not on the Jazz Harbor feed. I'll start reviewing footage from other establishments."

"Soup to nuts, Mitch. That's damn good work. You've been busy."

"With only a couple of Woody Woodpecker breaks." He smirked. "And there's more."

"Do tell."

"I heard from my buds with the Mississippi State Patrol about Tam…Ms. Espy."

"And?"

"Nothing official," Mitch said.

"Unofficially?"

"Criminal records check came back negative, but—"

"But what?"

"Both Tam…Ms. Espy…and Ms. Harrison are from the Jackson area."

"Not Tupelo?"

Mitch shook his head. "Not Tupelo."

"And?"

"Both Tam and Janelle have well-known parents."

"Oh?"

"Tam's mother is a member of the state legislature."

"Okay."

"And her daddy's the pastor of a mega-church in Jackson."

"Not the First Evangelical Baptist Temple, is it?

"You know it?"

"Reverend Doctor Efrem Zelphinius Espy," Betsy said. "A television preacher."

"Nothing wrong with that."

"Right. Nothing wrong with being a publicity-loving, sanctimonious son-of-a-bitch."

"And Janelle's old man is publisher of the Jackson *Clarion-Journal*."

"Newspaper?"

"Affirmative."

"Crap." Betsy stroked her chin. "A preacher and a publisher. Could be—"

"And a state legislator."

"Right," Betsy said. "And a mealy-mouthed politician."

"Reckon it could be worse," Mitch said. "It is what it is."

"Could you confirm that the girls are students at Ole Miss?"

"Affirmative. Sorority sisters."

"University have anything?"

"Negative." Mitch shook his head. "My friend checked with a contact in the Ole Miss Security Department. They haven't been reported missing yet."

"Not surprising. It's only Monday. Just means more loose ends, I guess."

"Right," Mitch said. "So I'm off to The John later to check on Tam and this Ian guy. Figured I'd start there and work my way down Frenchmen to Jazz Harbor. Connect with Ian before the start of his shift." He glanced at the window. "I'd hoped it would stop raining before I go."

"Looks like it's easing up," Betsy said. "I'm thinking of dropping by the local maritime workers' union hall off Tchoupitoulas."

"Oh?"

"Among other stuff, I've been researching reports of murders using sailors' rigging knives."

"Find anything?"

"Tons of bar fights and such…assault and battery type stuff."

"Any murders?" Mitch asked.

"Once I hit on the right search criteria, I identified three separate clusters of gut-slicing murders similar to the ones here."

"Where?"

"California…Long Beach area…seems the most similar," Betsy said. "Jacksonville, Florida, was another grouping. And then Baltimore, Maryland, and Norfolk, Virginia—both on the Chesapeake Bay—so I lumped them together."

"And you think they're the same guy?"

"Figure it's worth checking out."

"But the previous Sweeper killings here in New Orleans—before this year—didn't involve slashing wounds. At least not like the last two."

"And the ciphers were different, too," Betsy said. "I'm wondering whether the Sweeper's mixing it up to confuse us."

"Not hard to do at this point."

"True dat." Betsy's phone chimed. She tapped through to a newly arrived text. Same number as the calls from Hawaii. She bit her lip to keep from cursing as she read the message. Her heartbeat seemed to move from her chest to her throat. She swallowed hard.

"Something wrong?"

"Listen, Mitch." She inhaled deeply, then exhaled a cleansing breath. "Something's come up. Something personal. I need…to go."

"Something I can help with?"

Betsy shook her head. "If anyone's looking for me. Tell them I'll be back as soon as I can."

She stood and hastened toward the door.

Chapter Twenty-One: John Doe Number Two?

Monday, February 2, 2015 – 10:24 a.m.

Rain pelted the windshield of the RideShare as it approached the morgue. So much for Jonathan's thought that the front wouldn't roll through from the Gulf until early afternoon. Maybe it was a reminder about how unpredictable and off-kilter their investigation had been. Nearly thirty-six hours gone. Still within the proverbial "first forty-eight." So much undertaken. So little real progress.

He hit the End Call button on his iPhone. No luck reaching Susan Miller to see if Boris might be available to review the cipher. It was looking more and more like they might have to follow Max Jamerson's suggestion of visiting the NOPD analyst on paternity leave. Although they probably wouldn't hire a brass band. Maybe Cass Melançon could shed some additional light after the postmortem on the St. Louis Cemetery Number One victim.

"Here we are," the driver said.

"Thanks…" Jonathan looked at the "My Name Is" placard attached to the dashboard. "…Lawrence." Jonathan handed him a five-dollar bill. "They'll add seven percent as a tip when the invoice comes in. But here's a little extra."

"Solid." Lawrence smiled. "Appreciate you."

Jonathan dashed toward the front entrance. At least that was something smart they'd done. Awarding a contract to the RideShare company. Make a reservation using the Coroner's account information, and the bill got sent to the Parish. Sometimes reconciling records was an administrative pain. But the arrangement allowed staff to get around town without worrying about checking out a government car and paying through the nose for a parking space—if they could find one.

A seven percent tip seemed stingy, but the bean-counters objected to anything greater. Oh, well. Maybe Lawrence would be Voter Number One at next month's election. And five bucks seemed like a small price to pay for a potential vote—and totally legal under the circumstances. He'd have to take a lot more RideShare trips between now and St. Patrick's Day.

Jonathan entered the morgue's reception area and removed his coat. Water dripped onto the heavy vinyl mat embroidered with the office's distinctive logo—intertwined scales of justice and a caduceus resting under the overarching protection of a crescent moon. If his meeting with Bryan Whitcomb had ended a few minutes earlier, maybe he would have made it to the morgue before the downpour. Hopefully, Whitcomb was safe inside somewhere. Limping along with his cane in this mess wouldn't be pleasant.

"Morning, Dr. Gray." Carlton, their receptionist, smiled. "Looks like we got a real frog-choker outside."

"Just a friendly sprinkle." Jonathan put his still-dripping jacket on a coat rack near the door. "Dr. Melançon around?"

"Yes, sir," Carlton said. "Got one on the chopping block."

Jonathan remained silent. He bit his lip to keep from smiling. On the chopping block. Coroner humor. Sign of good morale, but not good form if the wrong person overheard the comment.

"Sorry, Doc." Carlton rolled his eyes. "I mean…she's in the autopsy space examining a cadaver."

"Got it. Headed that way now."

After a few steps, he hesitated in front of a bank of vending machines and focused on the unit offering Seattle's Best coffee. Some caffeine might be good right now. Best to wait, though, until after consulting with Cass. He chuckled, then made a mental note. He should have the support staff find out if French Truck had a vending program.

As he entered the examination area, Cass Melançon stood adjacent to a stainless-steel autopsy table. The table held a partially disemboweled male cadaver—Caucasian in appearance and skin tone—with the Greek symbols for Alpha and Omega carved into his forehead. Cass reached out with a long cotton swab and rubbed the tip on the cadaver's genital area. She placed the swab in a long glass tube, secured the contents with a lid, and handed it to Alma Montague, the autopsy assistant—diener—standing next to her.

"Good thought, Cass," Jonathan said.

Cass jumped slightly as if she'd been so deep in thought that Jonathan startled her. "How's that?"

"I assume you're looking for DNA."

"Wondering whether we can identify the witness who went missing. It's a long shot, but who knows?"

"It's a heads-up idea," Jonathan said. "Longshot or not."

"Thanks."

"We'll need to expedite the results. I'll approve the extra cost for a private lab if that will help."

"Appreciate the support." Cass turned to the diener. "Alma, run the latest samples to the police lab. Ask them to rush the DNA. Then drop off another set at Bayou Biologics—or whoever the Parish is using for private testing."

"Will do." Alma yawned.

"And then head home. Get some shuteye. I appreciate you doing double duty."

"Thanks, Dr. Melançon. Glad to help out."

Jonathan and Alma exchanged greetings as she exited the room.

"Double duty?"

"Jimmy Caplan didn't show up for his overnight. They called Alma to come in early and cover Jimmy's shift and hers. By the time she gets all the samples to both labs, it'll be early afternoon. She was already starting to drift off. I figured we could manage through the rest of her shift."

"Makes sense," Jonathan said. "That's not like Jimmy, though. Must have been something important."

"Probably."

"But I'm a little surprised to see you in the autopsy suite. Aren't you out of your normally assigned area of responsibility?"

"Well." Cass looked to her right, and her face flushed. "Like you said. One team. One fight." She shrugged. "My autopsy skills are a bit rusty…but it's sort of like riding a bike."

"Fair enough."

"So, I figured I might as well go for it."

"Good on you for that. Any revelations?"

"I was just wrapping up the external exam when you arrived."

"Between us chickens, I suspect the internal exam won't shed much light, given the injuries sustained."

"Right," Cass said. "But I'll do a complete autopsy. Make sure we hit all the wickets."

"Of course."

"But there are some interesting aspects of the external exam we should discuss."

"Okay, shoot."

"Cause of death seems obvious," Cass said. "Same as our John Doe Number One—the Washington Square Park victim."

"Gutted like a fish and bled out?"

"In layman's terms."

"No real surprise there."

"Right," Cass said. "And there's the forehead art."

"Done before death?"

"Affirmative."

"But no chest carving."

"Also affirmative."

"Hmmm. Got a theory?"

"Maybe the Sweeper took mercy on this one."

"Yeah, right."

"Agreed…not likely," Cass said. "Best guess is that the woman running away and police arriving spooked the killer. Not enough time for the chest work…simple as that."

"And he probably had the note police found already written." Jonathan crossed his arms. "What else struck you as odd?"

"The knees…or at least the left one."

"Another shattered kneecap?"

"Just like John Doe Number One."

"Theory on cause?"

"Could be from banging against some of the stonework in the cemetery."

"But you're not convinced?"

"No." Cass shook her head. "I'm thinking something like an ASP."

"Collapsible baton?"

"ASP's a brand name. I guess it's easier than saying collapsible baton. Same idea, regardless of brand, though."

"Makes sense," Jonathan said. "Sweeper could have taken it with him."

"Exactly."

"So, whack your prey over the knee with a steel baton to disable him?"

"Affirmative. Makes your victim easier to subdue."

"Especially if you're smaller than your victim."

"True," Cass said.

"Any info on the murder weapon?"

Cass pointed to an adjacent stainless-steel table. "Two items of interest."

"Looks like a sailor's rigging knife, same model as the first victim."

"Correct."

"And the thing next to it?"

"Looks like some sort of spring device to trigger the flash-bang grenade."

"Hmmm." Jonathan squinted as if that would make the item appear in greater focus. "Significance?"

"Simplest way to enable the grenade would be to pull the release pin and place the live flash-bang under the body."

"So it would explode almost immediately after the body was moved?"

"Exactly," Cass said. "Another way to trigger the flash-bang would be to loop some wire such that when the body was moved, it would simply pull the pin and activate the grenade."

"But this contraption—"

"More complex. Apparently designed to activate when the victim's weight shifted."

"An interesting development. Why would someone go to all that trouble? Another loose end."

"Maybe," Cass said. "But at least we know who the guy is."

"Oh? Kind of an important detail, don't you think?"

"Sorry." Cass blushed. "Probably should have mentioned it first thing."

"No worries." A lie, but confronting Cass wouldn't help the cause. "So, who's our guest?"

"Curtis Dowdy. From Minneapolis. At least that's what his driver's license indicated."

"Probably in town for a convention." Jonathan formed air quotes with his hands when he said 'convention.' "Booked himself on a special midnight cemetery tour. Got more than he bargained for."

"I'll send the info to Betsy."

"Good idea." Jonathan's phone vibrated. He continued talking as he read the incoming message. "See if we can access the Department of Defense DNA clearing house as well. John Doe Number One's, too. Maybe someone connected with this mess served in the military. Might increase our chances of a match."

"Will do. I made sure to take extra samples in case we needed a re-test, so there should be enough."

"Good move." Jonathan looked up from his phone. "Someone has a sense of humor."

"Oh?"

"Emma."

"Your wife?"

"Wants to meet at Felix's for lunch."

"Doesn't sound particularly humorous."

"Well, she sent this." Jonathn tapped on the screen and held the phone out toward Cass. He shook his head and chuckled as the room filled with a tinny version of "Twinkle, Twinkle, Little Star."

Chapter Twenty-Two: Men in Black

Monday, February 2, 2015 – 11:37 a.m.

Betsy Sprance stared out the window of the streetcar as it rolled along North Carrollton Avenue. A kayaker paddled across the peaceful waters of Bayou St. John. The streetcar, brakes grinding and wheels screeching along the tracks, slowed as it approached the end-of-the-line near the entrance to the New Orleans Museum of Art. Almost there. Just under ten minutes until the scheduled rendezvous. Despite the cool temperature, perspiration dotted her face.

She'd covered the four blocks along Martin Luther King Boulevard between Sixth District Headquarters and the streetcar stop on St. Charles Avenue as fast as possible, without drawing undue attention. A woman hurtling headlong down the street likely would have made someone take notice. Maybe call the police. She didn't have the inclination to explain her situation. Once she'd reached St. Charles, it was simply "hurry up and wait." At least the rain had stopped.

Too bad there wasn't a quicker way to have responded to Ranger's message under the circumstances. A cab or RideShare certainly was more direct, especially given the required transfers between streetcar lines and the often slow-as-molasses pace. But a cab or RideShare presented an unacceptable risk of having her name and face identified too easily. It would be much harder to trace her via the camera feed from the streetcar. She could pull her cap low, cover as much of her face as possible. Then rely on her experience from working casino security and other video surveillance to figure out the most likely blind spots.

And driving her personal vehicle or a city car was a no-go as well. Depending on what happened at the meeting, she might have to leave the car behind at NOMA. An abandoned vehicle—especially one belonging to the city—would surely raise too many questions.

Regardless, the text message—from the same number in the 808-area code as the previous calls—underscored that there was no time to waste:

Been calling. Meeting imperative. 1145 hours. RP Charlie. CV61.

Betsy refocused on the situation at hand. She exited the streetcar. The serene view across the bayou and slight breeze calmed her nerves, if only for a few seconds. "CV61." The hull number for the now decommissioned aircraft carrier USS Ranger. Their secret call sign for imminent danger. A play on her husband's Army nickname. No one knew the code but them. The text might have been from a different area code, but it could have only come from Ranger. And no one could force him to…Betsy's eyes moistened and her gut churned. She had to get to him.

She inhaled deeply, then let her breath out slowly as she crossed the street, entered the museum grounds, and traveled along the sidewalk adjacent to Lelong Drive. Ahead stood the museum's massive, fortress-like main building. In season, crape myrtles lining each side of the drive showcased a beautiful, yet eerie, combination of green leaves, magenta blossoms, and silvery-gray Spanish moss dangling from the branches. On a chilly midwinter afternoon, the trees seemed bland, uninviting. And under the circumstances, foreboding.

It had been easy enough to play along with Ranger's insistence on having a rally point—RP. Family safety and common sense dictated an emergency plan in the event of a fire at home or similar event. But insistence on a secret designation for messages seemed overkill. And what was with a safe-deposit box, prepaid debit cards, and burner phones paid for with cash—never a credit card? Perhaps it had been an outgrowth of Ranger's military assignment as part of a narcoterrorism response team. But he was retired from the Army. Why the continued need for such security procedures? Since retirement, he'd been taking part-time gigs as a "security consultant," whatever the hell that meant. Maybe...

She stopped. Two black SUVs raced toward her, down the wrong side of Lelong Drive. She moved to her right, angling for the cover of the crape myrtles. Two men, both dressed in black suits and both holding pistols flat against their chests, stepped out from behind the trees. She reached toward her sidearm.

The taller of the two men displayed his billfold badge, HSI in large block letters, plainly visible. "I wouldn't if I were you, Lieutenant Sprance." The second man raised his sidearm into firing position.

Betsy was a damned good shot. The Marines had trained her well. And time with NOPD honed her skills. She might be able to take one of them out before they returned fire, but probably not both. Time to put ego aside and let common sense control. Betsy extended her arms at a downward angle, her hands well away from her sidearm. What in God's name would Homeland Security want with her?

Tires squealed as the two SUVs stopped a few feet away. A female dressed in a black pantsuit emerged from the rear door of the first SUV. A badge dangled from a lanyard. Her suit jacket opened slightly as she moved, exposing a pistol in a holster clipped to her belt.

"We're here to take you to see Sergeant Major Sprance." She pointed to the open door of the SUV. "If you'd be so kind."

"Who the hell are you?" Betsy surveyed the area. No witnesses.

"My name's not important at this point, Lieutenant." She canted her head toward the open door. "Please...and I'll need your sidearm...and your phone."

Betsy looked at the two men standing by the crape myrtles, then back toward the woman in the pantsuit. Three to one. And probably two more armed HSI agents driving the SUVs. Five to one. Not the time for heroics, especially if she wanted to see Ranger—assuming he was still...She raised her arms toward her chest. "Help yourself."

Betsy entered the rear seat of the SUV. The woman didn't follow her. The door closed. Darkened Plexiglass barriers prevented her from seeing the driver or into the rear cargo area. The side windows—both tinted black—ensured she couldn't see where they were going. A small fixture in the back of the front seat illuminated the space with a soft fluorescent glow.

She pulled on one door handle, then the other. Locked. She lay on the seat, drew her legs back, and kicked the window of the driver's side door. Nothing, as if it were made of lead rather than glass. Same result with kicking at the passenger's side window. She planted her feet on the floorboard and pushed back against the cargo area barrier. No luck. Now exhausted, she slumped on the seat, then fastened the shoulder-and-lap harness. Better safe than sorry. Not much she could do but enjoy the ride and prepare mentally for whatever was about to happen.

Betsy's heart pounded at the sound of several car doors closing. The SUV moved forward. Two sets of bumps signaled that the vehicle had crossed the neutral ground between the lanes of Lelong Drive, apparently now going the correct direction of travel.

Her stomach churned as if a thousand miniature jackhammers were pounding away inside. She'd come so close to losing Ranger. And it would have been by her hand. Her fault. What had happened in the weeks since those people snatched him from his hospital bed? Where had they taken him? She mumbled to herself, "Goddammit, Ranger, what have you gotten us into?"

Chapter Twenty-Three: Now I Know My ABCs

Monday, February 2, 2015 – 12:07 p.m.

Jonathan opened the glass-paneled door of the Iberville Street entrance to Felix's Restaurant and Oyster Bar. He didn't have time to socialize. But Emma wouldn't have asked unless it was important. Besides, it was Monday. Some red beans and rice might be just what the doctor ordered.

As he approached the hostess station, his iPhone vibrated. He removed the phone from his pocket. A text from Emma, asking "Where 'yat?"

"Afternoon, Del. Rumor has it that my better-half is around here somewhere."

Delia, the restaurant's hostess, tilted her head toward a doorway about twenty feet ahead on the right, just past the lunch counter. "She's in the oyster room, Dr. Gray."

"Thanks, Del."

Jonathan covered the distance quickly, then entered the overflow dining area, where the restaurant also prepared oysters—both on the half-shell and for grilling. Emma, the only other customer in sight, sat at a four-top along the far wall. Charcoal smoke wafted from the area near the storefront window overlooking Iberville, where one of the cooks busied himself over the grill. Another staff member shucked oysters. Servers carried trays of oysters—some on the half-shell resting on beds of ice, and many grilled, still sizzling—toward the main dining area. Emma waved as Jonathan approached the table.

"Good of you to come." Emma raised a bottle of Sam Adams Lager as if offering a toast.

Jonathan smiled. It was true. You could take the girl out of Boston. But even after all these years in New Orleans, an Abita or a Dixie wouldn't do. It had to be a Sam.

She placed her bottle on the table. "Last time I saw you awake, you were going to rest your eyes and listen to the game."

"Sorry." Jonathan's face warmed as he sat down. "Something came up."

"Thought so. Got your note."

"Everything okay?"

"Just peachy. Figured this would be the only way I'd get to see you with your eyes open for a while."

"Fair enough. Ordered yet?"

"Assumed you'd be pressed for time." A server, holding a tray containing plates with food on them, approached the table. "Ordered your Monday lunch favorite."

"Red beans and rice?"

"And a fried shrimp half po' boy." Emma sipped her beer.

"You get me a Sam?"

She pointed to a glass on the table. "Unsweetened iced tea for you." She grinned. "You're a public servant. Can't have you drinking on duty."

They remained silent as the server delivered their lunches.

"What do we need to talk about?" Jonathan picked up his po' boy, then returned it to the plate.

"Couple of things." She reached into a briefcase on the floor near her chair and pulled out a blue file folder. "There's this."

"What's that?"

"Later. After we eat." She returned the folder to her briefcase.

"Okay." Jonathan sipped his iced tea.

They ate and talked—about everything except the Sweeper. Their triplets wanted to make a quick trip home for a few days to celebrate Fat Tuesday. An upcoming ribbon-cutting for one of Emma's architectural projects. Whether to renew the leases on a couple of the businesses renting space in the first floor of their building on Bienville Street. Normally important topics, but Jonathan couldn't engage fully. Worries about the Sweeper's next move weighed on him. The mayor's pep talk still echoed in his mind.

Emma probed about Jonathan's "inside joke" with Monsignor Rossignol, but Jonathan guided her away from the topic.

As predicted, the red beans and rice hit the spot. But he just picked at his po' boy, eating the fried shrimp, leaving the rest of the contents untouched.

"Not hungry?"

"Not really," Jonathan said. "Got a lot going on right now."

"I can imagine."

"You know, Fen, you could have told me most of this on the phone…or in a text." Jonathan inhaled a deep breath, then exhaled slowly. "I mean—"

"What, a loving wife can't see her husband for lunch every once in a while?" Her face reflected an odd mix of irritation and humor.

"Of course." Jonathan's face warmed. "It's just…" He looked toward a server carrying a tray of oysters-on-the-half-shell, then leaned toward Emma. He lowered his voice almost to a whisper. "I had to leave early this morning because the Sweeper apparently struck again just after midnight."

"I see."

"There was another coded note."

"To be expected, right?"

"And I got summoned to a meeting with Max Jamerson and Polly Bondurant."

"That couldn't have been fun."

"All I can say is that we're really feeling the pressure."

"Well." Emma pulled the blue folder out of her briefcase and placed it on the table in front of Jonathan. "*This* ought to put a smile on your face."

Jonathan perused the contents of the folder. His eyes darted back and forth between the documents in the folder and Emma. He looked around the room. His mouth moved as if he wanted to say something, but he remained silent.

"Don't worry, Del promised she won't seat anyone in here unless they get really busy."

"Is this what I think it is?"

"Well, yeah."

"When did—"

"I got bored watching the Super Bowl…alone. And you know how I like puzzles."

"You did this last night?"

"And some this morning."

"Don't you have work at the office?"

Emma grinned. "Being the boss has its advantages."

"Wow." Jonathan shook his head as if expressing his disbelief at the contents of the folder. "This is—"

"What you mean is, "thank you, Fen," isn't it?" Her countenance had softened, and her lips formed into something between a smirk and a grin.

"Of course," Jonathan said. "It's just…I mean…it's such a surprise…we've had so many loose ends."

"Like I said, a simple 'thank you' would be nice."

"Thank you." Jonathan forced himself to smile, but it probably didn't look sincere. His mind was elsewhere, planning the next move. "Now, can you tell me how you figured it out?"

"It took a while, but it wasn't that hard. Although, there were a couple of parts I couldn't translate."

"Oh?"

"The cipher has a lot of symbols. I think the plus signs represent the space between the words. And the other symbols—the heart, diamond, club, spade, and music note—I'm not positive. I think they stand for punctuation marks—like periods and commas—and articles or conjunctions, like 'a,' 'the,' 'and,' and 'but.' And there's no way to determine capitalization."

"Okay."

"Take out all the Is." She moved a copy of the cipher from the folder toward Jonathan. Let me know what letters are left."

"Let's see." Jonathan held his index and middle fingers together, like a pointer, and placed them on the cipher. He moved his fingers along the lines of the symbols. "That leaves 'A'…'F'…'E'…'D'…'G'…'V'…'C'…" He mouthed the various letters as his fingers continued to follow along through the document. "And…that's it." He looked at Emma. "Just those seven letters, right?"

"Wow, you sure know your alphabet."

"No use getting snarky," Jonathan said. "How does this help us track the Sweeper?"

"Fair enough. Are you up on your Roman numerals?"

"I may not be the brightest bulb in the pack, but at least I know Roman numerals."

"Okay, anything jump out at you?"

"All those 'I's' look like the Roman numeral for one."

"And?"

"The letter 'V,' that's five."

"Right."

"And there's 'C' and 'D.'"

"Let's stick with 'I' and 'V.' See any patterns?"

Jonathan again looked through the document. He cursed under his breath.

"Beg your pardon?"

"I see a series of ones—the letter 'I." Then, there are combinations of 'V' and 'I," and 'V' alone. So, the I's would be one, two, or three, depending on how many there are." And 'IV' is four. 'V' is five. And 'VI' is six. Am I close?"

Emma whistled the tune to "Twinkle, Twinkle, Little Star."

"Okay, you don't get extra points for making me look foolish."

"Remember your nursery rhymes?" Emma smiled. "The tune to 'Twinkle, Twinkle, Little Star' is the same tune as the 'ABC Song.'"

"So?"

"There are only six musical notes in the 'ABC Song,' each represented by a letter."

"Let me guess. That's 'A'…'F'…'E'…'D'…'G'…and 'C,' right?"

"Looks like the light bulb just turned on."

"Maybe," Jonathan said. "Is each letter of the alphabet identified by a combination of the six letters and Roman numerals?"

"Very good," Emma said. "You start with the mystery letter, then go along a line the number of spaces identified on a key."

"I see."

"The first letter in the note is 'AI.'"

"So, we look for the first letter in the A-Line?"

"Right," Emma said, "which corresponds with the English letter 'E.'"

"Okay."

"And the next letter in the cipher is 'FIII,' which corresponds with the English letter 'S.'"

"Seems easy enough once you have the key. Is there a copy of—"

"One of the documents in the folder has the grid."

"So, what does the first line translate to?"

"Esteemed mortals," Emma said. "Assuming that the plus sign is a space and leaving out the musical note at the end."

"Probably a colon or comma…something like that."

"Probably," Emma said. "Figured the non-letter symbols aren't important at this point. Needed to leave something for the NOPD techies."

"Got it."

"And the last part's icing on the cake."

"Don't keep me in suspense."

"Next to the last line translates to, 'yours truly.'"

"Jesus. And the last line?"

"Translates to 'the sweeper'…assuming my guess about the spade standing for an article—in this case, *the*."

"Looks like the Sweeper wants us to know it's him." Jonathan skimmed through the contents of the deciphered document again. "You know, Fen. I feel like I'm in a time warp. It's like he's taunting us again from his two previous visits."

"I wanted to deliver the good news to you in person."

"And I'm glad you did." Jonathan exhaled, as if he had been holding his breath throughout Emma's explanation. "And I—"

"And you hate to say it, but you need to get with your team." She smiled.

"So, it's 'See you later, Fen' time again."

"You know me pretty well, don't you?" He punched the speed dial number on his phone for Betsy Sprance.

"Like a book."

"Crap." His call rolled over into voicemail. "Betsy, it's Jonathan Gray. Call me as soon as possible. There's been a development." What a time for Betsy to go dark. "Fen, can you—"

"Don't worry. I'll take care of the check. Now, get out of here."

Chapter Twenty-Four: Ranger

Monday, February 2, 2015 – 1:19 p.m.

Betsy's seat belt tightened as the SUV skidded to a stop. Being effectively blind due to the blackened windows meant Betsy had to rely on her other senses. The trip from NOMA had taken just over forty-five minutes. Judging by their speed, the number of stops, and changes in the vehicle's pitch and angling, they had driven through town for several minutes and accelerated onto the interstate. Then they drove without stopping for about twenty minutes, exited, and stopped, with the engine still idling. Sounds of jet engines overhead suggested they were near the airport. After two minutes, the SUV started moving—seeming to reverse direction—heading back onto the interstate.

They drove for approximately twenty-five minutes after leaving their parking spot. The last few minutes were bumpier than the earlier part of the trip. Not the normal bumpiness of traveling across pothole-pocked streets. Gravel ricocheting against the underside of the vehicle hinted that they were on an unpaved road.

Perhaps their trip had been to disorient Betsy. Or maybe to ferret out anyone who might be following them. Probably both.

Echoes as the engine turned off indicated that the vehicle was in an inside space. Maybe a large garage or warehouse. Sharp odors of industrial lubricants and gasoline wafted into the vehicle. Multiple doors opened. Muffled voices and footsteps on a hard surface—probably concrete—

reverberated around the car. Betsy balled her hands into fists, then thought about the futility of resistance under the circumstances. Betsy blinked to acclimate her eyes to the brightness as the car door opened.

"We've arrived, Lieutenant Sprance." The woman from before motioned to Betsy to exit the vehicle.

"Thank you, Officer—"

"Special Agent," the woman said. "Special Agent Dismukes."

"Thank you, Agent Dismukes." Betsy clambered out of the back seat, entering a large space. External windows allowed sunlight into the area but were too high to see anything outside other than the sky, clouds, and an occasional bird. Three men and one woman stood guard—as if Betsy might try to make a run for it. Two of the quartet were the two HSI agents—the ones with pistols drawn—from NOMA. The other two must have been the drivers. "Is my husband here?"

"Yes, ma'am." Dismukes gestured with her arm. "Through that door."

"My sidearm and phone?"

"No can do, Lieutenant." Dismukes shook her head. "We'll return them once we're done."

Betsy moved forward, followed closely by Special Agent Dismukes and flanked by the rest of her entourage. The structure indeed appeared to be a warehouse. Betsy's nostrils flared at the musty odor. Rusting metal girders hinted that the facility was no longer in active use—at least as a warehouse. Faint screeching mews from seagulls outside suggested a location near Lake Pontchartrain. Of course, in New Orleans, almost everywhere was near the lake or other body of water where seagulls might flock.

Betsy stopped at a door with an alphanumeric keypad adjacent to it on the wall. A surveillance camera panned the area. Agent Dismukes nodded toward the camera. The keypad buzzed and clicked, as the door opened approximately an inch.

"Go ahead," Dismukes said. "It's okay."

Stepping through the doorway was like entering another world. The space inside was bright, almost pristine, like the clean room of a computer data center or medical lab.

"Second door on the left." Dismukes pointed. "Sergeant Major Sprance might still be sleeping, so don't be alarmed."

Betsy stepped toward the door. Ranger had been in such pain the last time she saw him in the hospital about three weeks ago. Two bullets in the back will do that. Thank God she and Mitch Broussard had fired so quickly at the figure in dark clothes and a ski mask. And thank God Ranger was so solid, a mass of muscle and sinew. Otherwise…Betsy's gut churned as she opened the door. Whatever condition Ranger was in would beat the hell out of the alternative.

Special Agent Dismukes called it right. Ranger was asleep. A medical device, apparently monitoring his vital signs, operated nearby. Good. He seemed stable.

Betsy approached the bed, then hesitated at the edge. She bent over and placed her left hand on the bed, then extended her right hand toward her husband's. She shifted her head downward as if readying to whisper something in his ear. "Oh my God, Ranger." Her voice quivered. "I'm so sorry."

"Thought you might be." Ranger's left eye opened slowly, and the edges of his mouth turned upward, almost a smile. "Been waiting to hear you say it."

"*Soc au' lait.*" Betsy pushed away from the bed and jumped back.

"Ow." Ranger winced, his voice somewhere between a laugh and a groan. "Not so fast."

"Jesus Christ." Betsy breathed in and out rapidly as if she were about to hyperventilate. "What the hell's wrong with you?"

"Nothing that a little sympathy wouldn't cure."

"Look." Betsy took a cleansing breath. "I said I was sorry."

"I know, Baby." He grasped Betsy's hand. "And I know you couldn't have known it was me."

"What in God's name were you doing at Sonny's in the first place?" She sat on the edge of the bed, slowly. "And the knife…"

"I can't say much." Ranger glanced toward a large mirror on the wall to his right. "Not now anyway."

Betsy had been on the other side of a two-way window watching interviews enough to know what was happening. "I understand. But why—"

"I told them that I needed to let you see that I was okay, on the mend." His eyes moistened. "You and Brandon."

"Them?"

"Let's just leave it at that for now." He looked toward the window. "I promise. This will all work out in the end. They'll read you into the program soon, when the time's right." He exhaled a cleansing breath. "Now come closer so I can give you a kiss."

Betsy leaned toward Ranger.

He angled in, as if to initiate a kiss, then moved his head toward her ear. He whispered. "Follow the rest of the plan."

"Okay, but—"

The door opened, and Agent Dismukes appeared. "Sergeant Major, you'll need to wrap this up for now."

Betsy stood up from the bed, being careful not to move it too much. "But—"

"Please follow me, Lieutenant." Dismukes motioned toward the door. "We'll continue to watch after your husband until he's a hundred percent… and make sure he's safe."

"Safe? From what?"

"Not what." Ranger coughed. "Who."

"That's all we can say at this point." Dismukes peered at Ranger as if irritated by his comment. "Lieutenant Sprance." Dismukes motioned to the door. "Time for us to take you home."

Chapter Twenty-Five: Ian and The John

Monday, February 2, 2015 – 3:56 p.m.

Mitch Broussard sipped coffee, nodded his approval to the manager of Jazz Harbor standing behind the bar, and turned his eyes toward the large plate-glass window overlooking Frenchmen Street. The manager, Tony, had been very kind to offer him a cup while he waited for Ian Wilkerson, the establishment's host—their *maître d'* as Tony referred to him—to arrive for his shift. The restaurant didn't open until five-o'clock, but Tony required Ian and other members of the service staff to show up an hour before opening to prepare for the evening's activities.

The building's interior blended exposed brick and wood from the nineteenth-century storefronts it occupied with modern lighting and amenities. An aroma of cayenne and filé gumbo filled the air. The cooks must have started their shifts long before the other employees. All in all, he could see why Janelle and Tam sought refuge and felt so comfortable in the warm, welcoming environment.

A man appearing to be in his mid-twenties passed the window and entered the restaurant. A touch under six feet tall, he was thin but muscular. Certainly, no ninety-eight-pound weakling. Probably capable of taking care of business if faced with a threatening situation. His flowing dreadlocks, neatly tied in a ponytail and adorned with beads on the ends, made him a dead ringer for the man Mitch and Betsy had seen on the security footage as he left Jazz Harbor—along with a couple of other men—just before midnight on Saturday.

The front door closed behind the man with a loud *thump* as he removed his jacket. Tony made a "come here" motion with his right hand. After a brief discussion, Ian, assuming that's who it was, dropped his jacket on a barstool and made his way toward Mitch.

"Tony says you want to talk to me."

The guy smiled. More of a tentative, show your teeth and grin sort of pose. Most likely, an attempt to compensate for being nervous as hell about an unannounced visit from a cop. An oval nametag above his shirt pocket identified him as "Ian."

"You're Ian Wilkerson?" Mitch displayed his badge and introduced himself. The guy was good-looking. Blue-green eyes. Easy to see why Tam had been attracted to him.

"Yeah…yes, sir…what's this about?"

"Have a seat." Mitch motioned toward the bar. "And don't worry. I told Tony this was about a hit-and-run you may have witnessed."

"I see. So, what's this about?"

"You were working last Saturday night, correct?"

"Yes, sir."

"You remember a couple of young women coming in around ten p.m. or so?"

"Well, we're usually busy…packed…on Saturday nights. And there were parades in the Marigny that night."

"These two were sorority sisters from Ole Miss. One a blonde. The other a brunette. Both real attractive."

"Um. We get a lot of attractive girls in here. Especially on weekends. Even more on parade nights."

Mitch removed photographs of Mississippi driver's licenses for "Bette Davis" and "Joan Crawford" from his portfolio and slid them across the table toward Ian. "Jog your memory?" Mitch leaned back in his chair, crossed his arms, and waited.

"Pretty common names, Joan and Bette. I mean, I'm not sure I can say for certain."

"Anything strike you as odd?" Mitch pulled a half-cheroot from his shirt pocket and clamped it between his teeth.

"I'm sorry Mister…Sergeant…Detective…Broussard we don't allow—"

He removed the cigar from his mouth. "Don't worry. I'm not going to smoke it. Now, anything strike you as odd about the licenses?"

Ian's eyes darted back and forth between the two photos. His olive-toned face flushed. Very subtle but nonetheless noticeable.

"Like both being from the same town?" Mitch pointed to the licenses. "Or having the exact same birthday? Both turning twenty-one the day they were in here? Anything?"

"We don't really question…I mean, as far as I could tell they were—"

"Twins from Tupelo?" Mitch chomped on his cigar. What fun, watching a witness squirm.

"Look, Detective, if Tony finds out—"

"I'm not here about two girls with fake IDs and some underaged drinking during Mardi Gras."

"Then what's this about?"

Mitch removed a photograph of the victim on the AIDS memorial from his portfolio and slid it across the table toward Ian. His eyes bulged, and his mouth moved, but no words came out.

Mitch spit out a couple of small pieces of tobacco. "One of the girls was assaulted in Washington Square Park around midnight. We think by this guy."

"You don't think that I had anything to do with *that*, do you?"

"Why don't you tell me what happened on Saturday night?"

"But it's nearly four-thirty, and we open at—"

"I know. Five." Mitch removed the chewed-up stogie from his mouth and dropped it into his cup. "You can either take a few minutes now and get me up to speed. Or I can drive you down to the Sixth District, and we can have a formal…conversation."

Ian shook his head and glanced toward Tony—and several members of the waitstaff preparing the restaurant to open. "Now's good."

Ian confirmed the basic details of his encounter with Tam and Janelle as outlined in Betsy Sprance's report of her interview with Janelle. The unknown details centered on his post-shift activities with Tam. She met him at The John sometime after midnight. They stayed there for a short time, then went to his place a few blocks away and spent the rest of the night together—in bed. He drove her to her car at the Marigny Inn the next morning in time for her to check out of the hotel.

"So, you didn't see Ms. Crawford—Janelle—after you left Jazz Harbor just before midnight?" Mitch asked.

"Right. I swear."

"And you don't know anything about Washington Square Park?"

"Rumors. No details. And nothing about the girl—Janelle."

"Do you know where Tam went after you dropped her off?"

"Back to Tupelo?"

"You haven't contacted her?"

Ian shook his head. "No, sir."

"Didn't ask for her number or email, anything."

"No, sir."

"And she hasn't contacted you?"

"No, sir. I swear."

"Okay, Ian. I think I have enough of your version, for now."

"What happens next?"

"We'll be in touch if we need anything else." Mitch placed the photographs back in his portfolio and stood. "Best of luck on your shift tonight." He turned toward the door. "And give my thanks to Tony for the coffee."

Chapter Twenty-Six: Visiting Mae's Place

Monday, February 2, 2015 – 6:22 p.m.

Jonathan entered the waiting area of Momma Mae's 24-Hour Gumbo and Poultry House in the Carrolton section of New Orleans, placed his sidearm in a locker, and pocketed the key. He probably could have insisted that he was on official business. But it was best to avoid any issues with carrying a firearm in an establishment that served alcohol.

"Hello, Mae." Jonathan greeted Mae Taliaferro, a longtime family friend and owner of several local restaurants. "Thanks for calling me."

"She's in the bar." Mae tilted her head to the left. "Been here about an hour…hitting it pretty hard the entire time…mumbling incomprehensible stuff about Ranger."

"Got it," Jonathan said. "You have some place out of the way I can bring her? Maybe one of the private dining spaces?"

"Of course. The Rodrigue Room." She pointed down the hall. "Should be comfortable enough."

"Thanks." Jonathan started toward the bar, then stopped. Betsy Sprance—occupying a table in a dark corner—stared into a nearly empty cocktail glass. Another drink, what looked like a newly poured Sazerac, rested on the table. "Mae, can you bring us a pot of coffee and two mugs?"

"I'll put them in the room," Mae said. "Let me know if there's anything else you need."

Jonathan turned toward the sound of clinking glasses, short bursts of laughter, and zydeco playing on the jukebox. Time to bring Betsy back from the brink.

"Need some company?" Jonathan sat in a chair across the table from Betsy.

"Suit yourself." Betsy finished her drink, placed the empty glass on the table, and reached for the next cocktail. "It's a cree…free…country."

"Didn't take you for a day-drinker." Jonathan picked up the empty glass, looked at it, then returned it to the table. "Something happen?"

"It's after working hours. Mormal…normal…working hours." She picked up her glass and swirled the contents. "Guess you've never been snapped… snatched…by the feds and stuffed in the back of a…" She sipped from her fresh Sazerac. "And have your husband dead…come back from the dead… not dead…but almost."

"Ranger?"

Betsy took a longer pull from her drink.

"Must have been tough. How many Sazeracs have you had?"

"A couple…maybe two."

Jonathan pointed to Betsy's drink, looked toward the bartender, and mouthed the words "how many." The bartender held up his hand, palm toward Jonathan, with all the digits showing.

Jonathan leaned toward Betsy. "More like five, maybe?"

Betsy looked toward the floor. "Could be."

Five Sazeracs in just over an hour. Jesus. Even if she just started number five, she'd already had four shots—about six ounces—of Rye Whiskey. And dashes of Absinthe and Peychaud's Bitters. She'd be lucky to make it to the Rodrigue Room without falling over.

Jonathan moved the partially consumed Sazerac—number five—out of Betsy's reach and held onto it. Her eyes reflected a combination of "screw you" and "thanks."

"Listen." Jonathan lowered his voice. "I can't imagine what you're going through right now. But I need you…sober…now more than ever." He slid the Sazerac toward Betsy. "I'll understand if you're not up to the challenge just now. But I need to know."

"Can't you space me…give me some space?" Betsy reached for the glass but stopped before grabbing it. "I need time to think."

"There's been a break."

"The maphis…manipest…the cipher?"

"Manifesto. Emma came up with a decent translation."

"Shit." Betsy inhaled and exhaled in short bursts, then took a long cleansing breath. She moistened her lips with her tongue. "That woman's a…a genie… a genus…she's incredible."

"And she'd never let us live it down if we didn't do something with the info."

Betsy placed her head in her hands and leaned forward over the table. She rubbed her face as if trying to stimulate the circulation. "Okay…so, what do we do now?"

"We're going hunting."

Betsy looked up. "Say what?"

"Tonight. Around midnight. We're going to cruise town to see if the Sweeper tries anything." He stood. "I'll fill you in over coffee. You can tell me about Ranger. And maybe we can ask Mae to send some food our way."

Betsy stood, keeping one hand on the table. "What did the cipher say?"

"More about that when we're in the Rodrigue Room…and you've had some caffeine." He moved toward Betsy and offered her his arm for support. "But I'll say this much at this point."

"Okay?"

"I deciphered the note from the St. Louis Cemetery victim."

"What'd it say?"

"Among other things," Jonathan whispered. "Cleo will pay twice the price."

Chapter Twenty-Seven: The Axeman Redux?

Monday, February 2, 2015 – 11:27 p.m.

Jonathan engaged the directional signal on an unmarked Ford Explorer with Orleans Parish license plates as the vehicle proceeded along Canal Street, then turned right onto North Rampart. Betsy Sprance sat quietly in the passenger seat. Her lips moved, but no words came out, as a flashlight beam highlighted Emma Gray's transcription of the note found in the left hand of the dead man from Washington Square Park, along with Jonathan's best guess of what the symbols in brackets meant:

esteemed mortals [:]

you thought you killed me [,] [but] i swam [with] fishes [.] you call me [the] sweeper [.] undoubtedly [,] you think me [a] most horrible murderer [.]

[but] i alone keep carnival clean [.] i strike [,] then i watch [.] when you fail [,] i must come back [and] finish your work [.] if you try [to] stop me [,] you will incurmy wrath [.]

until next we meet [,] adieu [.]

yours truly [,]

[the] sweeper

"Soup to nuts." Betsy drank from a bottle of water, then returned the bottle to a cupholder in the center console. "Esteemed mortals."

"Right," Jonathan said. "Wants to remind us of the New Orleans Axeman."

"Not surprised." Betsy drank more water. "Another part of the Sweeper's Eff-You calling card."

"Rubbing it in that no one caught the Axeman—"

"After almost a hundred years—"

"And taunting us that no one will catch the Sweeper, either."

"Egotistical son-of-a—"

"You ever known a serial killer who wasn't?"

"Suppose not." Betsy yawned.

"You doing okay? Feeling all right?"

"I've been better." She drank more water. "Coffee helped—"

"And Mae's chicken sandwich—"

"Hit the spot…a couple hours of sleep, shower, change of clothes…all good."

"Great. Keep pushing the fluids."

"Say, Doc, about earlier."

"Don't give it another thought. You've hit a rough patch. I mean, seeing Ranger like that and all."

"Yeah, right." Betsy stared out the front windshield. "Ranger."

"Don't count him out. He said it would all work out in the end, right?"

"Who the hell knows what that even means."

"Not much you can do, I guess," Jonathan said. "But listen. Maybe Tom Yarid can shed some light…I mean, the FBI must have some resources…insights."

"I suppose I could talk to Mandy Simpson in the U.S. Attorney's Office."

"Agreed. We'll dig into it first thing tomorrow. In the meantime—"

"Right. Keep my eyes peeled. You think we'll see anyone tonight?"

"Don't know. This guy's been unpredictable. Maybe we'll get lucky. If the patrol car had been just a minute earlier to St. Louis Number One…"

"I wonder," Betsy said, "why the Sweeper's not following his plan."

"Plan?"

"Didn't you say that the cipher on the streetcar translated to *vieux*.

"That's right."

"The Sweeper killed someone on the same night and same basic location as the Krewe du Vieux parade."

"Right," Jonathan said. "The Washington Square Park guy."

"And the chest carving on him translated to *Cleo*, right?"

"Cleopatra. Krewe of Cleopatra. Rolls Friday night."

"And all the previous Sweeper murders were along or near the parade routes."

"So, you wonder why he killed the guy last night at St. Louis Number One, right?"

"It's a puzzle, Doc." Betsy drank more water. "Especially since the note on the St. Louis Number One victim returned to the parade angle."

"Right. Cleo will pay twice the price."

"You think he was trying to throw us off the track?"

"Got me," Jonathan said. "But if this guy's deviated from the pattern once, maybe he'll do it again. And the clues in the rest of the St. Louis Number One letter give us a couple of hints."

"Listen, Doc, before we get into that. Looks like it's going to be another long night. And after all that water, I need to, well, you know."

"Understood. We're close to the Shell off Bayou St. John. Good enough?"

"It'll have to do."

The radio crackled. "This is Unit Two-Six-Three. We've got a dead body. On Tchoupitoulas. Just past Calliope…under the bridge approach. Cordoning off the area. Request advise next steps."

"Crap." Betsy picked up the handset. "This is Coroner One. Stand by. We're on our way." She replaced the handset. "Looks like I'll need to hold it a bit longer."

Chapter Twenty-Eight: The Lump

Tuesday, February 3, 2015 – 12:09 a.m.

Even on a crisp mid-winter night, New Orleans had its share of homeless who chose not to stay in designated indoor shelters. The roadway above and massive concrete support pilings where Tchoupitoulas Street passed under the approaches to the Crescent City Connection provided a natural location for a tent city. Just enough protection from the elements—especially the biting wind coming off the river—to make the area a magnet for the unhoused. Despite the city's best efforts to clear out the encampments—especially during Carnival season— the occupants melted into the surrounding neighborhoods during the day, only to return each evening.

Jonathan exited his vehicle and angled toward Mitch Broussard, who was talking with a uniformed officer. A few feet away from the pair lay a rectangular lump of ragged blankets and clothes. A shock of hair and partial view of a bearded face provided solid evidence that the lump was human. Lack of blood—fresh or dried—suggested that the head wasn't severed. And that he hadn't been shot or stabbed to death. More likely, his body had finally given out—no longer able to cope with the elements, with the persistent lack of adequate food and shelter, or with a loss of hope that things would get better.

On the other side of the yellow "Do Not Cross" tape, a dozen or so individuals—both adults and small children—congregated. Intermittent traffic noise from the highway above underscored the urban setting. Smoke from fires in metal barrels—and the telltale scents of marijuana and body odor—added a bizarre atmospheric twist.

"Evening, Mitch," Jonathan said.

"Howdy, Doc," Mitch looked at Jonathan and then at his vehicle. "Riding solo? Thought Lieutenant Sprance was with you."

"Pit stop," Jonathan said. "Dropped her at the Chevron. Should be here in a couple of minutes."

"Got it." Mitch smiled. "When nature calls, you best answer right quick."

"Been here long, Mitch?" No use commenting further on Betsy's bladder habits.

"Just pulled in myself. Been getting the rundown from Officer Goncalves."

"Evening, officer." Jonathan gestured toward the human-shaped mass on the ground. "You find the body?"

"Yes, sir." Goncalves said. "Me and my partner…that's her standing by the group over there…we saw a bunch of homeless…sorry…unhoused residents…hovering over something on the ground. Looked odd. So, we conducted a walk-through of the…of the encampment and saw him."

"Him?" Jonathan asked. "You got close enough to tell?"

"Yes, sir," Goncalves's face reddened as if he were embarrassed that he'd done something wrong. "Had to check to make sure he was dead…barely touched him, though."

"You followed protocol, Goncalves," Mitch said. "And you did a good job cordoning off the area…moving the crowd out of the way."

"Thanks, Detective." Goncalves smiled. "They didn't much care for it when we made 'em stand out in the cold, away from the fires. I was afraid they might interfere."

"Key thing," Jonathan said, "you didn't move him."

"Right…um," Goncalves's voice cracked. "You think he really could be wired? With explosives I mean?"

"That's what we're here to determine," Jonathan said. "Best not take unnecessary chances."

"True dat," Goncalves said.

A large tactical vehicle approached from the left and slowed as it got closer. Betsy Sprance stood on the running board, one hand grasping the side rail, the other hand holding a disposable coffee cup.

"We contacted EOD on the way here." Jonathan pointed. "Must be them coming now."

"Never worked with the bomb squad before," Goncalves said.

Betsy hopped off the running board and jogged toward Jonathan, Mitch, and Officer Goncalves. Behind her, the vehicle stopped. Several individuals dressed in tactical gear got out and assembled near the front bumper. One of them walked toward Gray and the others.

"Sorry I'm late." Betsy held up a cup marked "AM/PM Coffee"—the Chevron C-store's logo. "Had to empty out so I could fill up." She leaned her head toward the Explosive Ordinance Disposal vehicle. "And look who I ran into on the way."

"Glad you're here," Jonathan said. "We were just discussing next steps in dealing with our latest guest over there."

"Then I'm your man…Sergeant Willa Delacroix." She extended her hand to Jonathan. "Well." She motioned toward the officers assembled in front of the tactical vehicle. "Me and my team, that is."

Jonathan accepted the handshake. "Welcome to the party, Sergeant."

"You're worried the body might be fixed to blow," Delacroix said. "Like at St. Louis Number One?"

"Affirmative," Jonathan said. "Wasn't sure how much you knew."

"Hard to keep something like that off the fuzz buzz," Delacroix said. "You need to flip him over to see if he's wired, right?"

"True dat, Willa," Betsy said. "Recommendations?"

"Once you've determined the scene's been sufficiently documented." Sergeant Delacroix motioned toward her EOD team. "We'll clip on cordage…ropes…then hoist the body up using a series of frames we'll set up to act as a lift point." She looked toward the group on the other side of the crime scene tape. "And keep them at a safe distance."

The crowd grew noticeably louder as the officers continued their work clearing the immediate area around the body.

"Leave our homes alone." One of the people in the crowd gestured with his fist and pressed against the crime scene tape. "Let him rest in peace."

Officer Goncalves's partner shifted to her left, raised her baton, and placed it parallel to the ground, chest high. "Move back, sir. Let the officers do their work."

The man raised his middle finger, mumbled a profanity, then faded into the group. The crowd had doubled in size, up to at least two dozen people. Indistinct grumbling continued as EOD personnel attached four ropes to the dead man's clothing with large clips, then looped the ropes into their makeshift block-and-tackle arrangement.

Jonathan walked—somewhere between a purposeful march and a don't-cause-alarm saunter—toward the yellow tape and stopped a half-dozen feet from Goncalves's partner. A silent message to the increasingly rowdy residents: reinforcements have arrived.

Sergeant Delacroix raised her arm, then she surveyed the area. She looked at the four officers holding the ropes, then lowered her arm. "Go."

The EOD personnel tugged gently on the ropes, and the body moved slightly. Silence blanketed the scene—except for the sounds of the river breeze and vehicles from the highway overhead. As if they shared a common psyche in that instant, everyone inhaled, then collectively held their breath in anticipation. All eyes focused on the body and the ropes.

The team pulled their cords in tandem—slowly, deliberately, as if time stood still except for the team's actions. The body lifted an inch or two. No blood came gushing out. Still no apparent signs of injury. More important, no flashbang or other explosion. The team continued to tug at the lines, and the body's right side lifted, inch by inch. After a few more repetitions, gravity would take over, and the body would fall onto its back, mission accomplished.

Jonathan exhaled slowly as a single sheet of white paper with writing on it fell onto the pavement. Another manifesto? He cursed silently as the man's face came into view. Alpha and Omega on the forehead. The Sweeper had been here. No blood oozing from the carvings. So, they must have been made postmortem.

"The mark of the devil." The statement, direct but without emotion—more like a calm declaration of fact—came from someone in the crowd. A flash, then a loud bang—a gunshot—pierced the air.

Almost everyone—even the police—ran or ducked for cover. Screams mixed with excited gasps and angry curse words. The EOD team let go of the ropes, and the body fell back onto its front. Jonathan crouched as low to the ground as he could, his ears ringing from the noise. The sound echoed as the bullet ricocheted off one of the concrete support pilings. Thank God, the spent projectile—most likely a small caliber like a twenty-two—dropped harmlessly onto the ground. The shooter—pistol at his side—stood about four feet away.

Soon, probably within the next second or two, police would regain their composure and eliminate the threat—with weapons blazing. But there were civilians present—including children. No time for reflection, just impulse. Jonathan sprang forward from his crouching position. His shoulder crashed into the shooter just above the waist. Jonathan's heart pounded, and his head throbbed. As he yelled, "don't shoot," he tumbled forward and landed on top of the man. The pistol skittered across the pavement.

Jonathan's shoulder hurt like hell. His nostrils flared, and his eyes watered. The shooter stunk like he hadn't bathed or brushed his teeth in weeks. Regardless, Jonathan had to keep the guy pinned to the ground as the police rushed to assist. He gagged and held his breath as much as possible. Just a few seconds longer, and this part of the nightmare would be over.

Jonathan inhaled a deep cleansing breath, then exhaled, as Betsy helped him stand. Sergeant Delacroix placed the shooter in handcuffs. Jesus Christ. Why was everything so Goddamned hard? But the night wasn't a total loss. They'd located another of the Sweeper's victims along with a continuation of his manifesto. More clues to the Sweeper's plan, his thought process, his motives. But the greatest, most significant development to come out of their efforts? They'd saved a life.

Chapter Twenty-Nine: Beignets and Battleplans

"That was some pretty heroic shit you did back there, Doc." Betsy Sprance wiped powdered sugar from her lips and chin, then sipped coffee.

Jonathan stared into the darkness, across Decatur Street, toward Jackson Square and the illuminated façade of St. Louis Cathedral beyond. Raindrops pinged off the roof of a nearly empty Café du Monde. An increasingly intense downpour obscured his view and added a wintry chill to the open-air facility. He and Betsy were lucky to be protected from the worst of the storm. But what about those poor souls at the homeless encampment?

"No, really." Betsy drank more coffee. "It was soup to nuts, heavy-duty stuff." She bit into a beignet.

"Sorry." Jonathan jolted slightly, as if startled, then turned toward Betsy. "What?"

"Earlier…down off Tchoupitoulas…tackling the homeless guy."

"Yeah, well—"

"He was a trigger pull away from getting turned into mashed potatoes with a side of red gravy."

"Yeah, well—"

"What were you thinking?"

"Not much time for thought." Jonathan sipped his chicory-laced coffee and winced. Café du Monde's signature New Orleans treat. Supposed to be the perfect accompaniment for deep-fried beignets. But bitter as hell and heartburn-inducing. Yet, for some inexplicable reason, demanded by tourists as part of 'the Big Easy experience.' "Had to do something…no use letting the Sweeper chalk up another kill…even an indirect one. I mean, it seemed like a good idea at the time."

"Whatever. That guy was one lucky son-of-a-bitch."

"Maybe." Jonathan sipped more coffee. Seemed less bitter now. "He's *somebody's* son. And who knows how he found himself there? But a human life's a human life."

"Of course—"

"And the others…and the kids…"

"Got it." Betsy sipped coffee. "Could have been a real mess."

"Thank goodness Mitch and Sergeant Delacroix were there to handle the situation…the paperwork…take the guy into custody…all that."

"And let us escape so we could come here and eat some fat pills."

Jonathan managed something approximating a smile. "And plan our next moves."

"Starting with the message left at St. Louis Number One, right?" Betsy sipped coffee. "We got off track earlier. I mean, with the radio call and all."

"Yeah." Jonathan reached into the small portfolio on the chair next to him. "The one about Cleo paying twice the price."

"You have the full translation?"

"And I added my best guess of the symbols Emma couldn't figure out, like I did with the first one. That's the stuff still in brackets." Jonathan placed a single sheet of paper on the small table in front of Betsy. "Here it is:"

disappointing mortals[:]

[the] people must know that [the] entity you call [the] sweeper cleans [the] streets [for] them[.] keeps mardi gras safe [for] them[.]

police may fail [to] reveal my existence[.] [but] [the] times picayune must perform its function[.] [the] people must know me[,] so they can know peace[.] tomorrow[.]

accept this body as another warning[.] i pray none further will be required[.] keep me secret [at] your peril[.] cleo will pay twice [the] price[.]

yours [with] solemnity[,]

[the] sweeper

Jonathan again looked in the direction of St. Louis Cathedral. The rain had slackened, now more of a drizzle. Maybe it would end before they had to leave the café. Betsy concentrated on the document.

"Something going on in the Square, Doc?" Betsy waved her hand in front of Jonathan's face as if to get his attention.

"Sorry." Jonathan shook his head. "Just thinking about something Dan… Monsignor…Rossignol said." He returned his gaze to Betsy. "It's been kicking around in the back of my mind."

"Must be important."

"Remains to be seen. Might be nothing."

"Anything you need me to do?"

"Maybe," Jonathan said. "You have a camera in the car…one with a telephoto lens?"

"In my go-bag. Should I get it?"

"Not yet. Let me chew on it some more. Like I said, might be nothing."

"Okay." Betsy held up the translated document. "Well, this second piece of the manifesto isn't nothing. I mean, it's really something."

"True. What do you make of it?"

"More ego, that's for sure…and that thing about Cleo's worrisome."

"Sure as hell is."

"But what do you make of the comment about the *Times-Pic?*"

Jonathan leaned back in his chair and crossed his arms. "Best guess?"

"Best guess."

"Well." Jonathan looked around the restaurant. Other patrons. Probably none close enough to overhear. But he leaned forward, uncrossed his arms, and lowered his voice. "I think the Sweeper's pissed off at Bryan Whitcomb."

"The reporter?" Betsy asked. "What's he done to the Sweeper?"

"It's what he hasn't done."

"Which means?"

"The Sweeper sent a copy of the first document to the *Times-Pic*."

"The Washington Square Park manifesto?"

"But it apparently went unopened until just before I talked to Whitcomb yesterday morning."

"Interesting."

"And he hadn't deciphered it yet."

"Shit."

"Well, we hadn't figured it out either," Jonathan said.

"Did he have the one from St. Louis Cemetery?"

"Don't know. He didn't mention it. So, probably not."

"And you didn't tell him about it?"

"No. Figured I'd let things play out. The Sweeper might have changed his mind about telling the newspaper."

"So." Betsy looked at the floor then back at Jonathan. "The Sweeper's mad because he thought the *Times-Pic* would run with the story about his return?"

"That's my best guess."

"And the second message—the one from St. Louis Cemetery—expresses the Sweeper's anger…and has a warning that the *Times-Pic* needed to print something tomorrow?"

"Which was yesterday at this point," Jonathan said.

"So, the deadline's come and gone."

"Affirmative."

"Now what happens?"

"Not sure." Jonathan pulled another piece of paper from his portfolio.

"I'm thinking there might be something in the note on the homeless guy."

"Good thought." Betsy pointed at the document. "That the note?"

"Yeah. Copied it by hand before the CSIs showed up. It's a lot shorter than the others."

"Heads up move, Doc. You going to decipher it now?"

"No time like the present." Jonathan pulled another document from his portfolio. "Here's the translation key Emma gave me."

Jonathan looked back and forth between the cipher from the homeless encampment and the translation key. Slow going as he deciphered the note. As the message emerged—symbol-by-symbol, letter-by-letter—he occasionally looked up at Betsy and then went back to his task.

"Got it." Jonathan handed the handwritten translation to Betsy. "Take a look:"

despicable mortals[:]

this body is [a] gift[.] [for] both you [and] me[.] already dead [for] me[.] already dead [for] you[.]

[but] [the] paper failed[.] now [the] rat will die before sunrise[.] cleo will pay thrice [the] price[.]

[the] sweeper

"Soc au' lait." Betsy's eyes reflected a combination of fear and dread. "The rat. You don't suppose he's going after—"

"Mr. Whitcomb…Bryan…this is Jonathan Gray." He mouthed the word *voicemail.* "We think you're the Sweeper's next target. Headed to your place in the Bywater. Twenty minutes, tops."

"Just over an hour till sunrise." Betsy stood. "Let's hope we're not too late."

"Let's hope he gets the message. Too early for him to be in the office." Jonathan placed thirty dollars on the table. "That should take care of it."

"I'll head for the car while you gather your papers."

"Hang on a second." Jonathan looked toward St. Louis Cathedral. "That idea from before…I need you to do something."

"Okay. But won't you need backup at Whitcomb's?"

"You'll need your camera. I'll explain on the way to the car."

Chapter Thirty: Passing Desire

Tuesday, February 3, 2015 – 5:27 a.m.

Jonathan groaned when his vehicle hit yet another pothole as he traveled along Chartres Street on his way to Bryan Whitcomb's bungalow. According to the original GPS projection, he should have arrived at the Congress Street address three minutes ago. But the repeated slowing down, dealing with each pothole, then speeding up—only to slow down again—added delay after delay.

When in hell would the citizens elect a mayor and city council that knew how to fix the streets? Or maybe it was the neighborhood. Downtown, Chartres Street had issues. But nothing like the narrow, pockmarked ribbon of asphalt it became in the Bywater—on the edge of the Lower Ninth. And apparently on the edge of civilization—at least when it came to highway maintenance dollars.

His foot pressed down on the accelerator. Time was of the essence. A life at stake. Another hour to sunrise. But the horizon glowed with faint crimson, blue, and gray hues as dawn approached. He'd just passed Desire Street. About four blocks to go. Maybe he could make up a few minutes if he pushed it. Maybe—

Bam! He jolted forward, and his shoulder belt tightened. Then came a metallic grinding and hissing sound from the front of the vehicle. The car, listing to the right, stopped moving. Goddammit. Another pothole. More accurately, a hidden moon crater, waiting to swallow his supposedly indestructible SUV. He should have slowed down, paid more attention.

He turned off the engine and got out. He cursed under his breath as he inspected the damage. Right front tire flat. Damage to the fender and bumper. Perhaps a broken wheel rim or, worse, a cracked or broken axle. Another three minutes gone. Nothing to do now but head to Whitcomb's place on foot. He'd kept in reasonable shape. Probably couldn't sprint the entire way, but he could sure as hell try. At least it wasn't raining.

But he couldn't leave his SUV in the middle of the street. It'd be a hazard to navigation, so to speak. He got back in the vehicle. The engine didn't turn over. He cursed and slapped the steering wheel. Another minute lost. He closed his eyes and took a deep cleansing breath. He needed to stay calm. He tried the ignition again. No luck. Another cleansing breath, then back to the ignition—this time with a silent prayer. Success. The engine roared to life.

"Come on, old girl." Jonathan spoke to the SUV as if it were human. "Almost there. You can do it."

The injured vehicle creaked and groaned as he guided it past the sidewalk and onto the green space between Chartres Street and the flood wall. The engine sputtered, as if to say "I've given you all I can," then fell silent. He exited the vehicle and checked for his sidearm and badge. He cursed under his breath. More than ten minutes pissed away because of this one freaking pothole.

Jonathan sprinted along Chartres toward its intersection with Gallier Street. He was making good time now. Just another couple of…

He stumbled, then righted himself without falling. But the damage was done. A twisted ankle. He looked down. He hadn't seen the area, on the Chartres Street side of Elizabeth's Restaurant, where the sidewalk bulged upward. Not a large bulge, just enough to trip the unwary. And in the predawn haze, unnoticeable.

Potholes and unsafe sidewalks. It's as if the city wanted him to be late. As if the mayor and city council were on the Sweeper's side. He shook his head. What a stupid thought.

No time for placing blame. He had to get to Whitcomb's—*now*. He hobbled forward, stopping occasionally to shake out the ankle pain. After another two minutes of hobble-and-rest, he'd made it to Congress and turned left. Whitcomb's house, just over a block away—a few houses past Dauphine—came into view. The bungalow and the neighboring homes appeared calm. Maybe the Sweeper hadn't made it yet. Jonathan shuddered. Or, maybe the Sweeper had already been there and...

But he needed to be optimistic. Despite everything, he'd made it well before sunrise. He prayed his luck would hold.

He limped up the steps to Whitcomb's front porch. The one-story structure, long and narrow—similar to the common New Orleans shotgun house, but larger. The front door, flanked by five small windowpanes—sidelights—on each side, boasted a Mardi Gras themed—purple, green, and gold—wreath. No storm door.

Jonathan banged on the wall adjacent to the entrance. "Brian, it's me." A dog barked from a house on the right. "Jonathan Gray." More barking. He grabbed the doorknob. Locked.

The sidelight windows revealed a mostly dark interior. A dim glow, probably from a nightlight, provided faint background illumination.

Jonathan banged on the wall again. "Brian. We need to talk."

The dog stopped barking. Something—or someone—moved inside. Whatever—or whoever—it was didn't approach the front door and didn't respond. A noise, perhaps a muffled human voice, echoed from the back of the residence.

"Damn." Jonathan turned with his back to the house. He flattened himself against the wall on the right side of the door. "Brian, I'm coming." He extended his right arm forward, then reversed direction and crashed his elbow into the lowest of the sidelight panes. At the noise of shattering glass, a different dog barked—this one from somewhere across the street. The first dog, oddly, remained silent. Jonathan brushed bits of glass off his coat sleeve, then reached through the window to unlock the door.

The figure dashed to the left, possibly angling for one of the windows on the side of the house. Jonathan limped down the steps. The apparent intruder, dressed in black, a ski mask, and gloves, and wearing a small backpack, vaulted the chain-link fence marking the side yard, then collided with Jonathan. Both Jonathan and the figure staggered back from one another—as if they had both bounced off a rubber wall—wobbled, then fell to the ground.

Jonathan gasped for air as he pulled himself up. He reached for his sidearm. "Coroner's Office. Hands behind—"

Jonathan doubled over when a metal bar crashed into his abdomen. He groaned and collapsed onto his hands and knees. He gagged but didn't vomit. The intruder raced away on foot and turned right onto Dauphine Street, out of view.

He again dragged himself to his feet. "I'm getting too old for this." His ankle throbbed as he limped up the steps, removed his pistol from its holster, and entered Whitcomb's bungalow. He moved slowly, sidearm in a low-ready position. Glass crunched under his shoes. His nose wrinkled at an odor wafting from the kitchen.

"Brian. You here?" Jonathan stepped closer to a hallway leading to the back of the house. "It's Jonathan Gray." He surveyed the area, watching for signs of life. "It's safe."

Brian Whitcomb emerged, barefoot, dressed in pajama bottoms and a tee-shirt. "Thank God."

Jonathan lowered his weapon. "Sorry I'm late."

"No worries." Whitcomb exhaled a loud sigh. "I got your message and locked myself in the bathroom. I could hear the bastard…inside my house."

Jonathan returned his sidearm to its holster. "Don't come any closer…the door…there's glass."

"No problem. You okay?"

"I've been better, but I'll live." Jonathan put his hands on his abdomen and winced. "I think the Sweeper introduced me to his collapsible baton…his ASP."

"Thank your lucky stars he didn't go for your knees."

"Small miracles." Jonathan managed a chuckle. "But what's that smell?"

"Looks like my visitor left a calling card on the kitchen table. Damn. A copy of the *Times-Pic* and…holy shit…is that—"

"At least he has good taste," Jonathan said. "Redfish."

Chapter Thirty-One: Errands to Run

Tuesday, February 3, 2015 – 6:54 a.m.

Betsy Sprance sauntered along Bourbon Street toward St. Ann. In the distance—on the far side of Canal, upriver boundary of the French Quarter—gleaming skyscrapers in the Central Business District reminded the world that New Orleans was a modern city. A stark contrast with the smaller structures of the Quarter, the homely but powerful tourist magnet of the local economy. First rays of sunrise highlighted weathered facades—wood, stucco, and brick structures—that had seen their better days.

Thankfully, it wasn't a weekend. Fewer revelers—drunks—in the Quarter meant less odor from bodily fluids—mostly urine and vomit—fouling the morning air, waiting for city workers, or the rain, to wash them away. A steady breeze from the river helped. Then, the wind shifted. Her nose crinkled at the pungent aroma. Another benefit of life in The Big Easy.

Regardless, she needed to pick up the pace if she expected to reach Jackson Square in time to get settled in place without drawing attention. But her body—especially her digestive system—protested whenever she pushed too hard. No wonder. Beignets at Café du Monde with Jonathan. Later, a full breakfast at Clover Grill as she passed the time waiting to carry out her assignment. She was lucky to be moving at all. It was like having a bowling ball meandering its way through her gut, weighing her down.

And her assignment? A real puzzler. Jonathan had always been on top of things. But photographing people coming and going from St. Louis Cathedral? Maybe the pressure was getting to him. And the timing? Between seven-fifteen and eight-fifteen. You didn't have to be a genius to figure it out—just a practicing Catholic. Confessions were usually scheduled for the thirty minutes before each Mass. This morning, that would be from 7:30 a.m. until Mass started at eight. So, anyone entering or exiting during the designated one-hour window was likely a penitent.

Why in God's name did he want her to document people going to confession? And why the secrecy? "Don't let anyone see you." Jonathan had been quite insistent. "Act like a tourist." Odd. Weird, even.

What if Father Edward at Blessed Sacrament-St. Joan of Arc found out what she was doing? "Forgive me Father...I photographed faithful Catholics—who just might be potential serial killers—outside St. Louis Cathedral." Lord knows she didn't have time to worry about being excommunicated—or whatever—with all the other crap she faced. On forced admin leave from NOPD. The Sweeper back from the dead. Ranger and his "stick with the plan" nonsense. Buying burner phones. Doubling the cash in their safe deposit box. Purchasing prepaid debit cards. Making sure the key was where they agreed.

Besides, how could taking photos as part of your police duties be a sin, faithful Catholics or not? Maybe she wouldn't mention it to Father Ed. Even he would have to agree that catching a murderer and saving lives outweighed...

"Excuse me, Lieutenant Sprance."

The voice came from around the corner on St. Ann Street, so Betsy pivoted to her left. Her hand dropped toward her holstered handgun. Damn. How could she let someone get the drop on her? Too much daydreaming. She should have been paying more attention to her surroundings. "Agent Dismukes. Where did...how—"

"No need for alarm, Lieutenant." Dismukes held her hands out in front of her at about waist level, apparently to show that she was not reaching for her sidearm. "I just need to speak with you."

"Okay. But how did you find..." Betsy stopped in mid-sentence. "My God."

Her temples pounded, and her face warmed. "Has something happened to Ranger?"

"That's what we're hoping you can tell us."

"What the hell does that mean?" Betsy moved closer to Agent Dismukes, then lowered her voice. "I thought you had him locked up."

"Not locked up…he's in protective custody," Dismukes said. "Or at least he *was* in protective custody."

"What the fu—"

"Sergeant Major Sprance went missing last night."

"What do you mean, he went missing?"

"We made no secret about where his clothes were," Dismukes said. "He…" She looked to her right and stopped talking. A woman—petite, slightly stooped, and relying on a cane—hobbled toward them.

"Good morning." The woman smiled at Betsy and Agent Dismukes. "Wonderful day for a stroll, don't you think?"

"Yes, ma'am," Betsy said. "Headed to Café du Monde for coffee?"

"Oh, no." The lady smiled. "Off to services. Don't want to be late for Mass." She leaned on her cane. "Takes a lot longer than it used to."

"I understand." Betsy managed a smile, despite wanting to curse out loud. The woman was probably on her way to confession. Betsy needed to get into position. But first, she needed to find out about Ranger. "Take care."

"Good day, ma'am," Dismukes said.

"Thank you." The woman stepped toward St. Ann Street. "Have a blessed day."

"What do you…" Betsy kept her voice low, nearly at a whisper. "You mean he just got dressed and waltzed out of your facility without anyone noticing?"

"Sergeant Major Sprance is…resourceful…and determined."

"He *is* stubborn." Betsy managed something approximating a grin. "I'll give you that. But he's injured."

"He's almost fully healed. Some residual pain…he's on meds for that. And physical therapy. He's almost back to where he was before, physically. And he's probably stronger and in better shape than most men half his age—injured or not."

"Well." Betsy's face relaxed. Great. Ranger was almost healed. He was in the wind, whereabouts unknown. But at least he was okay. "He always was strong as an ox. I'll give you that, too."

"And he left us this." Dismukes held up her cell phone. A picture of a handwritten note:

Sorry. Errands to run. Back later. Sprance.

"That's his handwriting all right."

"You have any clue what errands he's talking about?"

"No."

"And you haven't seen your husband since—"

"Since you made me leave his bedside and drove me home in a blacked-out SUV?"

"Well…he told us—"

"No. I haven't seen…or heard from…him." Betsy cleared her throat. Still too early for Ranger to get into the safe-deposit box to retrieve the burner phone. "Now, if you'll excuse me, I'm on the clock, and I have a task to complete."

"Of course."

"And please don't tail me. I let my guard down this time…won't happen again."

"Yes, of course. You'll let us know if Sergeant Major Sprance contacts you?"

"Yes, of course." Betsy bit her tongue to avoid the smirk that the comment deserved. "You'll be among the first to know."

Chapter Thirty-Two: Heartbeats and Absolution

Tuesday, February 3, 2015 – 7:06 a.m.

Stryker strode along St. Louis Street, nearing the French Quarter, counting heartbeats. Fitness monitors were fairly reliable. But the best way to take your pulse and be certain of the result was the old-fashioned way. Fingers on your wrist or neck—your carotid artery. Eyes on the countdown timer. Even worked while walking. Stryker smiled internally. Sixteen beats in fifteen seconds. Heart rate of sixty-four. Not bad, all things considered.

Physical strength remained paramount. But the road back had been difficult. For months, survival hung in the balance. Chemo, radiation, experimental meds—and all the side effects that came along with them— had taken a toll. Baldness. Nausea. Being too exhausted to exercise. The worst part? Being alone. No one in your corner. The doctors and nurses were great, but it wasn't the same. Though perhaps he *was* there in a way. Funny how planning your revenge could give you a reason to live.

Ringing the bell made it all worthwhile. And the new crop of thicker hair signaled a return to a more normal life. Under most circumstances, maybe that should have been enough to let go of the past. But the Oncologist had seemed grim after the latest test results. So they'd done a more complete scan to be sure. Regardless, the thought of going through it all again…none of it mattered, really. The bastard responsible would pay. Final justice loomed, the plan coming together.

This morning had been another test. A visit to the lazy reporter's house. Prying his back door open, without making too much noise. Leaving a special gift—in a copy of the *Times-Picayune*—as a reminder that Whitcomb could end up sleeping with the fishes anytime Stryker desired. Not an actual threat. The reporter wasn't on the death list. Not yet. But he—and his newspaper—needed a final warning. Print the manifesto and announce the Mardi Gras Sweeper's return—or suffer the consequences.

And that son-of-a-bitch coroner. What a pain in the ass. But at least *someone* was doing their job. Thank goodness for expandable batons. A pound of metal applied forcefully to his torso served its purpose. The bite of the ASP. So what if the good doctor's interference required a sprint to the car parked blocks away? Stuff happens.

Stryker crossed Burgundy Street. Four blocks to go. At least now there was another voice that could urge the reporter to get his ass in gear. And after a shower, grabbing a quick bite to eat, and getting dressed for work, things were mostly back on track.

Too bad about the collateral damage. The first two earned what happened to them. The Sweeper at his street-cleaning finest. But last night's human detritus at the Tchoupitoulas Street encampment hardly deserved his fate. Death from so-called natural causes. Pickled liver. Heart giving out with the strain of life on the street. One dirty hypodermic needle too many. Whatever. His demise was as much a tragedy as the crimes visited upon the girl in Washington Square Park or the hooker from St. Louis Cemetery Number One. Even if the Sweeper didn't actually end his life, the homeless man served the plan. His otherwise mundane existence and unremarkable death would have some meaning after all.

Stryker exhaled. All in all, everything had been within tolerance. Some deviations from the plan, but nothing that hadn't been overcome. So, a pat on the back was well deserved. But now was not the time for complacency. Stay focused. Keep eyes on the prize. Remain resolute in what still needed to be done.

The triple spires of St. Louis Cathedral drew closer. Absolution would be icing on the cake. Nothing like having a silent partner to help carry the burden.

Chapter Thirty-Three: Message Received

Tuesday, February 3, 2015 – 8:07 a.m.

"You have any idea how long they'll take?" Bryan Whitcomb crossed his arms and leaned back against the hood of the CSI van parked outside his bungalow. "Seems like it's been forever already."

"Another hour or so," Jonathan said. "They need to be thorough."

"But the guy wasn't in there very long."

"I asked them to give it the fine-toothed comb for prints…contact DNA… anything the Sweeper might have left behind."

"I know, but—"

"Frustrating, I'm sure. But the CSTs need to take their time."

Got it," Whitcomb said. "It's just—"

"You had a chance to change clothes." Jonathan pointed to a briefcase slung over Whitcomb's shoulder. "And grab your laptop. Why don't you head for your office? Let the pros do their thing."

"I'd like to be here so I can lock up."

"Suit yourself. But I'm out of here as soon as NOPD can give me a ride."

"Car totaled?"

"Enough to be undrivable. Goddamn potholes."

"Amen to that, Doc."

Jonathan handed a file folder to Whitcomb. "I retrieved a couple of things before the city tows my vehicle away."

"What's this?" Whitcomb glanced at the contents, then cursed under his breath.

"Our best translation of the Sweeper's three messages."

"Three?" Whitcomb's eyes widened. "He left three?"

"The one from Washington Square was first."

"Jesus." Whitcomb leafed through the documents. "We never deciphered the one we got…and we haven't received the others." He looked at Jonathan. "When—"

"Second one's from a victim at St. Louis Cemetery Number One…late Sunday or early Monday—"

"Shit." Whitcomb continued to read.

"Third one's from a guy we found just after midnight…off Tchoupitoulas."

Whitcomb's face reddened as he mouthed the words on the manifesto. He closed the folder and looked at Jonathan. Whitcomb's face, now ashen, appeared as if all the blood had drained out and been replaced with ice water. "The rat will die before sunrise?"

"Well, we—"

"But he left a dead fish…a redfish for God's sake."

"The fish is probably a symbol," Jonathan said. "You know—"

"Like 'sleep with the fishes'…in concrete overshoes?"

"And that makes you—"

"The rat?"

"You and the *Times-Pic*."

"Jesus." The color had returned to Whitcomb's face, mostly.

"It's why I called…why I was on my way here. To warn you."

"I never said thanks, did I?"

"Don't give it another thought. I only wish we'd put two and two together sooner."

"Message received," Whitcomb said. "So, what do you need me…and the *Times-Picayune*…to do?"

Jonathan updated Whitcomb on the major points uncovered by the investigation to date, their theory as to why the messages threatened Whitcomb and his newspaper, and the potential link with Friday's parades—the Krewe of Cleopatra in particular.

"Okay," Whitcomb said. "I can bury something in the paper's online version later this morning. Hopefully enough to placate the Sweeper without causing panic. Then we can have a follow-on in the next print edition." He pulled out his car keys. "I'll head to the office now to coordinate." He looked at the CSI personnel swarming over his bungalow. "Your people can lock up, I hope."

"Thanks. Maybe it'll keep the Sweeper—" Jonathan's phone buzzed. "Where…when? Got it. Do what you can to calm them down. I'll be there as soon as I can."

"Can I drop you somewhere?"

"Yeah. Tulane Hospital…stat."

Chapter Thirty-Four: Look for the Union Label

"Appreciate you sitting outside with me while I burn one." Milton Wofford, President of Local Nine-Eighty-Seven of the International Maritime Worker's Union lit a Marlboro, inhaled deeply, and then exhaled a dusky-white cloud of tobacco smoke to his right.

"No problem, Mr. Wofford," Betsy Sprance said. "I appreciate you—"

"It's Milt." Wofford placed both hands on the weathered picnic table that served as the primary focal point of the union's open-air tobacco-use zone. Smoke from the cigarette resting between the fingers of his right hand rose a couple of feet straight up, then floated away in the breeze. "Call me Milt."

"Okay, Milt," Betsy said. "And I really appreciate you talking with me."

"Anything to help our boys…our officers…in blue." Wofford exhaled a series of smoke rings. "I would've been glad to come to the station."

"Roger that, Milt. Figured it'd be more convenient to chat at your place of business. Besides, the Coroner's folks would have probably frowned on you smoking anywhere within half-mile of their place."

Wofford's face lightened as if he were about to laugh. "Must be something about all them dead bodies." Any lingering hints of a smile evaporated. "But why the Coroner's office? Isn't this a police matter?"

"We always work hand-in-glove with the Coroner." Probably best to gloss over the unusual nature of her special assignment. Stick with business. Bare bones. Might help keep her mind off Ranger, too. "Especially in the more controversial cases…like this one."

"Because of the sailor's rigging knife?" Wofford took another drag on his cigarette.

"That's a large part of it."

"You said you had some pictures."

Betsy slid photographs of the sailor's rigging knives from Washington Square Park and St. Louis Cemetery Number One across the table. "Look familiar?"

Wofford stuffed his cigarette butt into a bucket of sand on the ground near the table. "Flotilla brand sailor's rigging knives." He pointed to his package of Marlboro Reds on the table. "Mind if I…"

"Feel free."

"That's the union's logo on the handles—crossed anchors and the initials IMWU." He placed a cigarette between his lips, then touched his thumb to the flint wheel of a Zippo lighter. "Used in a crime?"

"Two recent homicides."

"No shit?" Wofford flipped the cap on his lighter shut, placed it on the picnic table, and removed the unlit Marlboro from between his lips. "Bar fights or what?"

"Can't share too many details because it's an active investigation. But definitely not a bar fight. Both murders…" She looked to her right, then back toward Milt. "Both murders were rather gruesome. Let's just leave it at that."

"Well." Wofford placed the cigarette on the table next to the lighter. "Several years ago, the union negotiated a contract that required each shipping company to provide certain equipment."

"Like the rigging knives?"

"Exactly." Wofford rolled his eyes. "Embossed with the IMWU logo to make sure our members knew who to thank."

"You said 'years ago.' Still part of the contract?"

"Negative." Wofford picked up the Marlboro from the table, looked at it as if he were finally ready to light up, then placed it back on the table. "Couple of years ago…maybe longer…several of the shipping companies asked to negotiate an annual equipment allowance. Let members buy their own knives, work boots…that kind of thing."

"They give a reason for the change?"

"Not officially."

"Unofficially?"

"Scuttlebutt." Wofford looked to his left and then his right as if checking for someone close enough to overhear. He leaned forward and lowered his voice almost to a whisper. "Two reasons. There were a lot of knives disappearing. Members would take the knives home and claim they were lost at sea in a storm. Then they'd pawn them, sell them on the black market, whatever. And, of course, the company couldn't refuse when they demanded a new one. It was part of the contract."

"So, there's no real way to trace the knives? Sounds like there could be dozens floating around out there."

"Probably hundreds…maybe more."

"Sounds expensive. No wonder they wanted to renegotiate."

"You get the idea." Wofford placed the Marlboro between his lips, flipped the flint wheel on his Zippo, and inhaled deeply as his cigarette touched the flame.

"The second reason?"

Wofford blew another set of smoke rings. "Apparently, the knives—along with the union logo—were involved in an increasing number of barroom brawls…and other crimes." Wofford snickered. "Seems like the geniuses at national HQ concluded that having the logo in so many crime scene photos wasn't a good look for the organization."

"Seems logical," Betsy said. "But what did you mean by 'other crimes'?"

"IMWU's the premier organization representing individuals serving the maritime industry throughout this great nation. Our members work in a variety of specialties…merchant seamen…ship's engineers and officers… longshoremen…stevedores…you name it. If it's related to the maritime trade, we probably cover the waterfront, so to speak."

Wofford's Marlboro remained wedged between the pointer and middle fingers on his right hand, the ashes growing longer. He tapped the cigarette against the edge of the table. Ashes drifted to the ground. As if completing a mysterious tobacco lover's ritual, he raised the cigarette slowly to his lips and took a long drag. More smoke rings.

"All very impressive, Milt." So much for Milt's endorsement of the International Maritime Workers' Union. He really couldn't diss his employer in public. Understandable, but time to cut to the chase. "I'm curious about the 'other crimes,' though. Can you tell me more?"

"The union takes great pride in having so many quality employees—"

"Except for the ones killing people with sailors' rigging knives, I take it?"

"Can't get anything past you, I guess." Wofford buried his smoldering cigarette in the sand bucket. "That's right, we've had a couple of clinkers."

"Details?"

Wofford looked around. "Well, the lawyers—"

"Anything for the boys in blue, right?"

Wofford blushed. "Off the record?"

"As much as it can be. But you know how things are."

"Yeah. Police could never prove anything."

"But?"

"There's this one guy."

"Is?"

"He's still with us."

"Go on."

"Seems like they happened in spurts."

"Spurts?"

"You know, like groupings. Three or so killings in one port in a month's time. Then a long break."

"How long?"

"A year or so, and then—"

"Another cluster of killings with an IMWU sailor's rigging knife in another port, then a break?"

"That's right." Wofford's forehead wrinkled. "How'd you know?"

"Any of the groupings in New Orleans?"

"No…until—"

"Until the ones I showed you in the photos?"

"Listen." Wofford's voice sounded stronger, more demanding, insistent. "We cooperated with the authorities in each of the other cities. We always—"

"Right…the boys in blue." Betsy held both hands up at chest level, open palms toward Wofford as if in surrender. "No accusations. And you've been very helpful."

"Thanks. I—"

"Police have any suspects?"

"Like I started to say earlier. One guy, a union member. He'd been part of the ship's company—always on a different ship—in each port at the time of the killings. The police told us that it was an odd coincidence, but without any direct evidence—"

"They never could prove anything."

"True dat."

"So, where's the guy now?"

"We have a lot of members," Wofford said. "And it's hard to keep track."

"You mean you didn't keep a special eye out for a suspected killer?"

"Well, maybe—"

"Better," Betsy said. "The guy is?"

"Assigned to a break-bulk registered in Panama."

"Okay. At sea?"

"In port."

"Which one?"

"Port of New Orleans."

"Can you give me a name? Tell me which ship?" Betsy bit her lip to keep from cursing. A suspect in multiple murders still on the payroll? And the union hadn't done anything about it? Unbelievable. But maybe that was *good* luck. It took some digging, but at least now they were zeroing in on someone connected to the weapons used in two murders. And he was almost certainly in New Orleans, probably on board a ship berthed nearby. Maybe there'd be enough for a search warrant. This could break the case wide open.

"NOPD really needs your help."

"I know. Anything for our boys in blue." Wofford looked like he wanted to weasel out of saying anything else, but knew he'd talked himself into a corner. "Listen, when the lawyers find out, they'll—"

"*If* the lawyers find out."

"Right. If." Wofford picked up his pack of Marlboros and his lighter. "Let's go to my office."

Chapter Thirty-Five: The Parents

Jonathan hesitated before entering the conference room in Tulane Hospital, where he'd met with Betsy and Cass earlier in the week—just before Janelle's interview. A man wearing a white clerical collar spoke loudly enough for his voice to carry into the hallway. He gestured to a young woman sitting near him at the small conference table, then pointed toward Mitch Broussard at the head of the table. Mitch looked more like a whipped puppy than a grizzled detective sergeant. He didn't acknowledge Jonathan's presence. Another man and a woman sat across from the speaker. Their faces, pale and puffy around the eyes, reflected fear and exhaustion—tinged with a hint of anger, or at least irritation.

Jonathan angled away from the door toward a bank of vending machines. No use interrupting Mitch having so much fun. The voice of the man wearing the clergy collar increased in tone and venom. Jonathan typed a text message and hit send. Enough fun. Rescue time.

"Excuse me." Mitch's voice—polite but firm—drowned out the minister's entreaties.

Jonathan smiled. His texting ruse had worked.

"Sorry to interrupt." Mitch's tone left little doubt about who was in charge. "I need to respond to this. I'll be right back."

He closed the door behind him as he left. "Thanks, Doc." His eyes opened wide, and he shook his head as if he were recovering from being punched in the face. "Great timing."

"Figured you could use a break." Jonathan leaned his head toward the conference room. "The parents?"

"The nurse threw us out of Janelle's room."

"Too much noise?"

Mitch rolled his eyes. "The loud guy—the Reverend Doctor Efrem Zelphinius Espy—is here with his daughter."

"Tam?"

"Yeah."

"No Mrs. Espy?"

Mitch shook his head. "Legislative duties prevented her attendance…at least that's what the good reverend told us."

"Us?"

"The couple sitting across from Espy…that's Janelle Harrison's daddy and momma. They call her Nellie, by the way."

"The publisher and his wife?"

"Affirmative. Robert Francis Harrison. Goes by Bobby. And his wife, Melissa—or Missy, which is how she introduced herself."

"I see," Jonathan said. "Any landmines you need to tell me about before we go talk with them?"

"Reverend Espy seems to believe that his daughter wasn't involved in any way. Apparently, she drove home from New Orleans on Sunday—without Janelle."

"And never mentioned the fake IDs?"

"No, she did. But not how you might think." Mitch pulled a fresh cheroot from his shirt pocket, looked at it, then returned it to his pocket. "Ms. Espy—Tam—claims that everything was Janelle's idea. Coming to Frenchmen Street, the fake driver's licenses…the whole nine yards."

"What about Ian?"

"Apparently, no mention of Ian. At least to her parents."

"And Janelle?"

"Get this," Mitch said. "Janelle left her at the restaurant. Just ran out 'to meet a boy.' At least that's how Ms. Espy tells it."

"Guess we shouldn't be surprised. Wouldn't be the first time someone lied to make themselves look good."

"True dat."

"Didn't you track down Tam and Ian yesterday?"

"Yes and no. Got to Ian late afternoon—before his shift at Jazz Harbor. Tam had already gone back to Mississippi." His face flushed. "Sorry I didn't let you know."

"And?"

"He backs up Janelle's version. At least from what he could see at the restaurant."

"Anything about Tam?"

"She met him at The John sometime after midnight. They had a couple of drinks. Danced. One thing led to another and—"

"They hooked up?"

"Went to Ian's place. Put a sock over the doorknob. And did the nasty. Apparently for several hours."

"Were those Ian's words?"

"Not exactly, but that's the gist."

"Creative license on your part?"

"Don't worry, Doc. The official report's not quite as descriptive."

"Figured as much." Jonathan smiled. "Did you confront the parents with any of the information from Ian?"

Mitch shook his head. "Thought it best not to at this point."

"Good decision. Anything else from the parents before we go back in?"

"Espy said his next sermon would blast the city and its sinful ways."

"Typical."

"And Mr. Harrison promises an exposé and editorial about NOPD and its incompetence."

"Expected," Jonathan said. "Okay, Mitch. It's you and me, now. Let's do this."

Chapter Thirty-Six: Best Friends For Never

Tuesday, February 3, 2015 – 9:29 a.m.

"Good morning. I'm Jonathan Gray, Coroner of Orleans Parish. I apologize for not being here when you arrived."

Janelle's father stood and extended his hand. "Bobby Harrison. Nellie's…Janelle's…father." He tilted his head toward an attractive woman, probably approaching fifty, sitting next to him. "And this is my wife, Missy."

Jonathan accepted the handshake. "Mr. and Mrs. Harrison. Pleased to meet you…but, I'm sorry it's under such circumstances."

Jonathan turned toward Tamara and her father, both of whom remained seated. "And likewise, Reverend Espy."

Jonathan offered a handshake. Espy didn't extend his hand in return. Jonathan waited a couple of seconds. "I assume this is your daughter, Tamara."

"Doctor, how is it that you know who I am?" Reverend Espy's tone was sharp, with no hint of courtesy.

"Well, Reverend." Jonathan withdrew his proffered handshake. "I have acquaintances in Jackson. And your sermons are broadcast in New Orleans on a regular basis."

"Yes, I see," Espy said.

"I assume that Mrs. Espy's legislative duties preempted her accompanying you and your daughter."

"Yes." Espy cleared his throat. "Delegate Espy regrets that she could not be here just now…her constituents required her presence elsewhere."

"I understand, Reverend—"

"But I am here." Espy's voice rose several decibels. He looked at Bobby and Missy Harrison. "And I expect to uncover exactly what your office and the New Orleans Police Department have done to investigate this heinous assault."

"Excuse me, Reverend Espy." Jonathan looked at Bobby and Missy before turning back to Espy. "Mind if I have a seat?"

"If you wish." Espy's voice had returned to a more conversational tone.

Jonathan sat at the head of the table. Mitch pulled a chair into a nearby corner. Out of the direct line of fire, but close enough for a tag-team response if necessary.

"Thank you," Jonathan said. "I didn't realize that Tamara…that your daughter…was involved in an assault." He let the statement rattle around in Reverend Espy's head. "If you. I mean, if she has a complaint or details, I'm sure Detective Sergeant Broussard would be most eager to take her statement."

"Tamara has told her mother and I all the details about what happened," Espy said.

"Yes, of course," Jonathan said. "But I'm not aware she's ever given a statement to NOPD." He looked at Mitch. "Detective Broussard, are you aware of any?"

Mitch shook his head. "Negative."

"My daughter." Espy pointed to Tam. "My daughter traveled here with Janelle—a dear friend, one of her sorority sisters—to experience the joys of Mardi Gras. And as a direct and proximate result of the horror visited upon them, she has suffered the most grievous trauma imaginable."

"Yes, of course." A direct and proximate result? Sounded like a lawsuit in the making. Janelle's parents remained silent. No outward expressions or emotions. Nothing that would give a window into their feelings. "Once again, I wasn't aware that Tamara was present when the incident occurred."

He gestured toward Mitch. "Perhaps we should take a break and let Detective Broussard interview Tamara."

"We will do no such thing." Espy's voice again rose several decibels.

Had Espy been a lawyer in court during cross-examination, the opposing attorney would have likely appealed to the judge, "I object. Counsel is badgering the witness." But now wasn't the time for such histrionics. Best to maintain an even keel, a professional tenor and tone.

"Well, Reverend," Jonathan said, "I don't feel comfortable having Tamara give a statement in front of Janelle's parents. I mean, this situation involves a very serious personal matter."

"We're not about to let you divide and conquer, Doctor," Espy said. "My daughter has nothing to hide. And I'm sure that Mr. and Mrs. Harrison wouldn't mind if—"

"That's right," Missy crossed her arms across her torso. "We would be deeply interested to hear Tamara's views."

"Thank you, Mrs. Harrison…Missy," Jonathan said. "Perhaps we should start with what Tamara can tell us about Ian."

Tam closed her eyes, and her jaw tightened. She squirmed in her seat. She opened her eyes and stared toward a corner of the room as if she wanted to avoid eye contact.

"We don't know…we don't know about…anyone named Ian." Reverend Espy peered at Tam as he spoke. She looked at the floor.

"Ian's a person of interest," Jonathan said. "He's the host—the maître d'—at Jazz Harbor Bistro & Brews." Jonathan waited a few beats for a reaction from Tam. She continued to look at the floor. "We understand he showed quite an interest in Janelle and Tamara. We believe he's the one who checked their identification when they ordered alcohol."

Tam's eyes widened, and she looked toward her father. "Daddy…"

Espy held his right hand up, palm toward his daughter. "Be silent, child." He faced Jonathan. "Alcohol has never passed this youngster's lips." He looked at Bobby and Missy, then again addressed Jonathan. "I see what you are trying to do. And I won't let you. I don't care how rich and connected they are."

Espy stood. "Come, Tamara." He pointed toward the door and stood back as she passed in front of him and left the room. He placed his hand on the door handle and turned back toward the room. "The City of New Orleans and Orleans Parish will be hearing from my lawyers."

He closed the door with a loud bang. His voice carried in from the hallway but grew softer as he and Tam apparently walked away.

Jonathan's head jolted slightly. He turned toward Bobby and Missy. "I'm sorry you had to hear all that."

"We're not." Missy uncrossed her arms and placed both hands on the table.

"Who is this Ian character?" Bobby asked. "Do you think he had anything to do with this…incident?"

"And Tamara?" Missy asked.

"Well," Jonathan said. "Everyone's a suspect…until they're not." No use revealing that Mitch had talked with Ian. "It seems to me that Ms. Espy… Tamara…knows more than she's telling us."

"She's trying to blame everything on Nellie." Missy's eyes moistened. She intertwined the fingers of both hands together, almost as if in prayer. "You don't think—"

"We won't leave any stone unturned," Jonathan said. "If there's any reason to conclude that Tamara or Ian had any involvement, we'll uncover it."

"Yes, I see." Bobby Harrison placed a hand on top of his wife's. "What can you tell us about the events of that night?"

"Perhaps we can go to Janelle's room," Jonathan said. "I appreciate your thirst for an explanation. But I don't feel comfortable discussing too many details without her permission."

"Yes, of course." Bobby Harrison stood.

"Please." Jonathan opened the door. "After you."

Chapter Thirty-Seven: Nellie

Tuesday, February 3, 2015 – 10:27 a.m.

Janelle Harrison had already been through so much. Assaulted in Washington Square Park. Witnessing a gruesome murder. Suffering through an unfortunately invasive physical examination at the Tulane ER. Forced to recount the trauma of what happened in the park to complete strangers. And apparently abandoned by her sorority sister—someone who should be at her side in the hospital.

That her parents wanted to drag Janelle—Nellie—back into the horror seemed inappropriate. Likely, all it would do was add to her anguish. Perhaps Jonathan should have objected, declined to participate. But he could relate to what the parents must be feeling. Had this happened to one of his children, he'd want to learn as much as possible. Perhaps his presence would help make an awkward situation more bearable. Maybe the session would result in additional evidence, a new lead. Or, given the panicked expression on Janelle's face as the trio entered her hospital room, maybe it would send her deeper into a dark place. A place of no return.

"I don't want to talk about it, Daddy." Janelle wasn't panicked. Determined might be a better description. "Especially not in front of you." She pointed toward Jonathan. "Or *him*."

"But, Nellie honey," Bobby said, "it might do you some good to get it out in the open. What happened is terrible. And what Tamara Espy did is—"

"Leave Tam out of this." Janelle's calm demeanor belied anger—something approaching hatred—in her tone. "Tam didn't do anything to me." She glanced at Missy. "Mommy…"

Missy grasped Janelle's hand. "Bobby. Why don't you…and Dr. Gray… leave us alone?"

"Yes, of course." Jonathan opened the door.

Bobby peered at his wife but remained silent. He nodded and backed away from the bed. Not exactly with his tail between his legs, but he'd definitely been put in his place.

Missy didn't close the blinds covering a window in the door, so Jonathan, standing beside Bobby, watched as she and Janelle talked. Seconds passed into minutes. Not an animated discussion. A lot of active listening by a mother, obviously concerned with her daughter's welfare and not caring about what anyone else in the world thought. Thank God it wasn't, but it could have been Emma with Abby or Marjorie—their daughters—in the room. Woman to woman. Perhaps it was stereotypical that Emma was the consoler-in-chief for their children, especially the girls. Missy seemed to have that same quality.

Bobby perused the hallway. "What happened to the police officer who was guarding the room?"

"Not sure," Jonathan said. "I'll check with Superintendent Bondurant."

"You do that." Bobby's tone reflected anger and fear. "There's a murderer on the loose. Janelle saw him. He could come looking for her. You can tell the Superintendent that we demand that the police keep our daughter safe. And that I expect…"

Bobby's voice trailed off as Missy left Janelle's room and closed the door behind her.

"We need to take Nellie home," Missy said. "Where we can watch over her." She turned to Jonathan. "Dr. Gray, do you see any reason we can't take our daughter out of this place?"

"Not from my perspective," Jonathan said. "We have her information if we need to be in contact."

"Good," Missy said. "I'll find the discharge nurse. And then—"

"Did you tell Nellie that Tamara Espy was trying to put the blame on her?"

Bobby asked.

"Nellie's relationship with Tamara is…well…it's complicated." Missy glanced toward Jonathan, then back to Bobby. "We can handle that at home."

Missy took a single step toward the nurses' station, then stopped and turned around. "And Dr. Gray, when you find the person who killed Nellie's attacker—"

"Don't worry," Bobby said, "I've already talked to him about our concern that Nellie's in danger."

"Dr. Gray." Missy glowered at her husband. "When you find the person who killed Nellie's attacker, I want you to pin a medal on his chest. As far as I'm concerned, he's a hero. He did the world a favor."

Jonathan nodded. Not much to say. It wouldn't do any good to tell her the Sweeper's history. About the dead man in St. Louis Number One. Or the homeless guy on Tchoupitoulas. And she'd probably celebrate the dead fish left in Brian Whitcomb's house. Best just to let two worried parents take their daughter home.

Chapter Thirty-Eight: A Fish Out of Water

Tuesday, February 3, 2015 – 3:56 p.m.

Jonathan stood next to Betsy, near the open liftgate of an unmarked SUV from the Coroner's motor pool. Seemed surreal to be putting on police tactical gear at *any* location. Doing so in the parking lot of Riverside Children's Hospital added to the oddity.

"You sure about this, Betsy?" Jonathan tightened the Velcro straps on a set of black body armor covering his chest and torso. "How positive are you that we're dealing with the Sweeper?"

"The magistrate seemed confident enough when she issued the search warrant." Betsy removed a black police tactical helmet from the SUV and handed it to Jonathan. "Here. Try this on."

"Confidant that there was probable cause, we'd find evidence." Jonathan readjusted one of the Velcro straps. "Not that this guy was guilty beyond a reasonable doubt."

"The stuff provided by Milt Wofford at the IMWU was pretty solid."

"But all circumstantial, right?"

"The suspect we're after—Stanislaus Jankowski—fits the description of the guy I chased…and shot…two years ago before he fell, or jumped, off the Crescent City Connection."

"Still sounds circumstantial to me. No physical identification or other links to the crimes. That is, beyond looking like the person you thought you killed and who later may have been on cargo ships."

"You a gambling man, Doc?"

"Sorry?"

"Ever play the ponies…or visit Harrah's?"

"On occasion. Blackjack…Texas Hold 'Em, maybe. But what's that got to do with executing a search warrant?"

"Odds. Probability."

"Come again?"

"Nothing's certain," Betsy said. "But there's a hell of a lot of coincidences."

"I'm listening."

"What are the odds that someone assigned as part of the ship's crew is in port—in each of the cities and at the relevant times—when there are a series of murders involving a sailor's rigging knife with the logo of the International Maritime Worker's Union?"

"Well—"

"And the same guy assigned to ships visiting New Orleans during *both* of the Sweeper's previous visits?"

"But in the other times in New Orleans," Jonathan said, "the Sweeper didn't use a sailor's rigging knife."

"Look, nothing's a hundred percent. Maybe the Sweeper matured, changed his preferred method of killing. What we do know is that the current murders involved a sailor's rigging knife."

"Not the homeless guy on Tchoupitoulas."

"A cadaver of opportunity. Like the Sweeper's note said, a gift. Someone he found dead that he used to send us another message, without getting his hands bloody. But the first two? Both involved the knives."

"I guess you have a point."

"And now the guy's assigned to a ship docked at the Nashville Avenue Wharf?" Betsy shook her head as if signaling her disbelief. "Soup to nuts, Doc. You'd have a better chance of getting Ace-high Royal Flushes on two consecutive hands."

"So why can't we just pick up Jankowski on board his ship?"

"Union rules require a seven-day liberty while in port."

"Seems strange."

"Well, it means we don't have to jump through hoops to search on a foreign-flagged vessel. Hell, it took me long enough just to get the warrant." Betsy rolled her eyes and smiled. "And Milt at the union hall let it slip that Jankowski is shacked up in a flop house—Two-Two-Seven Alonzo Street. So, all we have to do is take a short drive, waltz up to the front door, and show him a copy of our search warrant."

"But still it—"

"You know, Doc. That's why they call it an investigation." Betsy smiled. "Don't you look dapper in your body armor."

"You showed me Jankowski's stats and photo. He's pretty damn big. What if he doesn't want to waltz?"

"Then you'll be damned glad you're wearing protection." Betsy tapped on Jonathan's body armor. "And when we start, don't forget your headgear."

"You know, serving search warrants isn't exactly my usual daily routine."

"Sorry I don't have a cadaver for you to carve…although if this guy puts up a fight…"

"Not funny." Jonathan put on his black police tactical helmet and snapped the closures on the chinstrap together. "I know I must look like a raging dumbass in this thing." He took the helmet off. "But I understand why I have to wear it."

"Soup-to…look…I know you're like a fish out of water here. But we don't have much of a choice, do we? Jamerson wants to keep NOPD out of this as much as possible. So, I can't exactly drag SWAT's ass up here. And we need to locate the Sweeper."

"All true. But—"

"You have any better suggestions?"

"No." Jonathan's voice reflected his resignation that he had little choice in the matter at this point.

"Okay." Betsy shut the liftgate. "Let's roll. Mitch is already in position to chase Jankowski if he jackrabbits. I'll outline the rest of the plan on the way."

Chapter Thirty-Nine: Open the Door!

Tuesday, February 3, 2015 – 4:28 p.m.

Jonathan adjusted the chin guard on his helmet as their SUV crept along South Front Street, then turned onto Alonzo. Betsy pumped the brakes and eased their vehicle to a stop two houses away and on the opposite side of the street from Two-Two-Seven.

Flophouse seemed like an overly kind description of the weather-beaten two-story duplex where they hoped to serve a search warrant on Stanislaus Jankowski. A faded sign above a garage door warned "Do Not Block Driveway," but said nothing about what would happen if they did. Noise from an air conditioning unit in a second-story window—an odd sound for a cool February afternoon—and overflowing trash cans signaled that at least part of the building was occupied.

Jonathan got out of the passenger side, grabbed one of the two 'O' ring handles on the iron battering ram resting on the floorboard, and pulled on it. The eighteen-inch-long, black-metal rod didn't budge. Using both handles, he lifted it out of the SUV.

Betsy left the driver's door open as she exited, then proceeded to the front of the vehicle. "I'll go in first." Betsy pointed to a gate in the chain-link fence surrounding the building. "You follow with the facility-breaching apparatus. Stay about five yards behind me, on my left side."

"You mean the battering ram?"

Betsy closed her eyes. "Right, the battering ram."

"Got it. But, Jesus, how much does this thing weigh?"

"About forty pounds." She pointed to an expandable strap attached to the ram. "Use that. Might make it easier to carry."

Jonathan adjusted the nylon sling and placed it over his shoulder.

"And one more thing, Doc. Watch the doors and windows. If you see even a hint of movement, get your ass on the ground—out of the direct line of fire—as fast as you can."

"Got it," Jonathan said, as Betsy turned and strode toward the house. He followed, approximately fifteen feet behind her. The strap on the battering ram dug into his shoulder. On the other side of Tchoupitoulas, Mitch stood next to his police SUV and waved.

Betsy stepped onto a small rectangular concrete pad—more of a stoop than a porch—moved to the left side of the door, and knocked. "Stanislaus Jankowski." Her voice remained calm, almost soothing. "This is NOPD. We have a search warrant. Open the door."

No audible response from inside the dwelling. A dog barked in the distance—probably a block away—drowning out the noise of cars driving along Tchoupitoulas.

She balled her right hand into a fist and banged on the door frame. "Stanislaus Jankowski." Her voice—louder, more forceful but not quite yelling—emphasized harsh consequences for disobedience. "This is NOPD. We have a search warrant. Open the door." Again, no audible response. A second dog barked, this one closer than the first. Curtains parted on a window at the house next door.

Betsy pivoted—her back now toward the house—and pressed herself against the wall. She looked toward the door, then shifted her gaze to Jonathan. "Doc, bring me the ram."

Still with her back pressed against the wall, she took the battering ram— the facility-breaching apparatus—from Jonathan. "Now stand back and be ready for some fireworks."

"Roger that." Jonathan removed his sidearm from its holster and shifted it into a low-ready position.

"Jankowski. Final warning. You've got five seconds to open the door, or we're coming in." Betsy inhaled then exhaled a cleansing breath. "Five. Four. Three. Two. Time's up."

Betsy, her hands firmly on the ram's metal rings, swiveled the eighteen-inch-long iron rod to her right side, then swung the device in front of her body to the left.

"Bam!"

The hammer-shaped end of the battering ram crashed into the door, just above the doorknob. The wooden door and frame cracked, but the door didn't open.

Betsy swiveled to her right and prepared the battering ram for another attempt. She inhaled and clenched her jaw as she again swung the ram across her torso.

"Bam!"

Small wood splinters flew past Betsy as the door gave way and opened approximately six inches. She dropped the battering ram and again flattened her back against the wall. She removed a flash-bang grenade from her tactical vest, pitched it into the house, and covered her ears with her hands.

Jonathan's temples throbbed when the charge exploded. If it was that bad from where he was, Betsy must really be feeling it.

A shower of sparks shot out of the door, followed by whiffs of light gray smoke. Betsy removed her sidearm from the holster and pivoted, bringing the weapon to a high ready position. Still no response from inside the dwelling. She shoved the door open, peered inside, and stepped forward.

A loud boom—sounding like a gunshot, but deeper than a pistol or long rifle—erupted just before Betsy crossed the threshold. She staggered backward and fell to the ground, as if she had been attached to a wire and yanked from behind without warning. She landed on her back and groaned.

Jonathan moved toward the door and brought his weapon into firing position. A male figure dressed in black emerged from the doorway, dropped what looked like a single-barreled shotgun onto the stoop, and catapulted himself toward Jonathan.

The collision forced Jonathan's pistol out of his hands. Jonathan staggered, but didn't fall. "Stop." He grabbed at the figure as it ran past—or more accurately over—him. "Jankowski." Jonathan curled his arms around the man's lower leg. "I said stop."

Smoke—darker and thicker than usual from a flash-bang—poured out of the doorway, followed by flames.

The man didn't respond to Jonathan. He kept moving forward, dragging Jonathan along with him. He grabbed onto the crossbar of a clothesline pole, steadied himself, and kicked at Jonathan with his free leg.

Jonathan let go and rolled away from the kicks. No use risking a concussion. Thank God Betsy made him wear a helmet.

The man looked over his shoulder—at something in the distance, not at Jonathan—then climbed over the chain-link fence. He sprinted toward the Nashville Street Wharf.

"You okay, Doc?" Mitch Broussard breathed rapidly. "Came as soon as I heard shots fired."

"I'm fine…but Betsy—"

"Go check on her. She's down, but alive. Body armor…thank God. Call for backup…NOFD, too." Mitch vaulted the fence as if it were a small hurdle in a track meet. "I'll get the son-of-a—"

"Mitch…watch out for the…"

Mitch cursed as he tripped over a garbage bin, somersaulted in a nearly perfect circle, then skidded face down onto the pavement. He stood, looked briefly toward Jonathan, and again ran after their now out-of-sight prime suspect.

Chapter Forty: Up From the Ashes

Tuesday, February 3, 2015 – 7:19 p.m.

New Orleans Fire Department personnel trained floodlights on Two-Two-Seven Alonzo Street—or at least what remained of it. Jonathan—dejected, exhausted, confused—sat on the hood of a police cruiser and stared at Betsy and Mitch standing nearby. Firefighters guided hoses, dousing hotspots when they flared.

Nothing like a failed attempt to serve a simple search warrant resulting in a two-alarm fire to make you feel as flat as a deflated pool float. A pungent mix of odors from charred wood, melted vinyl siding, and the other smoldering detritus associated with a house fire added to the headache-inducing atmosphere. What an absolute cluster.

NOFD's preliminary conclusion linking the blaze to the occupant—ostensibly Stanislaus Jankowski—igniting several flares, and not their flash-bang grenade, provided little consolation. Regardless of the cause, any evidence they hoped to find was likely destroyed or at least burned beyond recognition. Perhaps worse, Jankowski—or whoever the hell it was—escaped in the confusion. A potential serial killer on the loose. Not much else could have gone wrong.

Betsy leaned toward Mitch and said something Jonathan couldn't hear.

"Goddammit, it *is* my fault." Mitch stepped back from Betsy. "If I'd been just a few seconds earlier…and didn't go ass-over-teacups…I'd have caught him."

"Don't." Jonathan's voice left little room to doubt his irritation. "There's enough misery to go around." He looked at Betsy. "The EMTs give you a clean bill of health? How are you doing?"

"More or less."

"Meaning?" Jonathan asked.

"Sore as hell." She grimaced. "Some wicked bruises from the impact of the buckshot on the body armor. But fine...all things considered."

"Seems to me," Jonathan said, "that someone predicted how glad we'd be that we're wearing body armor."

"Damned glad." Betsy managed something resembling a smile. "At least that's how I remember it."

"Right," Jonathan said. "Damned glad."

"And the helmet," Mitch said. "Those were some wicked mule kicks."

"Right." Jonathan rolled his eyes. "Thank God for that dorky-assed helmet."

Betsy chuckled. "Ow." She held her breath, then exhaled. "Hurts to laugh."

"Sorry," Jonathan said. "Didn't mean to—"

"It's okay." Betsy smiled, but her eyes reflected pain. "But you did look like a dumbass in that get-up."

"So, what now, Doc?" Mitch asked. "We're not exactly batting a thousand these days."

Mitch sure as hell didn't pull punches. But it did seem like it had been two steps forward, one step back every day since the early Sunday morning visit to Washington Square Park. Not true, of course. They had made progress, learned a lot. They'd come so close. Disheartening, but they couldn't quit now.

"We've not yet begun to fight, so—"

"Come on, Doc." Mitch pulled a half-stogie out of his shirt pocket, moved it toward his mouth, then stopped. "It's bad enough without you playing the Navy card." He clamped the cigar between his teeth. "I swear to God if you tell us to damn the torpedoes, I'll—"

"Fair enough." Jonathan's face warmed. He held both hands up, open palms toward Mitch. "I just mean...we can't give up. We can't let the Sweeper get away."

"All right." Mitch spit out several small pieces of tobacco. "What's next?"

"Short term," Jonathan said, "we need to inspect the scene once NOFD tells us it's safe. Maybe we'll find something. Who knows?"

"Sounds like a long shot, Doc," Mitch said. "Wouldn't we do better to hit the street?"

"I can stay," Betsy said. "It shouldn't be much longer before they give us clearance. Then I can head home. Get a few hours shuteye before I have to get up at the crack of dawn to take photos at Jackson Square…of the churchgoers. Assuming you want me to be on spy duty again."

"Sounds like a plan…if you're up to it. I do need you at the Cathedral in the morning. Mitch and I can—"

"I'll manage," Betsy said.

"Good," Jonathan said. "Mitch, you up for another roving patrol? Like we did the other night?"

"I'm game." Mitch pitched the remnants of his cigar into the darkness. "Why don't I patrol—"

"Dr. Gray?" A firefighter approached the trio.

"Dr. Gray, name's Justin Powell. Lieutenant Powell. Incident Commander."

"What can I do to assist NOFD, Lieutenant?" Jonathan asked.

"If you'd come with me, I think there's something in the ashes that should be of interest to you…to the Coroner…to you as the Coroner. Sorry. I must sound like—"

"Like you've had a long day?" Jonathan asked.

"Probably not as long as yours." Lieutenant Powell motioned toward Betsy and Mitch. "Or theirs. But these last couple of hours *have* been kind of intense."

"Understood," Jonathan said. "What do you have for us?"

"There's a crap-ton of fire damage," Lieutenant Powell said. "Not a total loss, but…but among the debris, there's a body. Charred pretty badly. Curled up in the fetal position. Reminds me of pictures I've seen of people in the volcanic ruins at Pompeii. But it's human. Not an animal. I'm sure of that."

Jonathan cursed under his breath. That's what else could have gone wrong. Another dead body. "Okay, Lieutenant. Lead the way."

Chapter Forty-One: Insurance

Tuesday, February 3, 2015 – 11:46 p.m.

Betsy Sprance sat upright on the oversized sofa in the family room of her house on Plum Street. Horace—their tortoiseshell cat—leaped to the floor and scurried into a corner. He hunkered down, his tail curled around his body as if standing lookout, ready to attack. Betsy reached for her sidearm resting on the nearby coffee table and held her breath. She shook her head and rubbed her eyes to make sure she wasn't still in the middle of her nightmare about being chased by an angry Stanislaus Jankowski carrying a flamethrower.

The noise—a combined thump and scratch—had come from the back of the house, likely in the kitchen or adjacent laundry room. Shielded from neighbors' prying eyes by their backyard fence and shrubbery, that would be the most logical entry point. Lack of breaking glass must mean that the intruder had jimmied the lock. Or found where they kept the spare key—a rookie mistake. They might as well have left the door open with a sign: "Welcome, Burglars. Right This Way."

A muffled voice—deep, sounding more male than female—said something, perhaps a cuss word. Betsy slid off the couch, lowered her profile as much as possible, and waited. Ambient light from the house next door ensured that any intruder would cast a shadow if he—or she—moved into the family room. Betsy inhaled as quietly as possible. She exhaled slowly and hoped that her heart would stop beating so loudly. Adrenaline coursing in her body masked the pain from injuries she'd sustained during the Alonzo Street debacle.

The floor creaked as whoever was in the kitchen began walking. Then the creaking stopped, followed by a soft whoosh and clinking sounds. The refrigerator? This bastard must be stopping for a snack—often a hallmark of professional burglars. Show your dominance. Invade even the most mundane spaces with impunity, like counting coup against an adversary. Putting the cuffs on this asshole was going to be *very* satisfying.

A soft 'thunk' from the refrigerator door closing, followed by creaking floorboards, signaled that the intruder had finished his midnight repast and was ready to move to the rest of the house. Two or three more steps should bring Jankowski—or whoever in hell it was—into the light. Betsy raised her service weapon into firing position as the outline of a human figure came into view.

"NOPD." Betsy's heartbeat quickened. "Hands in the air…you're under arrest."

The footsteps ceased. Betsy kept her pistol trained on the source of the shadow and flipped the light switch with her elbow.

"That you, Baby?"

"*Ranger?*" Betsy blinked as the ceiling lights illuminated the intruder. She holstered her handgun. "What in the name of God?"

"Can I put my hands down?"

"What in the hell are you doing sneaking around in your own house?" Betsy's temples pounded. "I could have shot you."

"Again." Ranger lowered his arms.

"Yeah…again…and this time—"

"I know, Baby." Ranger moved toward Betsy. "This time you would have killed my ass."

"Damn you." Betsy balled her fists and shoved Ranger. "Goddamn you."

"I thought you remembered. It's part of—"

"Part of what?" Betsy shoved Ranger again, this time with only one hand, her palm open. "Part of your crazy-ass plan?"

"Well, yeah." Ranger sat on the couch. "You need to calm down, Baby."

"Claude Dubose Sprance. Don't you tell me to calm down. You scared me half to death…again."

"I figured they might be watching the front."

"They?" Betsy flopped onto the couch—on the opposite end from Ranger. "Who is they?"

"Special Agent Dismukes and that bunch."

"Why would HSI be staking out our house?" Betsy said. "I swear to God, Ranger, if you don't level with me about what you're up to, I *will* shoot your ass."

"Right." Ranger held his hands up, palms out. "I owe you that much."

"It's about Goddamn time."

"But first." Ranger held out a computer thumb drive. "There's this."

"What the hell is this?"

"Insurance."

"Insurance?" Betsy took the thumb drive from Ranger and looked at it. "What the hell does that mean?"

"Remember I told you that I took part-time work as a consultant after I retired?"

"Okay?" Betsy gave Ranger a sideward glance. "And?"

"Well, I…" Ranger took a cleansing breath. "I've been consulting with Homeland Security on some of the narcoterrorism stuff I was doing in the Army."

"Consulting?"

"Okay." Ranger closed his eyes, took a couple of deep breaths, and then looked at Betsy. "They actually call me a special government employee. Some kind of fancied-up title like that."

"So you're doing the same dangerous crap you were in the Army?"

"Not quite as dangerous. But, more or less, yeah."

Betsy held up the thumb drive. "And this is…what exactly?"

"Not quite sure I trust the HSI people. Too political for me."

"So, you're stealing government secrets?"

Ranger shook his head. "Been keeping a journal. You know. Names, dates, places. Things like that."

"And documents, too?"

"Some."

"Classified?"

"Some."

"*Soc au' lait*, Ranger. Are you crazy?"

"Well—"

"They'll put you under the jail." Betsy looked at the thumb drive. "And me, too."

"Don't worry, Baby. Ain't nothing classified on there." He smiled in a cat-ate-the-canary sort of way. "I got all that stashed away, just in case they try to scapegoat me. Insurance. Like I said, I don't exactly trust HSI."

"So, what *is* on it?"

"I got my notes…my operational diary, so to speak," Ranger said. "And enough other stuff—nothing classified—that'll help you and your doctor friend deal with that creep Jamerson."

"But why?"

"Let's just say I didn't like how Washington interfered with the Mayor's case. And this is just my way of, well, you know…"

"Seeing that justice is done?"

"And watching out for you, Baby."

"Ranger, you can be such a dick."

"All my Army training coming through."

"So, what will you do about leaving your…hospital?"

"I left a note. Said I had some errands to run. That I'd be back."

"That's it? Errands?"

Ranger surveyed the room as if he were looking for someone who might be eavesdropping. "I'm going to tell you something." He cleared his throat. "I'm about to go on another op."

"Soup to nuts, Ranger. You took two bullets in the back."

"Weeks ago. I'm fine. Besides, we'll have a period of time for final workups before we deploy to the field."

"Jesus." Betsy closed her eyes and exhaled a long, cleansing breath. She opened her eyes, but didn't make eye contact. "I thought when you retired, this would stop."

"I know you did, Baby."

"And why in hell would you agree to go on another mission if you don't trust HSI?"

"Listen, Baby, the money's good. Real good."

Betsy's jaws tightened.

"When Dismukes first asked me about this new op, I told her that I missed you. And needed to well, you know…"

"No, I don't know."

"I said I needed me some lovin' before I got back into the business end of things. So, I left a note."

"And they'll buy that? Jesus Christ, Ranger. You're really full of yourself."

"You didn't want me to tell them I needed to give you the thumb drive, do you?"

"Guess not."

"You be sure to make several copies and stash 'em away."

"Okay."

"Maybe give one to Dr. Gray."

"All right."

"And in the meantime, how about you help me with my cover story?"

"About?"

"Needing some lovin'."

Betsy shook her head. "You're a sick one."

"So, how about it? Might be a while before I'm back."

"Jesus, Ranger. After the day I've had?"

"Sure thing, Baby." Ranger reached out his hand to Betsy. "Why don't you come tell me all about it?"

Chapter Forty-Two: A Priestly Editorial

Wednesday, February 4, 2015 – 8:32 a.m.

Jonathan hesitated in front of Café Pontalba, drank the rest of his coffee, then threw the cup away in a nearby trash can. Early morning fog masked the triple spires of St. Louis Cathedral. A touch of melancholy and mystery to mark his upcoming meeting with Dan Rossignol, perhaps.

Or, more likely, just another overcast morning in the French Quarter. Street vendors prepared their stalls so they could hawk paintings, jewelry, and other souvenirs. A smattering of others—likely tourists heading for Café du Monde and some locals heading to work, or perhaps home after a long, sleepless night—meandered in the public space in front of the cathedral.

Near the still-locked gate to Jackson Square, Betsy Sprance adjusted a camera on a tripod. She appeared to be setting up a photo of the Cabildo—a museum adjacent to the cathedral. And she had stayed past the one-hour window he'd asked her to, as she recorded foot traffic in and out of St. Louis. Good. A couple of simple, heads-up moves. Betsy's expertise as an investigator came through. She'd made herself look like just another photographer working for a travel magazine. Not someone on a spy mission to record comings and goings of parishioners—potential penitents and, God forbid, possible suspects in their hunt for the Sweeper.

Jonathan stepped off the banquette—the sidewalk—and angled toward St. Louis.

"Excuse me, sir." An elderly gentleman, unshaven and dressed in clothes that appeared to have been slept in, stood a couple of feet away. "Can I ask you something?" The odor of alcohol wafted toward Jonathan.

"Morning, Boats." Jonathan attempted a smile. Hard to act happy seeing a Navy veteran—or anyone else for that matter—overcome by life's travails. "You're up early."

The man blinked and rubbed his eyes. "I didn't recog…recom…see…it was you, Captain Gray."

"Well, I am far afield from my office, you're right about that."

"Yes, sir." He coughed a wet, wheezy cough. "We don't know where circum…circus…life…might lead us."

"True that. And how can I be of service to a fellow Navy vet?"

"Well, Captain." Boats moistened his lips with his tongue. "You see…I'm—"

"You hungry?"

"Yes, sir. I could eat a bite."

"You need a couple of dollars?"

"Ain't asking for charity, now. I'd like to earn it by making a prognosti…a procrastination…a prediction."

Jonathan glanced at the open doors of St. Louis. "Sure thing."

"For ten dollars." Boats smiled. "I can tell you where you got your shoes. The date. The time. And the place."

"Come on now, Petty Officer Sinclair, you can do better than that." Jonathan chuckled. "I've got my shoes on my feet, and—"

"I know," Sinclair—Boats—said. His eyes sparkled. "I know. I can tell you how your name's spelled on your granddaddy's birth certificate."

"All right." Jonathan's name on his grandfather's birth certificate? This should be entertaining.

"Well, on your granddaddy's birth certificate, your name is spelled, y-o-u-r-n-a-m-e."

"Okay." Jonathan rolled his eyes and chuckled. "That's worth breakfast." Jonathan placed a twenty-dollar bill in the haggard street comedian's hand. "But you've got to promise me something."

"Yes, sir. Anything." He put the money in his pocket.

"Promise you'll get some real food."

"Yes, sir."

"Stop by Meena's or Daisy Dukes."

"Yes, sir. Been hankering for some shrimp and grits."

"Good enough. Now, if you'll excuse me."

"Yes, sir. Off to church with you." Boats smiled and coughed another wet, wheezy cough. "And you promise to put in a good word with the Lord about me."

"All right." Jonathan placed his hand on the man's shoulder as he turned to leave. "Consider it done."

What a place for a beggar to ply his trade. The Catholic church had enough money to buy Newton Sinclair—former Boatswain's Mate Second Class, U.S. Navy—and others like him breakfast a thousand times over. No, beggar wasn't the right term. Boats, like so many of the denizens of the French Quarter Jonathan had come to know by name, was simply doing his best to make a living. It might be to fuel a need for an intoxicant to keep him going. But it was an honest attempt to deal with a system that often presented insurmountable hurdles. That it happened to someone who had served his country in uniform made it all the more regrettable.

That was a cause and a complaint for another day. Jonathan looked toward Betsy just before he entered the cathedral. They had a job to do. The Sweeper might be cleaning the streets of miscreants like the guy in Washington Square Park. But he was also targeting down-on-their-luck people. Whatever one thought about killing rapists and whoremongers, Boats and the others didn't deserve the hand life had dealt them, much less being fodder for a vigilante serial killer.

He arrived at the penitent's door to the confessional just as Dan Rossignol approached from the front of the church. Jonathan entered, closed the door, and sat down. He had a lot to accomplish during their conversation. He was there to act as a sounding board and confidant for Dan as he struggled to cope with his guilt over a parishioner using the crucifix he'd given him to stab someone in the neck. And Jonathan needed to pry about the parishioner who confessed—or at least hinted—at killing someone with a knife. It probably wasn't the Sweeper, but what if it was? What if it was Jankowski? What if—

"Morning, Jonathan." Dan opened the small window divider between the Priest and Penitent sections, then lowered the screen.

"Same, Dan." No tobacco odor. Good. "How've you been?"

"Better. But there's been a development."

"Oh?"

"Something potentially very disturbing."

"Can you tell me more?"

"Tuesday morning, one of the nuns reported a woman taking pictures in front of the Cathedral."

"Doesn't seem unusual." Jonathan's face warmed. "Don't tourists take photos all the time?"

"Of the Cathedral, Jackson Square, sure."

"But the nun thought this looked different somehow?"

"Well, the woman stayed at the corner of Jackson Square, like she wanted to remain hidden. And she was only photographing parishioners entering and leaving the Cathedral." Dan remained silent for several seconds, as if waiting for Jonathan to comment. "And it was around the time of the eight o'clock Mass…or maybe closer to confession."

"Does seem odd." Jonathan's gut churned. "Any idea who it might be?"

"No. Sister thought she looked like a parishioner she's seen at Blessed Sacrament."

"In Carrollton?"

"Yes, that's right," Dan said. "And Sister reported that the same woman was outside the Cathedral again this morning."

"Hmmm. Any thoughts on who would be photographing parishioners?"

"Today, the woman had the camera on a tripod, like she was a professional photographer."

"Seems to put things in context. Probably just someone doing a spread for a travel brochure."

"Perhaps. I don't suppose she was still there when you arrived, was she?"

"Maybe." Jonathan hesitated as he searched for the right words to acknowledge that he saw Betsy, without also admitting he knew who she was or why she was there. "Now that you mention it, I may have noticed a photographer."

"I see."

"But I didn't pay that much attention. I was in a hurry...and someone stopped me to ask for money...so I may not be the best one to comment."

"Yes, of course. We're all distracted with one thing or another."

"And I'm sorry you have to deal with another controversy—along with guilt about a penitent who misused the crucifix you gave them."

"Yes. That is a worry. But the thought that someone may be targeting our faithful is rather disturbing, don't you agree?"

"Yes, of course."

"And my personal drama pales into insignificance alongside a threat to our parishioners."

"Well—"

"Or something of concern to someone who is not a parishioner. An old friend."

"Well—"

"And I don't want to pry, Jonathan, but you seem distracted. Is something wrong?"

"I can't really comment about—"

"Is it the item in the Jackson newspaper?"

"What item?"

"An acquaintance forwarded me a link to this morning's *Clarion-Journal Online* because it involved New Orleans."

"An editorial by Bobby Harrison?"

"Yes, that's right, Robert Francis Harrison. Are you familiar with the editorial?"

"I'd been expecting it...it's a long story."

"He was quite derogatory about your office and the police."

"Like I said. It's a long story."

"I can only imagine what he and Mrs. Harrison are going through, with his daughter's assault and so little progress."

"I don't suppose he mentioned the mutilated body they found next to his daughter."

"That's right. There's nothing about that."

As if a verbal dam had broken, the words flowed from Jonathan in a torrential stream of consciousness. Janelle Harrison's apparent assailant gutted with a sailor's rigging knife, the chest and forehead carvings, and the encrypted note. And then the rest of the sordid mess. A total of four dead bodies, three men and one as yet undetermined victim from the fire on Alonzo Street. Dan listened. Mostly, his countenance remained blank, a priestly poker face. As Jonathan discussed the most recent event—the failed attempt to serve the search warrant—Dan's expression changed, as if he had finally connected the dots.

"Now I understand why you seem so distracted," Dan said. "And why you were so interested to hear about my dilemma with the penitent who talked about killing someone with a knife."

"And if the Sweeper keeps it up, there'll be more to come."

"But you know I can't say anything."

"Perhaps. But which is more precious? Your duty to keep secrets or your responsibility to protect innocent human life?"

"The Law of the Church—"

"Shouldn't serve to protect a murderer who will strike again."

"It's in the Lord's hands."

Jonathan bit his lip to avoid cursing. He exhaled a deep cleansing breath. "Dan, in the name of all that is Holy, can't you give me a clue? Something for us to go on to stop this monster before he strikes again?"

"The Lord works in mysterious ways."

"Very mysterious." Now wasn't the time to challenge Dan's commitment to the sanctity of the priest-penitent relationship. He seemed smug, but there was something about Dan's expression. Maybe a seed of doubt. Maybe if given a little more time, he'd come around. "But I appreciate your position. Perhaps we can talk again later."

"Perhaps." Dan started to stand but stopped. "Let's talk again on Friday. I'll pray that you will have resolved this Sweeper matter by then."

"Yes, of course." Not exactly the help from Dan he had hoped for. "Until Friday."

"Oh, and Jonathan. Please pay my respects to Detective Lieutenant Sprance. I'm sure Father Edward at Blessed-Sacrament—St. Joan of Arc looks forward to seeing her at Mass on Sunday."

Chapter Forty-Three: Charred Remains

Wednesday, February 4, 2015 – 10:47 a.m.

Gathering clouds symbolized Jonathan's mood as his RideShare neared the morgue on Earhart Drive. So much for his stroke of not-so-genius to have Betsy stalk parishioners on their way to confession. Dan Rossignol hadn't said anything directly, of course. He was too savvy. His mention of Betsy and a reminder to attend Mass this Sunday was Dan's not-so-subtle way to broadcast "I know what you did." He might as well have presented Jonathan a combined award for Dumbest Idea and Worst Kept Secret.

But desperate times called for desperate measures. More than three days had passed since the first murder in Washington Square Park. Their strongest lead—Stanislaus Jankowski—seemed to have vanished without a trace. Beyond Emma's translation of the Sweeper's ciphers, what else did they have as events hurtled headlong toward Friday's parades and the promise that "Cleo will pay thrice the price"? Four dead bodies—one burned beyond recognition. A request through an encrypted phone app for a couple of teenagers to tag streetcars with graffiti. Tam and Ian as potential co-conspirators. The editor of a Mississippi newspaper and a television preacher on separate crusades to expose the incompetence of the Coroner's Office and NOPD. Beyond that, crickets.

Asking Betsy to surveil the church might have been a Hail Mary, but they had to do something—anything—to blast their investigation off dead center.

Maybe Betsy's two days of photographing uncovered a clue. Maybe Ronnie Mohan would turn up critical evidence during her autopsy of the body from the fire at the Alonzo Street flophouse. Ronnie—Dr. Rajamahendri Mohan, his Deputy Coroner for Forensic Examinations—had autopsied several burned cadavers in the past. Knock on wood, her unique skills and experience would lead to a breakthrough.

As if to underscore their failures thus far, a light rain started as Jonathan dashed from the RideShare to the morgue. More of a drizzle than a major downpour. But just enough to make the situation seem even more miserable. He entered the reception area, put his jacket on a coat rack, and headed for the autopsy suite.

"Morning," Jonathan said as he entered the examination area. Betsy Sprance stood several feet away from the autopsy table. Dr. Mohan, assisted by Jimmy Caplan as Diener, hunched over the charred remains of their latest victim.

"Morning, Doc." Betsy crinkled her nose. "Grizzly work, isn't it?"

"Morning, Ronnie," Jonathan said. "Thanks for taking point on this one. Jimmy, thought you only worked overnights."

"Morning." Dr. Mohan's voice was slightly muffled because of her surgical mask. "I'm to blame for Jimmy being here. Thought he might benefit from seeing this particular postmortem."

"Got permission to cut one of my pre-med classes," Jimmy said. "Prof agreed it would be a great experience."

"Not often we get a burn victim." Ronnie lowered her mask. "Thank God."

"Jimmy, what's your number one takeaway?" Jonathan asked.

"Hard to say, there's so much." Jimmy lowered his mask. "If I had to choose, probably how the body curls up."

"Boxer pose," Jonathan said. "Depending on age and other factors, the body is somewhere between fifty and sixty percent water. Once the fire evaporates the water, all sorts of strange things happen. Skin tears. Fat and muscle shrink. As muscles contract, the joints flex. Look at how the cadaver's arms are drawn up toward its face."

"Like a boxer protecting himself in a fight," Jimmy said.

"Exactly," Jonathan said. "Great observation. Hope you won't see another one like it for a long time."

"True dat," Jimmy said.

"So, Ronnie," Jonathan said, "can you give us an overview of the results?"

"And not too graphic," Betsy said.

"Of course. I'll keep the gross parts to a minimum." Dr. Mohan smiled, then covered her mouth with her mask. "If you and Dr. Gray want to mask up and come closer, I'll share some highlights."

Jonathan and Betsy donned surgical masks.

"We've noted the Pugilistic Pose of the body," Ronnie said. "But look at the posterior of the skull."

Jimmy adjusted the lamp to illuminate the cadaver's skull.

"The entire skull's charred, of course. Hair, skin, and so forth, mostly gone." She pointed to an indented area in the rear of the skull. "There's what appears to be a gash in the area covering parts of the parietal and occipital lobes."

"Blunt force trauma?" Betsy asked.

"Best guess at this point," Ronnie said.

"Cause of death?" Betsy asked.

"Probably not," Ronnie said. "Death was almost certainly due to smoke inhalation—"

"But the victim was probably incapacitated by a blow to the head," Jonathan said.

"Exactly," Ronnie replied.

Interesting," Jonathan said. "Can you identify the victim…fingerprints?"

"Not likely." Ronnie shook her head. "Fingers were burned pretty badly, so we haven't been able to find any usable prints."

"DNA?" Jonathan asked. "Despite the fire damage?"

"A better chance—but not much better. We've taken specimens from various parts of the remains," Ronnie said. "Best chance is teeth and bones."

"Dr. Mohan," Jimmy said, "asked me to drop samples at the police crime lab."

"And at the private lab we use," Ronnie said. "I assumed you'd approve the extra expense."

"Good call, Ronnie. Time estimate on results?"

"Added rush requests to both," Ronnie said. "I'd be surprised if we get the NOPD results anytime soon. Private lab can turn them around in a day or two."

"Gives us something to hope for," Jonathan said.

"And we need to talk about a couple of developments," Betsy said.

"The editorial in the *Clarion-Journal?*" Jonathan asked.

"That's one thing," Betsy said. "And the Mayor's called a press conference at four o'clock to address it."

"Crap. Just what we need right now."

"Oh," Betsy said. "There's more."

"Okay. Maybe we can grab some lunch and go over things."

"Sure thing," Betsy said.

"But first," Jonathan said. "Jimmy, some stuff's come up about last Saturday night. You got a minute?"

"Sure, Doc," Jimmy said. "I need to drop off samples. But I don't have class until two o'clock, so I don't need to leave quite yet."

"Great," Jonathan said. "Let's grab a cup of coffee."

Chapter Forty-Four: The Man in the Flannel Shirt

Wednesday, February 4, 2015 – 11:37 a.m.

Jonathan swiped his credit card in the coffee vending machine near the morgue's conference room. Hard to imagine that Jimmy Caplan could be the person who killed Janelle Harrison's attacker in Washington Square Park. No. Not hard to imagine. Impossible to imagine.

But Jimmy had been placed near the scene of the murder at the right—or wrong—time. On video no less. He fit the description of the guy talking to Janelle at The Bunker. And his military service before becoming a pre-Med student at Tulane. A Navy Corpsman serving with the Marines in Afghanistan. Physically fit. Strong as an ox. All the right training and experience to know how to handle surgical instruments—including scalpels and knives. And the stories he'd related, in confidence, about hand-to-hand combat—killing another human, albeit in self-defense, in the line of duty.

And there was the St. Louis Cemetery Number One victim—Curtis Dowdy. Jimmy was scheduled to work as diener on the overnight shift Sunday night. That would have given him a virtually unassailable alibi. Normally, someone missing a shift would get chewed out by their supervisor or be referred to Human Resources. But two murders definitely took this out of the purview of an ass chewing or counseling by HR.

So, Goddammit, he *had* to talk with Jimmy. Just like Jonathan told Janelle's parents. "Everybody's a suspect. Until they're not." One of Betsy's favorite sayings. Better Jonathan deal with Jimmy. Navy vet to Navy vet. Medical professional to medical professional. He'd understand the necessity. And, hopefully, appreciate that it was Jonathan asking the questions.

Jonathan walked into the conference room.

"Howdy, Doc." Jimmy, seated at the room's massive conference table, smiled.

"Two Seattle's Best café mochas. Just what the doctor ordered."

Jimmy accepted his cup from Jonathan. "Much appreciated." He sipped from the cup. "So, what's this all about?"

"A formality, really." A small untruth under the circumstances. No reason to make Jimmy panic or get defensive at this point. "Need to ask you about something that happened on Saturday night."

"Oh?"

"But before we get to that, Dr. Melançon told me you missed your overnight on Sunday."

"I." Jimmy's face reddened. "I had something come up. Thought I'd arranged for someone to cover my shift. But it must have fallen through."

"Who?"

"No names." Jimmy shook his head. "My shift. My responsibility."

"Understood."

"And Alma was great to jump in for me."

"She did you quite a favor."

"I'm taking her day shift on Thursday to help make amends."

"Good on you." This explanation sounded more like the Jimmy he knew. "But doesn't that interfere with your class schedule? Day shift's eight a.m. to eight p.m."

"Yes and no," Jimmy said. "I can miss a couple of non-medical classes—history or whatever—no problem. My pre-med professors are pretty flexible—like attending today's postmortem on the burn victim. And I talked my anatomy professor into letting me skip Thursday's class in return for me giving a lecture on autopsy procedures."

"Well done." Jonathan smiled. "When's your next shift after Thursday?"

"I'm on the overnight Sunday night."

"Day after Chewbacchus?"

"Affirmative. I'm sure I'll be sober by eight p.m." He shifted in his chair as if sitting had become uncomfortable. "So, about Saturday night?"

"Right. Sorry." Jonathan cleared his throat. "A female student from Ole Miss was assaulted in Washington Square Park around midnight."

"Heard something about it. Mostly about someone carving up the guy who did it."

"I see." Jonathan sipped his café mocha. "The woman…a student at Ole Miss—"

"Right. I remember talking to her at The Bunker before all the…before what happened in the park."

"Name's Janelle Harrison."

"Sounds familiar. First name, anyway."

"Any insights? What did you talk about?"

"Just general stuff. Kept it light. Thought I might ask for her number. But she seemed a bit young—although she and her friend were doing tequila shots."

"Good call."

"Told her about Chewbacchus. And how dirty the bathroom at The Bunker was."

"Did she say anything about her friend?"

"Not really. Not that I can remember, anyway."

"Definitely not her name?"

"Right."

"Her name's Tamara, by the way. Janelle calls her Tam."

"Okay. Tam."

"Anything else?"

"Later. Around midnight."

"What happened?"

"Saw the girl—Janelle—and her friend…Tam…at Jazz Harbor as I was walking up Frenchmen."

"Inside the restaurant?"

"Correct. They were at a small table in the bar. In plain sight through the plate-glass windows."

"And?"

"I noticed a guy in a nearby alley. Looked like he was watching the restaurant."

"Dressed in a flannel shirt and a baseball cap, like you?"

"Affirmative. Down vest, too." Jimmy sipped his coffee. "Gave me the creeps. I sort of developed a sixth sense in Afghanistan. You kind of learned who looked most like the next suicide bomber. Certain tics and tells. You'd get this sensation in your spine. Not sure how to describe it."

"Sounds like a valuable skill to have."

"Maybe. Well, anyway, I dropped back into the shadows and waited. The guy just stayed there."

"Hmmm."

"When Janelle and Tam got up, apparently to leave, the guy disappeared."

"Odd."

"Agreed," Jimmy said. "I watched the pair leave Jazz Harbor. They appeared to be arguing. Tam headed up Frenchmen toward Burgundy, like she was in a hurry."

"Burgundy. That's where The John is, right?"

"That's right. I was about to leave when I noticed the guy from the alley come off Royal Street like he was following the friend. Following Tam."

"The guy wearing the flannel shirt and ballcap?"

"And a down vest," Jimmy said. "Looked like he was following her up Frenchmen."

"And Janelle stood outside Jazz Harbor, alone?"

"I still had that feeling, so I followed them. I made sure to stay on the other side of Frenchmen. Tam walked into The John. The guy behind her kept going. I waited a couple of minutes, then turned around and ran back down Frenchmen. By the time I got to Jazz Harbor, Janelle was gone."

"Anything else?"

"Next thing I knew, there were sirens up around Washington Square Park."

"Did you check it out?"

Jimmy shook his head and looked at his coffee cup. "No."

"Something wrong, Jimmy?"

"I should have stayed to watch Janelle. Or done something."

"You couldn't have known."

"Well, Doc, maybe I could have—"

"Done what? Go to the park and maybe get yourself killed?"

"Maybe it would have saved Janelle."

"Don't do that to yourself, Jimmy. You know the answer. You made the best decision you could with the facts you had. You addressed the most direct threat—Tam apparently being stalked on her way to The John. What if you hadn't followed Tam? What if Tam had been the one who was attacked?"

"Doesn't make it any easier to deal with it."

"Maybe not, but—"

"Listen, Doc, I need to drop Dr. Mohan's samples at the labs." Jimmy stood and grabbed his cup. "And get to class. So, unless there's something else, I should get started."

"Understood. Thanks for your time, Jimmy. Be safe."

Jimmy held his coffee up as if he were making a toast. "Thanks for the joe."

Chapter Forty-Five: Photographs

Wednesday, February 4, 2015 – 1:17 p.m.

"Sorry we couldn't go out for lunch." Jonathan scooped a spoonful of gumbo out of a Styrofoam take-out container and blew on it. "Glad Two Brothers' delivers."

"Roger that," Betsy said. "Eating at the morgue's not exactly on my bucket list, but I understand the time crunch." She bit into a fried oyster po'boy. "Jimmy shed any light on Janelle's assault?"

"Acknowledged meeting her at The Bunker." Jonathan ate the gumbo and maneuvered the spoon for more. "Man that's good…they talked a while."

"Details? About the girl. Not the gumbo."

"Just general chit chat. Kept it light. Thought he might ask for her number, but didn't want to come on as too creepy. He warned her about the dirty bathroom."

"Like Janelle claimed."

"And he told her about Chewbacchus…also like Janelle said."

"Anything about Tamara Espy?"

"Some vague mention of a friend she was in town with." Jonathan ate another spoonful of gumbo.

"Did you mention the security camera footage?" Betsy took another bite of po'boy.

"Didn't have to. Jimmy told me he saw the girl and her friend later, at Jazz Harbor, as he was walking up Frenchmen."

"He also saw a guy in a nearby alley. Looked like he was watching Jazz Harbor."

"Dressed in a flannel shirt and a baseball cap?"

"Affirmative," Jonathan said. "And down vest. When Janelle and Tam got up, apparently to leave, the guy disappeared."

"Strange."

"He watched them argue. Didn't hear what it was about. Tam left and hurried up Frenchmen toward The John, like she was in a huff."

"Verifies Janelle's version, more or less," Betsy said.

"More or less. And Jimmy was about to leave when he noticed a guy in a flannel shirt and ballcap turn off Dauphine Street like he was following Tam."

"Shit."

"So, he followed them up Frenchmen."

"And left Janelle behind, alone?"

"Yeah. Tam walked into The John. The guy behind her kept going. Jimmy says he waited a few minutes, then ran back down Frenchmen. By the time he got to Jazz Harbor, Janelle was gone."

Betsy leaned back in her chair. "Damn."

"Next thing he knew, there were sirens up around Washington Square Park."

"Jesus. You don't believe Jimmy is the one who killed the guy, do you?"

"Don't think so." Jonathan inhaled deeply, held his breath for a couple of beats, then exhaled slowly as if giving himself time to think before saying anything else.

"There's a 'but' in there somewhere."

"Wish we had more extensive video or a witness…"

"Because?"

"Well." Jonathan crossed his arms, then raised his right fist to his chin. He tapped on his chin as if sending himself a message in Morse Code. "It's just…Jimmy's a complex guy. And his experiences in Afghanistan…"

"And that makes you think what? That Jimmy could have butchered someone?"

"Listen, I hate myself for thinking it. Much less saying it." Johnathan shook his head. "But I…but I can imagine Jimmy coming across Janelle being assaulted and—"

"*Soc au' lait.* Jimmy?"

"Well, he's got all the right training. Those years in combat as a Corpsman. He knows his way around knives and scalpels. How to make incisions. He's physically fit. And…"

Jonathan's face warmed. He'd just nominated one of their autopsy techs as someone capable of carving up Janelle's attacker. And he hadn't even mentioned Jimmy's unexplained absence from the morgue overnight on Sunday into Monday morning—during the timeframe someone butchered Curtis Dowdy in St. Louis Cemetery Number One. Or his not being on the schedule at all when they were dealing with the incident at the homeless encampment on Tchoupitoulas.

"I just wish we had something else to put Jimmy in the clear. We need to get Mitch, or someone, to review the rest of the video we have."

"On it," Betsy said. "Already asked Mitch to prioritize his review."

"Thanks."

"Some pretty heavy stuff to think about. Maybe we should change the subject."

"Agreed." Jonathan sipped his iced tea. Jimmy might be a valid suspect. Time would tell. But Betsy was right. They needed to move on—at least for now. "Listen, Dan Rossignol busted me today about your photographs."

"Soup to nuts."

"I talked around everything," Jonathan said. "But he nailed me."

"How's that?"

"Asked me to give you his regards and remind you that Father Edward's probably looking forward to seeing you on Sunday."

"Jesus, Doc, *soc au'*—"

"Right. A real bag of milk. Sour milk at that."

"You'll get my ass excommunicated."

"Doubt that," Jonathan said. "That was just Dan's way of telling me he wasn't pleased."

"But still—"

"I told him all about the Sweeper. The dead bodies. The secret cipher. The whole nine yards…or at least enough to let him know we're facing a real evil son-of-a—"

"Did it work?"

"Not yet. But we'll see." Jonathan drank more iced tea. "In the meantime, did you get any good info from the photos?"

"Maybe. Most appeared to be locals. We can run them to ground as time allows. But a couple of people stood out. One in particular."

"Okay. And?"

"I recognized one of the card dealers from Harrah's. One of our seasonal employees. She was there both yesterday and today. Today, she was wearing what appeared to be her dealer's clothing."

"Appeared to be?"

"Standard outfit is black shoes and black pants. They change into their dealer's shirt at the facility."

"Dealer's shirt?"

"It's a requirement for dealers. Shirts have a single pocket for tips. Helps us monitor payments by the players. You know, potential bribes and all that."

"Skywatch?"

"Right," Betsy said. "Anyway, she was probably on her way to or from her shift. I'll drop by the casino and see if I can get into her personnel file."

"Got it. Is that the one who stood out?"

"No. I have a better image on my computer at the office." Betsy tapped through to a photograph on her phone. "But thought you needed to see this ASAP." She placed her phone on the table and slid it toward Jonathan. "Taken this morning."

"Is that Jankowski?"

"Looks sort of like the photo Milt at the union office gave me. But you got a better angle—"

"As he was dragging my butt across the yard?"

"Affirmative."

"Sure as hell does look like the guy who ran over me."

"And the timing fits," Betsy said. "If he's the Sweeper and telling Monsignor Rossignol about stabbing someone."

"Too bad we don't have photos from Monday or before," Jonathan said. "Any more clues on Jankowski's whereabouts since the fire?"

"No."

"And you didn't arrest the guy?"

"Based on what?" Betsy's voice reflected more than a hint of sarcasm. "My split-second look as I was flying backward from taking a shotgun blast to my body armor? Or your lengthy view of his boot heading for your tactical helmet?"

"Good point. Next steps?"

Betsy's phone alarm chimed. "The press conference."

"Right. Maybe we should drop by and make sure Max and Polly don't step in it too badly."

"My thought exactly."

Chapter Forty-Six: The Presser

Wednesday, February 4, 2015 – 3:47 p.m.

Jonathan drove slowly as he weaved around four mobile television-broadcasting trucks, their associated equipment, and several support vehicles near the parking garage at City Hall. "Looks like the Mayor's press conference is turning into a circus." He guided their vehicle into the garage.

"Afraid so," Betsy said. "The *Times-Pic Online* article yesterday about the Sweeper's return may have something to do with it."

"Brian Whitcomb did a decent job of burying the story, though. Bobby Harrison's editorial must have made people go digging."

"Over there." Betsy pointed to a lone figure standing near a sign: **Reserved for Coroner Vehicles**. "Isn't that Whitcomb?"

"Yeah." Jonathan waved as he pulled into an open parking space. "Wonder what he's doing here." Jonathan lowered the car window. "Brian. Surprised to see you."

"Took a chance you'd be here. Hoped I'd catch you before the press conference."

"Sure," Jonathan said. "We can talk on the way."

Whitcomb stepped back as Jonathan and Betsy clambered out of the vehicle.

"Lieutenant." Whitcomb nodded toward Betsy.

"Afternoon, Mr. Whitcomb," Betsy said. "Seems like your article stirred up a hornet's nest."

"About that." Whitcomb looked at Jonathan. "One of my colleagues with *The Advocate* seems to have latched onto the Sweeper angle."

The atmosphere became louder and more electric as the trio approached the press briefing room adjacent to Max Jamerson's office. Jonathan shared as many additional details about their investigation he felt comfortable revealing. Whitcomb, in turn, advised Jonathan and Betsy about the few facts he had been able to uncover. They stopped at a door labeled "Official Personnel Only."

"Here's where we part company." Jonathan opened the door and stood back as Betsy walked through.

"Right," Whitcomb said. "Best no one see us together."

"Roger that." Jonathan closed the door.

"You trust Whitcomb?" Betsy asked.

"Not much choice. We need his help to keep this from getting out of hand."

"Well—"

"Dr. Gray." Claudine Guiteau stood in the hallway about twenty feet away. "Glad you and Lieutenant Sprance are here. I believe the Superintendent has been trying to reach you."

"Sorry, Claudine," Jonathan said. "Didn't receive any messages."

"Yes, of course, please follow me." Claudine opened the door. Max Jamerson's voice resonated. Jonathan looked at his watch. Three-fifty-seven. Max must have started the press conference early.

Jonathan and Betsy entered the press room and sat in empty seats on the side, hidden from view of the audience by a curtain. Max Jamerson—still speaking—and Polly Bondurant stood on a small stage, behind a podium with the City of New Orleans seal on the front.

"That concludes my prepared remarks in response to the regrettable editorial denigrating our efforts to investigate a very serious offense in a thoughtful and respectful manner." Max looked at Polly, then back toward the audience. "I believe Superintendent Bondurant and I have time for a follow-up question or two."

The attendees raised their hands and shouted questions.

"One at a time, please." Jamerson seemed delighted at the opportunity to demonstrate his control. He pointed. "The attractive young lady in the front row."

"Thank you, Mr. Mayor. Miranda Rashid from *The Advocate*. Our readers are very interested to learn more about the possibility that the so-called Mardi Gras Sweeper has returned."

Apparently, the question hit Max out of the blue. His eyes flashed surprise—a true micro-expression—definitely there, but barely noticeable. So many years performing in the public arena—some might say so many years *prevaricating* in the public arena—meant Max had honed the art of hiding his emotions. So, his facial expression—regardless of how quick it had been—seemed even more telling.

"Yes." Max cleared his throat. "Thank you for the question, Miss Rashid."

"Ms."

"Of course, *Ms.* Rashid…but, as you know, the subject of the presser was to be limited to the unfortunate, and inaccurate, editorial in the Jackson *Clarion-Journal*. So, I'm—"

"Are you saying there is not a serial killer on the loose?"

Ms. Rashid seemed skilled at her craft as well. She waited long enough for the words to sink in but not long enough to give anyone else an opportunity to interrupt the flow of her cross-examination.

"Or do you believe that *The Advocate's* readers don't deserve to know whether they're safe at home…safe as they go about their daily lives?"

Murmurs from the audience signaled that Max would really have to dance to get out of the corner he'd been painted into by an attractive, young—and apparently tenacious as hell—female reporter. Still shielded from the audience by a curtain, Jonathan and Betsy remained silent.

"Yes, of course, the well-being of your readers…and all of the good citizens of this city and parish…remains of paramount importance. And our administration is, and always has been, committed to a level of transparency in matters of public interest."

"So what is it, Mr. Mayor?" Ms. Rashid angled her head to the side as if illustrating her skepticism of the response. "Is the Mardi Gras Sweeper on a murder spree again?"

"I'm loath to discuss investigative matters that fall within the Superintendent's jurisdiction. Perhaps you can direct your inquiry to NOPD's press liaison."

"Well." Ms. Rashid didn't let up. "Superintendent Bondurant is standing right there." She tilted her head toward Polly. "Won't you have her address the Sweeper situation?"

Ms. Rashid's hook had taken hold. Time to reel in the big fish. The audience murmured as if predicting how Max would react.

"An excellent point, Ms. Rashid." Max had apparently climbed behind the wheel and was about to drive the proverbial bus right over his Superintendent of Police. "Polly, would you care to share your perspective on this important question?"

"Of course, Mr. Mayor." Polly stepped to the podium. "I can't comment on the details of ongoing investigative matters."

"So, you *are* investigating a serial killer?" Ms. Rashid angled her head slightly sideways as if craning to hear the response.

Now it was Polly's turn to dance. "As you may recall, two years ago, one of our detectives, acting in the line of duty, discharged her firearm at the person we believed to be the Sweeper as that person jumped off the Crescent City Connection."

"Yes," Ms. Rashid said. "That was then. This is now. What about the present day?"

"We're supremely confident that the individual from two years ago couldn't have lived. I mean, the odds of survival would be astronomical."

"You're still not answering the question, Superintendent Bondurant. What about today?"

"This past weekend," Polly said, "NOPD responded to an incident bearing remarkable similarity to the previous visits by the individual some have called the Mardi Gras Sweeper."

Jonathan's face warmed, then became clammy. Another ice water for blood transfusion. There was something in Polly's tone. Jonathan's gut churned. Polly was about to climb on the bus with Max.

"So, Mayor Jamerson and I…"

At least she was going to make sure that Max couldn't wash his hands of the mess.

"…decided to form a task force under the lead of the Coroner—assisted by NOPD—to ensure that this incident was investigated thoroughly and expeditiously."

"Why the Coroner?" The question came from a person out of view.

Polly held her hands out, palms open toward the attendees, as if to push them back, at least figuratively. "Having a separate, specialized group to drill into the unique medical aspects of this matter has allowed us—Mayor Jamerson and I—to concentrate our efforts to ensure that this year's Carnival will be the safest ever."

Good dodge. No doubt Polly had pulled it out of her backside on the spur of the moment. At least Jonathan could leverage the comment to press for more support from the police. No need to keep the Sweeper's apparent return—or Jonathan's direct involvement in the hunt—secret.

"As a matter of fact, I invited Dr. Gray, Parish Coroner, and Detective Lieutenant Sprance from NOPD to consult with me after the press conference." Polly turned her head and motioned with her hand in a "come here" fashion. "Perhaps they will provide whatever details they can under the circumstances to outline their efforts."

Nothing like being put on the spot after being thrown under the bus.

Polly backed away from the podium as Jonathan and Betsy stepped forward.

"Thank you, Superintendent Bondurant, Mayor Jamerson," Jonathan said. How satisfying it would be to say "eff you" to the pair of bureaucrats. But now wasn't the time to give in to personal feelings. A simple "thank you" was the only safe acknowledgment. "I'm pleased to provide clarification, where I can. But as you might imagine, we can't discuss details."

Jonathan answered various general questions from the crowd. He reminded them that the so-called Sweeper had never targeted participants in Mardi Gras. So, the bottom line was that Carnival parades and other activities should be safe, especially with the assurances and extra security directed by the Mayor and Superintendent. He didn't share that the body count was up to at least four, that their prime suspect was probably wandering free in the city, or that the "manifesto" warned that "Cleo will pay thrice the price."

Jonathan surveyed the group. "So, if there are no further questions, we can conclude this briefing."

No such luck. Miranda Rashid raised her hand.

"Yes, Ms. Rashid. Final question."

"Thank you, Doctor. Can you comment on Mayor Jamerson's executive order setting a special election for March seventeenth? Or that Cassandra Melançon, one of your Deputy Coroners, has filed as a candidate?"

So there it was. Cass had already thrown her hat in the ring. Can't fault someone for trying to better themselves. Still, Cass should have had the common decency to say something. Time to remember rule number one of combat medicine—and politics—keep your cool. Dive into the blood-and-guts with gusto—and latex gloves wherever possible. And, especially in politics, never let 'em see you sweat.

"Deadline to file is almost two weeks away," Jonathan said. "And March seventeenth seems like it's on the other side of the galaxy at this point. As you might imagine, my concentration is elsewhere right now."

He let the comment sink in for a few seconds and ignored the two or three reporters who raised their hands. Only Ms. Rashid spoke.

"Excuse me, Dr. Gray, does that mean—"

"So, ladies and gentlemen, if you'll excuse us, Lieutenant Sprance and I have pressing duties elsewhere."

Chapter Forty-Seven: Ask, and Ye Shall Receive

Wednesday, February 4, 2015 – 11:42 p.m.

"Driving around staring into the darkness isn't exactly what I'd call pressing duties elsewhere," Betsy said. "It's almost midnight. How much longer we going to keep this up?"

"You have a hot date?" Jonathan engaged the left turn signal at the intersection of St. Charles Avenue and First Street.

"Guess not. But some meaningful shuteye might be nice."

"Right." Jonathan executed the left turn onto First Street. "Thought we might take another pass through the Lower Garden District. Swing by Lafayette Number One and Number Two. Then maybe we can call it a night."

"You really think the Sweeper has a penchant for cemeteries?"

"No," Jonathan said. "I think people in this town seem to have a penchant for having sex in dark cemeteries and parks. And the Sweeper has a penchant for doing violence to people engaged in such activities."

"I see your point."

Jonathan turned right on Coliseum Street. "This'll take us by Number One."

"Maybe we can stop by Commander's Palace for some takeout on the way."

"Your treat?"

"Of course." Betsy removed a thumb drive from her pocket and handed it to Jonathan. "And speaking of treats, I forgot to give you this."

"A thumb drive? What's this about?"

"Ranger paid me a visit last night."

"I thought he was in some kind of Homeland Security facility getting patched up."

"Long story. But he gave me the thumb drive. Told me to make copies and give one to you."

"Oh? What's on it?"

"Apparently, HSI has some intel on Max Jamerson that the U.S. Attorney didn't have when they got the mayor indicted."

"Don't tell me Ranger stole this. Jesus, Betsy. Taking stuff from a federal investigation's pretty serious. Probably a felony."

"Ranger promises me there's no classified info on the drive."

"Well, that's fine, but—"

"Says it's mostly his notes and some open-source data. Thinks it might help you deal with Max Jamerson. You know, maybe get him to reconsider calling for an election."

"Blackmail? Are you out of your mind?"

"I'm planning to take a copy to Mandy Simpson at the U.S. Attorney's Office."

"And that's supposed to make me feel better?"

"Shouldn't you at least review what's on it, first?"

"Fair enough," Jonathan said. "And we've cruised around the cemetery twice now. Looks like there's nothing doing at Lafayette Number One."

"Off to Lafayette Number Two?"

"I don't know. Why don't we hang it up for the night? We'll do a quick drive-by of the cemetery on the way back to…where should I drop you? Your house?"

"Car's at the Sixth District HQ."

Jonathan turned right on Seventh Street and headed toward St. Charles Avenue. "Sixth District it is."

"Crap. I hate days like this," Betsy said as they drove toward the Sixth District Police building at the Corner of Martin Luther King and South Rampart. "Things are shaking like crazy. Then all of a sudden, nothing. Waiting for test results. Witness leads drying up. And—"

"Could be worse," Jonathan said.

"It could?"

"You could work full-time at the Coroner's Office."

"Oh, and how's that?"

"It's always dead at the Coroner's Office."

Betsy groaned. "Please, Doc, no more corny-assed humor right now."

The radio crackled to life. "Dispatch. This is Unit Four-Oh-Seven. We need an ambulance on North Prieur, near St. Louis." The conversation continued, but the transmission became garbled. "…stab wounds…symbols carved…applying emergency measures…officer in pursuit…Lafitte Greenway toward I-10. Request backup."

Jonathan turned on the vehicle's blue flashing lights. "Ask and ye shall receive."

Chapter Forty-Eight: A Proposition

Thursday, February 5, 2015 – 12:38 a.m.

Jonathan and Betsy arrived at the intersection of North Prieur and St. Louis seconds behind an ambulance. Two NOPD cruisers, empty of occupants, doors open, sat partially on the street and partially on the wide expanse of Lafitte Greenway. Jonathan and Betsy rushed toward a playground about twenty yards ahead. Two uniformed NOPD officers knelt beside a male lying on the ground. One officer applied pressure to wounds in the man's torso. The other dabbed the man's face with a gauze pad. He moved the pad long enough to reveal the Sweeper's hallmark—Alpha and Omega—etched into the victim's forehead.

The officer cleaning the forehead wound signaled to the EMTs. "Over here." One EMT jogged forward with an emergency medical kit. The second EMT lagged behind, pulling a gurney.

The victim, probably in his mid-twenties, appeared to be unconscious, his breathing shallow. Along with the Alpha and Omega, the victim's torso bore slash marks, as if he'd resisted, and the Sweeper had to flee before finishing the job. A bloody sailor's rigging knife lay a couple of feet from the victim, on top of a folded sheet of paper.

As the EMTs arrived and took over care of the man, the officers stood and removed their latex gloves. One of the pair walked toward Jonathan and Betsy.

"Corporal Evans," Jonathan said. "Were you first on scene?"

"No, sir. Me and my partner arrived within a minute, though. Pascal—my partner—joined in the foot pursuit."

"The other officer from the first unit to arrive?"

"Yes, sir."

"Any indication of what happened? Beyond the obvious, I mean?"

"Looks like maybe a drug transaction gone bad. Victim's a known dealer. Not sure beyond that."

The EMTs rolled a gurney carrying the victim toward the ambulance.

"Excuse me." Jonathan displayed his badge. "Status?"

"Serious, probably not fatal," one EMT replied. "Taking him to University Hospital."

"Got it," Jonathan said. "Thanks." He turned toward Corporal Evans. "We'll need to take a photo of the piece of paper over there by the knife."

"I don't know, sir. The CSTs aren't here yet. Protocol requires us to—"

"I'll take responsibility," Betsy said. "We can't give a serial killer any more of a time advantage."

"Yes, ma'am," Evans said.

Betsy removed two pairs of latex gloves from her tactical vest and handed one pair to Jonathan. "Okay, Doc, let's see what the Sweeper wants to tell us."

Betsy took photographs on her phone as she "processed" the note, showing it as they found it, various steps in unfolding it, and then placing it flat on the ground. Jonathan photographed the document as well once it was unfolded.

Jonathan pulled out a notepad and his translation key. He sat down at a nearby picnic table and located the clearest photograph of the document he'd taken on his phone. "Betsy, shine your flashlight over here while I work."

Betsy sat on the other side of the picnic table. She pulled out her phone. "Light's brighter on this."

"Right." Jonathan shifted his gaze back and forth between the photo on his phone, the translation key, and the notepad, writing on the pad as he did so. Occasionally, he'd cuss under his breath or look at Betsy and shake his head before returning to the documents.

Jonathan handed the newly translated manifesto to Betsy:

disorganized mortals[:]

finally[,] you recognize my prowess [in] your newspapers [and] elsewhere[.] this pleases me[.]

in return[,] i offer you this proposition as [a] showing [of] my infinite mercy[.] i am very fond [of] carnival[.] [and] i swear by all i hold dear[,] that any person who shall be watching [a] parade this morrow[']s night [and] anyone [in] whose home [the] sweet fragrance [of] king cake exists[,] shall be spared[.] for others [in] [the] box[,] beware[.] my wrath exists [in] [the] shadows [of] cleo[.]

until next we meet[,] adieu[.]

yours truly[,]

[the] sweeper

"Jesus, Doc. What the hell does it mean?"

"Among other things, it means the Sweeper's playing with us. This crap about "a proposition" is straight out of a letter someone claiming to be the Axeman of New Orleans sent over a hundred years ago. And, if we hadn't figured as much by now, we're dealing with an intelligent, calculating bastard."

"So, next steps?"

"I'll drop you at your car. Not much we can do today." I'm betting tomorrow will be better." He smirked. "Can't be much worse."

Betsy yawned. "Hope not."

Chapter Forty-Nine: Two Steps Backward

Jonathan ate the last of the gumbo he'd ordered from Two Brothers' Trolley Stop Café, a small restaurant a few blocks from the Coroner's Administrative Offices in City Hall. "Man, that's good. The brothers have mastered the roux, that's for sure."

Betsy wadded up the paper wrapper from her andouille sausage po'boy and pitched it into a small waste basket in the corner. "Two points."

"Double our score for the day."

"Sad, but true," Betsy said. "Seems like we've been taking one step forward and two steps backward."

"I'll say this, the Sweeper—"

"Or whoever the hell we're chasing—"

"Right. Whoever we're chasing is a combination of the smartest and luckiest suspect I've ever seen."

"True dat," Betsy said. "No prints, no surveillance camera images, no reliable witnesses, no—"

"No forensic evidence from the autopsies leading to an identification of the Sweeper, either."

"Even when we have a witness, they disappear or don't know anything very helpful."

"Well, if it was easy, anybody could do it."

"You know, Doc, right now I'd settle for easy." Betsy smirked. "Or at least a more supportive Superintendent and Mayor."

"Maybe we should focus on what we have…what we know."

"Glass half full, I guess."

"That's one way to look at it," Jonathan said. "First, we know that Janelle Harrison was sexually assaulted, but not raped."

"And that someone…maybe the Sweeper…dispatched her attacker."

"Affirmative," Jonathan said. "And, it seems unlikely they're involved, but we can't entirely rule out her sorority sister—Tam—and that guy, Ian, until—"

"Jimmy Copeland, either."

"Right," Jonathan said. "Until we look through all the video evidence we've collected."

"I'll see where Mitch is on the review."

"Great," Jonathan said. "Best thing is that we're inside the Sweeper's mind to a certain degree, with the manifesto."

"Thank goodness for Emma," Betsy said.

"Roger that."

"So far, the Sweeper's operated in a manner similar to his visits two and four years ago."

"And," Jonathan said, "consistent with what's in the various iterations of his manifesto."

"Which means that we should be able to concentrate our efforts during Friday's parades. I mean, NOPD will still cover the main routes like always."

"And you, Mitch, and I can lead a small team to flood The Box. Surely Polly can spare a dozen officers for a special detail."

"Still leaves us a pretty large area to cover," Betsy said. "From St. Charles on the lakeside to Tchoupitoulas along the river. And from Napoleon to Canal Street."

"Right. Gives us the core of a plan for tomorrow. And the best part is that the Sweeper will have trapped himself in The Box as well."

"Should almost be like shooting fish in a barrel."

"Let's not get ahead of ourselves." Jonathan's phone vibrated. "This is Gray." He looked toward Betsy as he listened. Maybe he should have put the phone on speaker so Betsy could hear the news for herself. "I see…you're sure?…no, that's okay…it is what it is. Thanks, Ronnie. I'll spread the word."

Jonathan lowered his phone to his side and closed his eyes. He inhaled deeply, then exhaled a series of cleansing breaths. He opened his eyes and stared blankly at Betsy.

"Okay, Doc. Don't keep me in suspense."

"Ronnie Mohan." Jonathan spoke slowly, his voice subdued. "Ronnie Mohan got the results back on the victim from the house fire on Alonzo Street."

"And?"

"It was Stanislaus Jankowski."

Betsy's eyes widened, and her jaw dropped open. "What? How? Who shot me and ran over you?"

"Exactly. Seems like we just took a half-dozen steps backward."

Chapter Fifty: Time for Rock 'n' Bowl

Thursday, February 5, 2015 – 3:42 p.m.

"Thanks, Milt. Appreciate the info." Betsy squeezed her desk phone's handset between the side of her head and her shoulder. "Sure. I'll ask Homicide to contact you once they open a formal case." She nodded. "Understood. I'll send the referral this afternoon. They'll probably want next-of-kin info so they can notify the family." Betsy wrote on her notepad as she listened. "Right. We were as surprised as you were. But you should wait until you have a formal go-ahead from NOPD before you announce…yeah, should be this afternoon, tomorrow morning at the latest. But if you haven't heard from someone by noon tomorrow, give me a ring." Betsy rolled her eyes. "All right, Milt. That's fine. Yeah, you too." Betsy returned the handset to the phone cradle.

"Anything of value?"

"Not really." Betsy shook her head. "Wofford—Milt—said that he didn't know anyone who might want Jankowski dead."

"I didn't overhear everything. Did you provide him a lot of details?"

"Barebones stuff. Made it sound like the fire was probably an accident, pending NOFD's investigation and referral to Homicide for their review. Death from smoke inhalation. Didn't mention the chunk missing from the back of his skull. Told him I was just tying up loose ends."

"Makes sense."

"Did you talk to Dr. Melançon?"

"I did," Jonathan said. "She sent me a preliminary draft of her autopsy report—including tox results."

"And?"

"Jankowski had metabolites of marijuana, fentanyl, and maybe alcohol in his tissues."

"Metabolites?"

"Fancy term for residue. The chemical compounds left after substances—like fentanyl—are digested or absorbed into blood, internal organs, or even fatty tissue. And heat from the fire may have had an effect."

"Damn," Betsy said. "I *must* be getting tired. I've been involved in enough investigations involving narcotics that I should have remembered."

"I know the feeling."

"Was it fentanyl or one of the new knock-offs we've been seeing?"

"The real deal," Jonathan said. "Test results showed norfentanyl—characteristic of prescription fentanyl. Analogues—knock-offs—yield different metabolites, depending on the version."

"Think the weed might have been laced with it?"

"Possibly. Fentanyl—prescription fentanyl—is a valid analgesic, like oxycodone, so he may have ingested it separately."

"Got it," Betsy said. "And *maybe* alcohol. Why just maybe?"

"Jankowski's tox screen revealed alcohol in his system. But could have been endogenous, not consumed."

"In English, Doc."

"The body can produce alcohol postmortem. During decomposition, microorganisms—especially yeast and bacteria—can ferment any sugar—think carbohydrates—in the body to produce ethanol."

"So even if Jankowski hadn't been drinking, his tox screen may have listed alcohol?"

"Ethanol," Jonathan said, "but right. And that's why it's only maybe."

"Got it. But didn't Dr. Melançon say that cause of death was smoke inhalation?"

"Affirmative," Jonathan said. "But it's part of the picture."

"Understood. Using drugs, and maybe alcohol. Blunt force injury to the back of the head. And a fire started with signal flares."

"Not a pretty picture of Jankowski and the company he kept."

"You thinking a drug deal gone bad, Doc?"

"Could be. Gambling debt. Mob enforcer. Who knows? Not sure it matters to our investigation, though."

"Because?"

"Doesn't fit the Sweeper's pattern."

"But," Betsy said, "what if Jankowski *was* the Sweeper?"

"Then it sounds like tomorrow's parades will be very boring."

"But you don't think so?"

"No." Jonathan shook his head. "The Sweeper's been too focused, too organized. Doesn't seem to be the kind to get himself into a situation leading to being bludgeoned and his house set on fire."

"But if Jankowski's not the Sweeper, then who was it?"

"I'd prefer not to speculate."

"That's how investigations work, Doc. Identify people with means, motive, and opportunity, then see what the evidence shows. Speculate. Rule people in or out. Whittle down the list of suspects. So, besides some total stranger we haven't identified, who's left after Jankowski?"

"Well," Jonathan said. "We don't have a lot of people to choose from."

"Ian?"

"I just can't see it. Tam gives him an alibi for the Washington Square Park victim."

"And if he and Tam were in cahoots?"

Jonathan shook his head. "Motive? And what about the other victims? Seems awfully coincidental that Ian would hook up with Tam, kill the guy in Washington Square Park, and then start on a murder spree."

"Scratch one—or two—suspects." Betsy hesitated as if she didn't want to say something. "That seems to leave us with either a complete stranger or—"

"Don't. Go. There." Jonathan frowned. "It's not Jimmy."

"But you said—"

"Don't care what I said. "It's not…has Mitch reviewed any more video?"

"There's nothing, yet, that would exonerate Jimmy."

"Looks like we're back to a complete stranger." Jonathan leaned back in his chair and crossed his arms. "So, there's got to be something we've missed. We need to go back to square one and review everything again. Rethink our—"

"I agree. But time's running out." Betsy frowned. "Maybe we need a break. I think I'll go to Rock 'n' Bowl, grab a burger, and roll a few frames. Something about pounding the pins clears out the cobwebs."

"You're right. We've hit a wall—mentally at least. We should come at it fresh tomorrow. Maybe I'll go for a run." Jonathan stroked his cheek. "And I should spend some time with Emma. Make sure she hasn't served me with divorce papers."

Chapter Fifty-One: Something Extra

Thursday, February 5, 2015 – 4:19 p.m.

Stryker finished her first shot of bourbon and thought about pouring another. Maybe it was too early in the day. But it was five o'clock somewhere. And under the circumstances, a dram or two would be understandable, almost expected.

A telemedicine visit was one hell of a way to confirm that the cancer had recurred. And spread. But thank goodness the Veterans Administration had at least made that option available. Otherwise, it would have been necessary to gas up the CR-V and trek to the VA Hospital in Houston. Not the most convenient time for an unplanned side trip.

Latest estimate was that it would be at least a year before the new VA Medical Center in New Orleans—replacing the facility destroyed by Katrina—would open. But the Oncologist thought they could arrange for treatment—radiation and chemo—in New Orleans because of an agreement between the VA and the Ochsner Hospital Group. Another gracious lagniappe—a little something extra—for an Army vet from a grateful nation. And a fitting reason to have a second shot of bourbon—in celebration.

Would it really matter after this weekend? Assuming everything went exactly as planned—especially her escape—there'd be more reason to run the medical gauntlet again. But the worst-case scenarios? The most likely results of the next hours? Dragged to the Orleans Parish Jail in handcuffs. Or lying dead in a pool of blood, filled with lead. Either way, there'd probably be no bourbon in her future.

So if she wanted to play the odds, now was the time to call it all off. Cut her losses and fade into history. Hope that she'd covered her tracks well enough to avoid being caught and punished for the crimes already committed. But that wasn't in the cards, either. All the more reason for a third shot—a final toast before entering the arena. *Morituri te salutant. Those of us who are about to die, salute you.*

Best not to get drunk, though. Still a lot of heavy lifting. Stay sharp. As always, stay focused. Finish final preparations for tomorrow, then get plenty of sleep. Friday, and the next critical steps in the plan, would come soon enough.

Chapter Fifty-Two: The Gallery

Thursday, February 5, 2015 – 8:15 p.m.

Jonathan clicked on the remote control to increase the temperature on one of the two electric space heaters standing on their second-floor gallery overlooking Bienville Street. Unless the wind or rain made it untenable, the units allowed year-round use for meals or, as tonight, relaxing and reveling in the gumbo ya-ya of voices, traffic noise, and jazz notes from the streets below. A reminder of how much he and Emma enjoyed living and being property owners in the French Quarter—despite the challenges.

"Not sure you should have been so harsh on Betsy." Emma sipped her wine—a Pinot Noir. Bon Jovi, a calico cat belonging to Emil Morrisette—proprietor of a shop on the ground floor of their building—rubbed against her leg."

"You cat-sitting again?" Jonathan sipped his Pinot Noir. Maybe he could change the subject.

"I told Emil I'd watch him for a couple of days."

"Morrisette have a hot date?"

Bon Jovi jumped onto the gallery's wrought-iron railing, hissed in Jonathan's direction, then sauntered away. He jumped down from the railing and curled up near the space heater.

"Emil and Victor have some Krewe events they're attending the next couple of nights."

"I see." So far, so good. Maybe Emma had forgotten already. "Did Emil ever fix the computer issue with his lease payment?"

"Come on, Gray. Don't think you can avoid talking about Betsy." Emma poured wine into her glass. "She's just doing her job."

"I probably shouldn't have said as much as I did about the Sweeper investigation."

"Well, you did. So why give Betsy such a hard time?"

"Jimmy. Betsy shouldn't have—"

"Shouldn't have what? Listed the reasons Jimmy might be a suspect?"

"Well—"

"Even you were thinking that he might be involved."

"That's different."

"How?"

"We don't have time to futz around with dead ends." Jonathan gulped down the rest of the wine in his glass—about three ounces or so—as if that might make things better. He poured more Pinot Noir. "We don't have a shred of direct evidence against Jimmy. It's all circumstantial."

"Look, I can imagine how frustrated you must be."

"Goes with the territory."

"And our wonderful mayor calling for a special election has to be tough to bear."

"Can't we just change the subject?"

"Gray, this isn't like you."

"What's not like me?"

"Tucking your tail between your legs and—"

"I'm not—"

"And giving up."

"I haven't given up."

"You could have fooled me."

"What's that mean?"

"The Jonathan Gray I know wouldn't stop, no matter what, until he'd cleared Jimmy or seen him convicted."

"Fen, that's—"

"Unfair?"

"No." Jonathan inhaled deeply, then released a long cleansing breath. "I guess not."

"I get it. Things look bleak. But I can't believe you don't have anything to go on. What about that document I translated?"

"I've probably said too much already." Too late for that. Emma was right. She deserved to know more. "But I could use a new set of eyes and ears."

"Okay."

"The document you translated was the first of four we've come across."

"Each one attached to a dead body?"

"Three dead. One still alive." Jonathan drank more wine. "And we recovered charred remains of someone killed in a fire. But no note."

"Oh my. Five victims. No wonder you're bummed."

"We think the documents are all parts of a manifesto."

"I see," Emma said.

"And everything points to tomorrow night's Cleopatra parade."

"Okay. That's something. Like what?"

"Latest note said 'Cleo will pay thrice the price'."

"Jesus, Mary, and Joseph. You expect there to be three murders during the parade?"

"Afraid so."

"And you don't have enough evidence to detain—"

"Jimmy?"

"Wouldn't that stop the murders?" Emma asked. "Or rule him out as a suspect if they continue?"

"Probably could make some excuse to lock him up, but—"

"But if you're wrong, it would destroy Jimmy emotionally."

"That's the idea."

"But what if you're not wrong? What if it *is* him?"

"It's not him."

"And you're willing to stake your reputation—and other people's lives—on that belief?"

"I am." Jonathan drank the rest of his wine.

"Okay. I understand. You know I'm behind you, whatever you decide."

Jonathan stared into the Quarter. He nodded slowly, but remained silent.

"Why don't we go upstairs and change the subject?"

"Upstairs?"

Emma reached her hand toward Jonathan. "The bedroom."

Chapter Fifty-Three: Havoc the Wolf

Dan Rossignol had always been punctual. So his failure to appear in the priest's box of the confessional precisely at eight-forty-five raised concerns. Had their discussion on Wednesday morning presaged Dan's decision to avoid further contact? Another two minutes. He'd give Dan another two minutes to show before…

The faint odor of tobacco arrived just before the door to the priest's box opened. Dan must have been having another early morning cigar. The door clicked shut, and the screen between the priest and penitent sections slid open. Jonathan's nose crinkled. Alcohol? Surely, Dan hadn't been drinking. Being a few minutes late was one thing. But day-drinking…worse, morning-drinking…something else entirely.

"Good morning, Jonathan. Sorry I'm late."

"Is everything okay, Dan?" Dan's words were clear, enunciated well, and not slurred. But something seemed off. "I know we didn't leave on the best of terms on Wednesday."

"Wednesday? Don't give it another thought." Dan cleared his throat. "I guess I'm just disappointed about last night's game."

"Last night's game?"

"Of course, you probably don't follow the Wolf Pack. Loyola lost to Belhaven."

"Sorry?"

"Basketball. Eighty-one to seventy-one."

Loyola University basketball? What the hell did Loyola University of New Orleans—or its basketball team—have to do with Dan's interpersonal issue about his Crucifix being used to stab someone? Or the Sweeper? Or anything of consequence for that matter?

"I'm sorry, Dan, I didn't realize you were such a Loyola fan."

"Oh yes, of course I am. Always have been. Helps keep my mind occupied."

Really? In all the discussions they'd had over the years, Loyola, much less its basketball team, had never been a substantial part of the conversation. Maybe a casual mention, but nothing like Dan's current obsession with Loyola sports. How much had Dan had to drink?

"Oh, I see. I don't recall you being so enthusiastic."

"And Havoc the Wolf." Dan chuckled. "What a clever name for a mascot, don't you think?"

"Yes. Of course. Havoc the Wolf." Jonathan leaned toward the small opening between the two sections of the confessional. "I guess you've gotten over the issues we've been talking through."

"Not entirely. But, earlier, I spoke with a woman…a soldier. Or at least she was a soldier for many years. She's medically retired."

"Oh, I see."

"Cancer."

"Well, that's a tragedy."

"Yes," Dan said. "A tragedy. And how she was mistreated by her superior officer. And the Army command structure."

"Mistreated? How?"

"She helped me to see more clearly about how insignificant my problems are in comparison. I mean, a woman in what's predominantly a man's world."

"You mean the Army?"

"Yes."

"Well, I served with plenty of females in the Navy."

"Yes, I know. You've talked about your experiences. But the Navy seems altogether different to me."

"Different? How? And Betsy Sprance was in the Marines."

"I don't know. Maybe it's just me, but it seems like there shouldn't be women in the Army. That's all."

Before Jonathan could answer, a loud buzz filled the confessional.

"Yes. This is Monsignor Rossignol."

A phone call in the confessional? Jonathan shook his head at the oddity. Who'd have thought a priest would bring a cell phone into a supposedly sacrosanct location?

"Excuse me, Jonathan. Something's come up. I must go now. Shall we plan to talk again on Monday?"

"Well…"

The door to the confessional opened. As footsteps echoed in the distance, Jonathan sat in silence, stunned. What the hell had he just experienced? Maybe he should speak to Archbishop Fontenot about a priest who seemed to be coming unhinged. His cell phone vibrated. An incoming text. Crazy Dan Rossignol would have to wait. Betsy needed to meet. Stat.

Chapter Fifty-Four: Hasta La Vista

Friday, February 6, 2015 – 10:02 a.m.

"Sure you don't want some coffee while we wait?" Betsy let go of the *portiere* covering one of the sidelights on the front door of her house on Plum Street. "Thought he'd have been here by now."

"I'm good." Jonathan shook his head. "You sure you want me here for this?"

"Ranger does."

"Do you know what it's about?"

"Not sure," Betsy said. "I have an idea, but I can't really say anything."

"Or why I need to stay out of sight?"

"Same."

"Okay."

A black SUV, its general outline visible through the sheer curtains covering the front window, pulled up to the curb. A figure emerged from the back seat on the driver's side and spoke to someone, perhaps the driver or another passenger. The figure closed the door and walked toward the house.

"He's here," Betsy said.

Jonathan stepped to his left and shielded himself behind a china cabinet.

The door opened. Ranger. Odd. He stepped into the house and embraced Betsy while the door remained open. Nothing unusual about hugging your wife first thing. But it was as if he wanted to ensure that whoever was in the vehicle saw their interaction. After several seconds—and an Academy

Award-level performance aimed at…whoever—he led Betsy further inside and shut the door behind them.

"Sorry. Don't have much time. We're wheels-up from Belle Chasse in just over an hour." Ranger looked around. "Dr. Gray make it?"

Jonathan stepped out from behind the china cabinet. "Ranger."

"Dr. Gray." Ranger extended his hand. "Thank you for coming."

"Sure." Jonathan accepted the handshake. "What's this about?"

"Not sure what all Betsy's told you."

"Wasn't much to tell," Betsy said.

"Yeah, well," Ranger said. "Best that you don't know a lot."

"Then this is a perfect situation." Betsy frowned.

"Fair enough," Ranger said.

"Not to interrupt your personal time," Jonathan said. "But can you give me the thirty-thousand-foot view of why I'm here?"

"Since I retired, I've been consulting with a government agency about some sensitive matters I dealt with in the Army."

"Consulting?" Jonathan asked.

"Let's just leave it at that for now," Ranger said. "And we have an operational deliverable coming due."

"An operational deliverable?" Jonathan asked. "What the hell does that mean?"

"Bottom line is that I won't be around for a while, and I need to take care of a few loose ends before I leave."

"And I'm one of the loose ends?" Jonathan's forehead wrinkled.

"Listen, Doc, last time we were together wasn't exactly a tea party."

"Agreed."

"I can't tell you why I was at Sonny's place, but I promise it wasn't to kill Sonny." His eyes darted between Jonathan and Betsy. "Or his lady friend…or you."

"Right," Jonathan said. "You were there for a knife-throwing exhibition?"

"You did have a gun aimed at me."

"You blame me?"

"No." Ranger shook his head. "But you need to understand that if I had really wanted, I could have—"

"Cut out my heart and shown it to me before I died?"

Ranger grinned. "One of my special skill sets."

"Got it," Jonathan said. "Throwing a knife at my face—nothing personal, right?"

"Something like that, Doc."

"Message received," Jonathan said. "I'll need to chew on it for a while."

"Thanks, Doc." That's all I can ask. "And I hope that the stuff on the thumb drive might be—"

"Like a peace offering?"

"More like my way of helping to make things right. The people I'm working…or, I mean, consulting with, had a lot of info on Jamerson that didn't make it to the U.S. Attorney. Maybe this additional stuff will help put Max where he needs to be."

"And if it helps with my election campaign, so be it?"

"Right."

A car horn sounded.

"I need to split." Ranger handed an envelope to Betsy.

"What's this?" Betsy asked.

"For Brandon."

"Nothing for me?" Betsy frowned.

"Couldn't. They monitor all outgoing comms."

"You mean Dismukes looked at your letter to Brandon?" Betsy's eyes narrowed as if to signal her skepticism.

"And they would have reviewed anything I wrote to you, Baby. Told them I needed to deliver the letter personally and say goodbye."

Betsy maintained a poker face.

Ranger removed a pen from his shirt pocket, located a notepad on a nearby table, and wrote something. He folded the note and handed it to Betsy.

"What's this?"

"Secret word. So you'll know it's me."

"Of course." Betsy rolled her eyes. "Another secret."

Jonathan cleared his throat. "Why don't I step into the kitchen and give you two some privacy?"

"Not necessary." Ranger smiled at Betsy. "We said our goodbyes the other night."

Betsy didn't return Ranger's smile. "I guess I'll see you when I see you." Her eyes seemed to add a silent "here we go again" comment.

Ranger opened the door, stepped onto the porch, then turned back toward Betsy. "Hasta la vista, Baby." He winked and pulled the door closed.

Chapter Fifty-Five: The Helmet

Friday, February 6, 2015 – 1:19 p.m.

"Morning, First Sergeant." The military guard, a Marine Corps Corporal, handed Stryker's retired ID card to her through the open car window. He pressed a button to raise the security barrier. "Welcome to MCSF New Orleans."

"Thanks, Corporal." Stryker smiled. "Floats still in the staging area next to the MARFORRES building?"

"Yes, ma'am." The guard pointed. "Through the gate, then right. Follow the road around to the other side of the HQ. You can't miss them."

"Got it." Stryker hit the button to close the car window and proceeded forward.

Warriors of Ares. Three floats carrying active duty and retired military personnel, throwing beads, drinking Jello shots, and generally having a good time. Hard to call them a Mardi Gras krewe, though. But it was a low-budget way to participate in Carnival without the expense usually associated with being in top-of-the-line parading organizations such as Orpheus or Endymion.

Formed only a couple of years ago, they'd searched each parading season to find a real krewe to take them in. The Warriors of Ares floats would meld into the main parade, almost like a dancing group or marching band. Neither fish nor fowl. Not part of the "real" krewe, but the fans lining the streets wouldn't care. A throw was a throw, regardless of the source.

This year, they'd struck gold. The Warriors of Ares would parade as part of the Krewe of Loyola on Saturday. Wedged in between Choctaw and Freret, the Loyola parade was a great placement for both the Warriors of Ares, as the group struggled to establish itself, and for the overall plan.

Funny how circumstances sometimes came together. Who'd have thought that running across an article in *Army Times* would lead to becoming an out-of-town member of the Warriors of Ares? And even more serendipitous that—after several years following him around across the country—the object of her personal campaign for justice would step into the picture and present this opportunity. An unsuspecting, but not so innocent, lamb to the slaughter. It might not be for the right reasons, but people would remember this year's Warriors of Ares parade.

Stryker parked, got out of the car, and shouldered a backpack. She angled toward the three floats, lined up one behind the other. Only a couple of people were around, surprising considering that the parade was tomorrow.

"Yo, Stryker." The voice came from the third float in the line. "Here to load throws?"

"Some, Gunny. But I've got a couple of last-minute maintenance items to check on." Stryker waved. "Semper Fi."

"Ooorah." Gunnery Sergeant Maxson, "Float Lieutenant" for the haze-gray, battleship-themed float reserved primarily for Navy, Marine, and Coast Guard riders, returned the wave. "You on The Helmet?"

"Bingo." Stryker grinned. "Better than the wild blue yonder thing the Air Force came up with."

"Roger that," Maxson said. "Crazy assed zoomies."

Stryker shoved her backpack onto the float crafted to look like a giant green army helmet from World War Two—complete with combat netting. She stepped onto the rickety steps attached to the float, grabbed metal handholds on each side of the opening, and climbed aboard. Time to make sure the devices were still in place.

The float designed to honor the U.S. Army left a lot to be desired. Most Mardi Gras floats were constructed by longstanding experts like Kern Studios. The three floats for the Warriors of Ares, however, were built by krewe-member volunteers. In keeping with standard practice, the Warrior of Ares floats were constructed on thirty-foot flatbed trailers. Some additional metal framing was involved, especially for multi-level floats. But mostly, they were wood-heavy fire traps. Floors and walls were cheap plywood. And the various themed designs—a helmet for the Army, a jet for the Air Force, and a miniature battleship for the "seagoing services"—were generally crafted using four-inch-thick Styrofoam sheets, covered in chicken wire and papier mâché. Add artwork, the right color and type of paint, and, voila, a Mardi Gras float.

But there were two items of special interest. This year's "Patriot on Point," the Warriors of Ares equivalent of a Grand Marshal, was an active-duty general. So, he would stand at a place of honor—an elevated platform constructed on the front part of the Army's float that included a set of springs to allow for additional resilience and comfort. The other area garnering Stryker's attention? The suspension system of the trailer upon which the entire float rested.

Stryker busied herself placing her parade throws in plastic garbage bags. The weather didn't call for rain, but in New Orleans, it was always better to be safe than sorry. And the excuse of bagging up her throws and conducting a last-minute maintenance check covered her real mission. She needed to ensure that the explosive devices she'd positioned under the Patriot-on-Point's platform earlier were still in place. Similar, but smaller, devices, disguised to look like they contained large amounts of explosives, had been placed in critical locations on the frame of the float.

All was in order. Stryker climbed down off the float, latched the access door, and headed for her vehicle.

"Hey, Stryker, where you think you're going?" Gunny Maxson approached. "You not sticking around for the VIPs?"

"Sorry?"

"The Colonel's bringing our distinguished visitor around for a look-see in a few."

"Norsworthy? General Norsworthy's coming?"

"Yeah." Maxson grinned. "Figured you'd want to rub shoulders with a fellow snake eater."

"Sounds like fun." Stryker's heartbeat pounded. Not a good time for a meeting. "But I gotta run some errands." Not a total fabrication. But the so-called errands involved tonight's parades and making the Krewe of Cleopatra "pay thrice the price."

"Suit yourself." Maxson shook his head. "You riding the float to the staging area on the East Bank in the morning? Or meeting us there?"

"Figured I'd meet you there."

"Got it."

Stryker hastened to her car. Good timing. She pulled out of the parking lot just as Lieutenant General Javius Norsworthy, current Commander of Special Operations Forces, U.S. Southern Command, arrived.

They *would* meet—again. But not today. Tomorrow. Just as Stryker had planned.

Chapter Fifty-Six: Out With a Bang

Friday, February 6, 2015 – 5:55 p.m.

Mardi Gras—a season beginning each year on January 6th, the Twelfth Night, and continuing until Fat Tuesday—no doubt shone as the greatest party in the United States. Perhaps the world. To a casual observer, Mardi Gras parades likely represented a devil-may-care free-for-all. But to a participant, or anyone involved in bringing everything together to make it happen, each parade represented a highly regulated, logistically complex evolution. An only half-joking rumor spread each year that purchases by parade planners of antacid, ibuprofen, and bourbon skyrocketed during Carnival.

Only three parades scheduled in the city on Friday—Krewe of Cork, Krewe of Oshun, and Krewe of Cleopatra. Thank God for small miracles. Jonathan and Betsy had been fine-tuning their plan for Friday night in the hours since the unexpected encounter with Ranger. Resolving his status—at least learning that he was healthy enough to go on another "can't tell you where or what" adventure with Homeland Security—had to be a relief. At this point, if they weren't ready for Friday night's activities, they'd never be.

Unless the Sweeper had decided to chart a new course, Cork—an afternoon walking parade of wine and food lovers in the French Quarter—wasn't a worry. Polly Bondurant had agreed to assign a small group of plainclothes officers to follow along the parade in case something happened. But the Sweeper had always concentrated on the larger, float-centric parades.

And there had been no reason to suspect that he would change horses in mid-stream.

Oshun and Cleopatra. Two parades. Myriad security problems. Their overall route—starting from different locations in the Garden District, but mostly proceeding along St. Charles Avenue toward Canal—was over four miles long. And the parading krewes themselves, massive. Oshun boasted more than three hundred riders. Interspersed between floats, the associated marching bands, dancing troupes, and such, meant there'd be easily fifty individual parade units and nearly a thousand parade participants to monitor as Oshun rolled.

But the Sweeper's latest missive hovered in the background like one of Harry Potter's Dementors. *Cleo will pay thrice the price.* Cleopatra. An all-female "mega-Krewe." One of Carnival's most popular and well-attended. Nearly twelve-hundred riders on two dozen floats. Combined with bands and so forth, the number of units participating as part of Cleo ballooned to almost seventy-five, along with an additional two-thousand band and marching group members.

And worse, both parades got underway after sunset. Oshun at six. Cleopatra at six-thirty. Darkness brought with it the most daunting challenge. Plenty of places for the Sweeper to hide, come out to unleash his mayhem, and then fade away into the shadows among thousands of fans watching the activities.

Not much to worry about for the safety of the parades themselves—under normal circumstances. NOPD had "security in depth" protocols in place, well-honed and practiced after decades of guarding participants and revelers. But the addition of the Sweeper's threat meant that this year's parades would be anything but normal.

Fortunately, the Sweeper had never attacked krewe members, others in the parades, or people in the crowd. Each float had passed a rigorous inspection process for safety and fire issues. Bomb-sniffing dogs had passed through each group of floats as they assembled at the merge point of their respective parades. They'd worked with each krewe to screen members who'd be riding on each float.

And the Sweeper had telegraphed where his activities would take place—in "The Box," an area bounded by the streets along the parade route. Generally, that meant the large urban rectangle formed with St. Charles, Canal, Tchoupitoulas, and Napoleon as its sides. Better yet, the Sweeper had further limited his target pool by exempting people watching the parades or whose house contained the "sweet fragrance of King Cake." Too bad NOPD didn't have a cadre of King Cake-sniffing dogs.

Polly Bondurant had detailed eight NOPD officers, in plain clothes to blend in with the crowd, to assist Jonathan's so-called "Box Team." They'd even been assigned a special radio frequency for communications purposes. "Box Command," Betsy and Jonathan, rode together in a small electric utility vehicle designed for use on the narrow streets and alleys of the French Quarter. Short of canceling the parades—something not done in over thirty years—they'd covered all the possible bases.

"Box Command." Jonathan's radio crackled. "This is Broussard. Riding with Air One."

"Roger, Mitch," Jonathan responded. "What's the view from above?"

"All systems go. Crowd seems mighty thin for a Friday parade."

"Roger that, Mitch," Jonathan said. "Fear of the Sweeper?"

"Maybe," Mitch replied.

"No issues on the ground, yet. Keep us informed."

"Roger that, Box Command. Broussard out."

Smaller crowds. Sounds like people weren't taking the Sweeper at his word. They should be thronging the parade route to avoid being a victim. Maybe they were staying at home eating King Cake.

"Parade Control reports delays with Oshun," Betsy said. "They haven't started yet.

"Finally." Jonathan smiled. "Something normal."

Jonathan and Betsy monitored radio chatter as they continued patrolling. Oshun was almost thirty minutes late getting started. Then, one of the floats broke an axle, and the parade had to be halted as authorities evacuated the riders. The krewe didn't clear the intersection of Magazine Street and Napoleon—to allow Cleopatra to roll—until almost eight o'clock.

It would likely be another thirty minutes before the last of Cleopatra's floats turned the corner at Tipitina's and started along the parade route in earnest. As the minutes ticked by, the night seemed to become darker. Betsy and Jonathn continued their patrol in "Box Command." Jonathan guided their utility vehicle along Prytania Street. Maybe they'd dodged a bullet. Or, maybe, the Sweeper had moved his operation to somewhere else in the city.

"Eight-fifteen," Betsy said. "Why don't we check on Cleo?"

"Roger. Another four blocks to Napoleon. Should be there in no time."

As Napoleon Avenue came into view, a loud boom, sounding similar to a shotgun blast, reverberated among the floats still present. Fluttering bits of silvery metal floated in the air. The street lights within approximately a two-square-block area went dark. The parade halted.

"Soup to nuts," Betsy said. "Some asshole must have fired a Mylar confetti cannon."

A scream echoed behind them, on Prytania along the route they had just covered. Jonathan executed a U-turn and accelerated the underpowered vehicle as much as possible.

"Stop." Betsy pointed to her left. "Under that tree. A body."

Jonathan and Betsy jumped out of the utility vehicle and sprinted toward a male victim lying on the ground, writhing in pain.

"Looks like someone mugged him," Betsy said.

Jonathan knelt beside the man. "Or hit him with a collapsible baton."

"The Sweeper?"

"Look at the marks on his forehead." Jonathan checked for a pulse. "Alpha and Omega. But in marker, not carved. No blood. He's unconscious; labored breathing. Concussion, maybe." Jonathan handed a piece of paper to Betsy. "And look at this."

Betsy shone her flashlight on the document, studying its contents. "Holy Mother of God."

Another boom echoed in the distance, several blocks deeper into The Box.

Jonathan grabbed his radio. "Box Team. This is Gray. Sweeper moving toward Canal Street. Shooting a confetti cannon to cause localized blackout. Repeat. Shooting a confetti cannon to cause localized blackout. Check for assault victims in the blackout area. Gray. Out."

Looks like a final note from the Sweeper," Betsy said. "In the clear. No cipher." She shone her flashlight over the contents as she re-read the typewritten note:

Newly Relieved Mortals:

You have obeyed. This pleases me. My work here is done. Let there be no death at my hand until two years hence. But you can delay my return by cleaning up your streets.

I will slither away to my peaceful haven and leave this flawed place to its citizens. I pray that our next meeting shall never become necessary.

Yours truly,

The Sweeper, as you call me

A third boom. This one, barely audible. The Sweeper must be really deep in the Box. Jonathan cursed under his breath. He turned to Betsy. "Thrice the price."

Chapter Fifty-Seven: Night Terrors

Saturday, February 7, 2015 – 3:27 a.m.

Stryker's body shook. Her eyes opened so forcefully that she feared they might pop out of her head. But she couldn't move. The night terrors and immobility had ended, or at least hadn't recurred for several weeks. But learning that the cancer had returned—and spread—must have been an emotional trigger. As always after an episode, she lay in bed, covered in sweat, breathing labored, for what seemed like an eternity. Then, as if connected to a switch she didn't control, her psyche released the trauma, and she could move again.

She'd been working so long for revenge. No. Not revenge. Justice. To ensure that the person who'd raped her…who'd infected her with HPV—the human papillomavirus—that led to her cancer…who'd ensured that her military career would end in shame…would finally be held accountable for his actions. And his rationale that he merely wanted to show her how an enemy would treat her if captured? Garbage. His way of driving Stryker—and other capable women like her—out. Reminding them that special forces was a man's world. Females need not apply.

And to watch as that misogynistic bastard prospered. Promoted to Brigadier General, Major General, and then Lieutenant General. Awards and accolades. Nominated by the President and approved by the Senate as Commander of Special Operations Forces, U.S. Southern Command. Each promotion, each award, simply added fuel to Stryker's internal resolve.

How long she'd planned for this moment. Not this precise moment—awakened by another nightmare, reliving the sexual assault. But for rendering justice whenever the fates aligned. And now they had aligned. She'd searched and failed to find a way to bring him down. Roaming the country in a motorhome. Stopping for seasonal jobs at casinos. Researching, calculating, and waiting for the right opportunity. A couple of near misses, but something always seemed to come up at the last minute to thwart the mission.

And then learning that Norsworthy would be coming to New Orleans. Delving into the history of the Axeman. Identifying a pattern of killings using a sailor's rigging knife. And the ultimate cover for her scheme—previous visits to Carnival by the so-called Mardi Gras Sweeper. Maybe Norsworthy's luck had finally run its course. Maybe this time...

But at what cost? Killing twice—a rapist and a whoremonger. Maiming a drug dealer. Thank God they'd deserved what happened to them. Three more men taking advantage of women or peddling death in the form of adulterated pills. And the poor soul at the homeless encampment on Tchoupitoulas? A sad commentary, but useful for the plan. Despite the rationale, the crimes—especially the killings—ate at her soul. Like the cancer might soon enough be eating at her physical being.

Stryker sat up and swung her legs off the bed. She licked her parched lips, then steadied herself as she stood up to get some water. She couldn't lose heart now. Her personal fate seemed preordained. Chemotherapy, radiation, hospice, death. But she still had her wits. Her body hadn't yet turned on her. Maybe she could ring the bell again. So now was not the time to give up or give in. Now was the time for action.

Stryker filled a glass with ice cubes and water, then sat down at her small dining table. The water tasted so good. It would be the simple things in life, like ice water, she'd miss most.

Perhaps it was good she had awakened so early. Enjoy as much of the day as possible. Have a good breakfast. Check that all her weapons were in order. Run over the details of the plan—to include her escape—yet again. Maybe pay a final visit to St. Louis Cathedral.

A sojourn to the Cathedral would definitely be in order. Not for confession. She'd already confessed to past transgressions and been forgiven in the eyes of God. No priest could offer absolution for a sin yet to be committed, though. She'd go to pray. Pray that the God of the Old Testament would give her strength. The strength to see justice through to the end. The strength to ensure an eye for an eye.

Chapter Fifty-Eight: Jonathan's Plan

Saturday, February 7, 2015 – 7:42 a.m.

What a cluster Friday night had been. Like chasing a ghost. And the Sweeper's "never mind" message had really thrown a monkey wrench into the works. Max Jamerson wasted no time in spreading the word. The crisis had passed. The Sweeper was gone. Mardi Gras was once again safe. All, thank you very much, due to Max's heads-up move of forming a specialized task force to meet the challenge. His Honor had dubbed it "Operation Sweeper Nix."

"Goddamn Max and his press conference." Betsy pitched her notepad onto the table of the conference room in the Coroner's administrative office in City Hall. "I'm not buying the 'It's all over. See you in two years.' What a line of bull."

"Agreed," Jonathan said. "Especially given Dan Rossignol's hints."

"I'm almost ready to say 'screw it' and let Max suffer the consequences if something happens."

"You've discussed that thought with Polly Bondurant?"

Betsy shook her head. "I'm still on her naughty list. So, let's just say she's not a member of the Betsy Sprance Fan Club."

"Understood," Jonathan said. "But we won't be able to do much without her cooperation."

"Yeah, well. We don't have a lot of time. First parade launches at one."

"Pontchartrain?"

"Right," Betsy said. "And they're probably already lining up."

"Got it. Which parades are on tap for today?"

"Chewbacchus is tonight in the Bywater and Marigny."

"Jimmy Copeland's in Chewbacchus."

"Right," Betsy said. "And it's a walking parade, so we're not worried about it, are we?"

"Affirmative. We're just looking at the rolling parades. All are on the St. Charles route."

"Schedule?"

"Like you said earlier, Pontchartrain goes at one. Choctaw at one-thirty. Loyola at two. Freret at two-thirty."

"No doubt, there'll be delays," Betsy said.

"Of course. That's why they built a long break after Freret. Knights of Sparta goes at six and Pygmalion at six-forty-five." Jonathan exhaled a long sigh. "Jesus. That's six parades we need to cover."

"Right. But you could almost look at it as one really long parade. Because once they get started—"

"Got it," Jonathan said. "So, do we have a plan?"

"Figured we…or, actually, *you*, could approach your friend Polly—"

"*My* friend?"

"She's sure as hell not *my* friend."

"And exactly what am I asking Polly to do?"

"Well, the law enforcement assets are still in place."

"So?" Jonathan asked.

"Which means that we should just have to make sure they are aware to be on the lookout for the Sweeper…or a copycat, just in case."

"A copycat?"

"Figured that would be the best way to keep Polly in the loop. She can tell Max that she appreciated his role in getting rid of the Sweeper. You know, he was right, but—"

"Good thought," Jonathan said. "Stroke Max's ego and let Polly show that she's still on top of things."

"Affirmative."

"Okay. I'll talk to Polly. See if I can brief the area supervisors again, this time about a potential copycat Sweeper."

"Great," Betsy said. "And maybe we can ask them to put a special emphasis on Knights of Sparta and Pygmalion…and the tail end of Freret—"

"Because?"

"The Sweeper's been operating after dark since day one. Sparta and Pygmalion won't start until after sundown. And Freret will probably still be on the parade route."

"Logical." Jonathan crossed his arms across his torso and stared into the distance. His right hand tapped rhythmically on his left arm. "Makes sense…" His words trailed off. His lips moved as if he were preparing to start speaking again.

"But?"

"I…I just can't get Dan Rossignol's words from yesterday morning out of my mind."

"What did he say, exactly?"

"Well, out of the blue, he started talking about Loyola. The university, not the Mardi Gras krewe. Loyola basketball, of all things.

"Basketball seems an appropriate topic this time of year." Betsy shook her head. "But a Catholic Monsignor mentioning Loyola University of New Orleans…talk about weird."

"Sarcasm noted," Jonathan said. "But I don't think I've ever heard him say more than two words about Loyola or basketball."

"Okay. Monsignor Rossignol's showing off his inner sports nerd. That doesn't mean much, does it?"

"Maybe not in isolation," Jonathan said. "But then he went on this diatribe about whether women should be in the Army."

"The Army?"

"Right. Whether women should be in the Army."

"Not the Navy or the Corps?"

Jonathan shook his head. "I reminded him that I served with lots of females in the Navy and that you were in the Marines."

"Well." Betsy rolled her eyes. "The Army *is* different."

"That's exactly what Dan said."

"So, what do you think we ought to do?"

"I know it sounds crazy." Jonathan looked into the distance. "But Dan wouldn't have kept mentioning Loyola, unless he had a purpose. Maybe he was just trying to avoid discussing the parishioner who talked about killing someone with a knife. But still…"

"And that leads you to conclude, what?"

"It's not exactly a conclusion…more of a hunch."

"We're operating on instinct now?" Betsy asked.

"Well. Dan Rossignol wouldn't—"

"Given the Krewe of Loyola parade's start time, there's no way it'll still be rolling after sunset…after dark."

"I know," Jonathan said. "The Sweeper's been operating under the cover of night."

"So, what makes you think he'll do something in the light of day?"

"I can't shake the feeling that something'll happen during the Krewe of Loyola parade."

"We're back to feelings?" Betsy said. "Okay. You trust your gut. I trust your gut, too. Thoughts on how to approach security?"

"NOPD's in place for the other parades. We can let Mitch Broussard be liaison with the overall effort, starting with Pontchartrain. The two of us can concentrate on Loyola."

"The floats line up on Tchoupitoulas pointed upriver," Betsy said.

"At Tchoupitoulas and Napoleon. By Tipitina's."

"Affirmative. And the bands and marching groups approach the merge point across Napoleon, facing downriver on Tchoup."

"Right," Jonathan said. "Think we can arrange for another pass through the floats with the bomb-sniffing dogs beforehand without panicking anyone?"

"I'll put out word to Krewe leadership that NOPD's training a new batch of canine officers. They can put "Working Dog In Training" vests on them, and no one will be the wiser."

"Too bad we don't have the resources to check out the bands and marching groups, too."

"Agreed." Betsy nodded. "But given the Sweeper's use of explosive devices, the floats are the more likely target."

"Roger that."

"And," Betsy said, "I'll assign someone to review the krewe rosters again to make sure there aren't any add-ons to worry about."

"Great idea. Will NOPD have plainclothes officers trailing along the route?"

"Affirmative. Usual complement is one officer for three floats. So, counting the ones with the Royal Court, Grand Marshal, and all that, there should be around eight or nine designated walkers who'll be paying special attention to the Loyola group, along with us."

"Plus, the officers normally stationed along the route?"

"Affirmative. Mostly for crowd control."

"So, we can observe the merge of the floats and the marching groups onto Napoleon…and we still have the "Box Command" vehicle, right?"

"Right." Betsy stood. "I'd better get started coordinating things."

"Good thought." Jonathan breathed deeply, then exhaled slowly as if doing so would slow his racing heartbeat. "And as much as I'd hate to let Max take a victory lap, I hope like hell he's right that the Sweeper has folded his tent and gone home."

Chapter Fifty-Nine: Showtime

Saturday, February 7, 2015 – 2:37 p.m.

Jonathan and Betsy walked along Tchoupitoulas Street, nearing its intersection with Napoleon Avenue—the so-called merge point for the day's parades. To their right, the lead float of the Krewe of Loyola—followed by over a dozen more, all fully loaded with riders—pulled up to the krewe's staging point on the corner, adjacent to Tipitina's. Ahead, as far as the eye could see, bands, dancing krewes, and other marching groups lined up along Tchoup on the other side of Napoleon.

Perhaps Mayor Jamerson's "Ding Dong the Sweeper's Dead" missive had worked. Or maybe it was simply the normal enthusiasm generated by participating in a Mardi Gras parade on a clear, unseasonably warm Saturday in early February. Regardless of the reason, the atmosphere could best be described as electric. No apparent worries about serial killers or mad bombers. Reports from Mitch Broussard indicated large crowds, five or six people deep, all along the parade route.

"Already over half an hour behind schedule," Jonathan said. "Any word on delays?"

"Mitch said something about one of Mr. Mudbug's claws getting stuck in a live oak when Pontchartrain cornered from Napoleon onto St. Charles."

"Only in New Orleans." Jonathan shook his head. "Mr. Mudbug."

Betsy pressed her hand to her right ear. "Parade Control reports that Pontchartrain is well along St. Charles, nearing Lee Circle. And Choctaw's last float just passed Magazine."

"So, it should be—"

"Now," Betsy said. "Loyola just got the go-ahead."

"Let the games begin."

The first three floats—carrying the krewe's Captain in the lead float, the King and Queen in the second, and the Princesses and their escorts in the third—turned right onto Napoleon Avenue. Technically, krewe members weren't supposed to start throwing for a few blocks—when the parade passed Magazine Street. It was a rule honored more in the breach than in the observance.

Officials directing the merge signaled for the first marching organization—the red, black, and white-clad Belle Chasse High School Cardinal Band—to turn left onto Napoleon. And so the merge continued: a float turning right, followed by one or two marching units—bands, dancing troupes, or walking krewes. The music from the bands added to the joyous atmosphere. Just another Mardi Gras parade moving forth without incident.

"That's what, nine floats down?" Jonathan asked.

Betsy looked at her phone. "Ten, according to my list."

"Looks like another four to go."

Betsy checked her list. "Right, four more Loyola floats." She pointed to her right. "And that's Freret, maybe three blocks down Tchoup coming up."

"I'm beginning to think that my gut feeling isn't very trustworthy." Jonathan pointed to the left, toward the marching group staging area. "What the hell is that helmet-looking thing."

Betsy's eyes widened. She closed her eyes and dropped her head. "Shit."

"What does—"

"*Soc au' lait.*" Betsy's eyes reflected both surprise and shame. "I forgot about 'em."

"Who?"

"Warriors of Ares."

"I didn't realize they were a krewe."

"Not a formal krewe," Betsy said. "Working on it. So, the city approved them as a marching unit."

"So we haven't vetted—"

"No. I recognize the jaybird on the raised platform at the front of the helmet-shaped float. The guy dressed in the fancy blue uniform and green beret. Lieutenant General Javius Norsworthy, Army Special Forces. Must be their Grand Marshal. But other than that, we never identified members, or—"

"Searched for explosives?"

Betsy shook her head. "Right."

"Dammit. Can we get the dogs back?"

Betsy spoke into her phone. "Great. We'll meet you at Magazine Street."

Jonathan drove their utility vehicle, while Betsy maintained comms. They fell in behind the third of the three Warriors of Ares floats—a mock-up of an Air Force F-16 Eagle—their primary fighter jet.

"If the dogs start at Magazine," Betsy said, "we'll only have about six blocks before St. Charles. Once the parade turns, it'll be nearly impossible to pull any of the floats out."

"Thank God they're moving at a snail's pace." Jonathan steered toward the side of the parade route and angled up Napoleon past the floats. "It'll give us a few extra minutes."

"And if the dogs hit?"

Jonathan steered the utility vehicle toward two NOPD SUVs at the intersection with Magazine Street. "Canine Units just arrived."

"Great," Betsy said. "Lead Warriors of Ares float's still a block back."

As the two bomb-sniffing dogs deployed, one on either side of the approaching floats, Betsy communicated their situation to Parade Control.

"There's a park on Napoleon about six blocks up from St. Charles," Jonathan said.

"Samuel Square?" Betsy asked.

"Right. Let's direct any float positive for explosives there. Tell people we have a medical emergency…have NOPD cordon off a one-block radius around the square. Keep the crowds back. No sirens. Have the EOD unit meet us there."

"Maybe we'll get lucky. Maybe the dogs won't find anything."

"Don't buy a lottery ticket anytime soon." Jonathan pointed toward the floats. "Looks like our luck's run out."

The canine on the far side of the floats alerted on the first one—the float designed like a giant World War Two Army Helmet. The second dog continued on to inspect the other two floats. It circled around the back of the third float and continued up the other side. The second dog also alerted on The Helmet.

"Looks like we have our target," Jonathan said. "I'll direct the driver to cross St. Charles and head up Napoleon to Samuel Square."

"Got it. I'll coordinate clearing the way for you and getting NOPD in position."

"Officer." Betsy motioned to a uniformed NOPD patrolman stationed a few feet away. "Get in. I need you to drive."

Jonathan jogged off toward The Helmet. He caught up to the float as it neared Chestnut Street. Only four blocks to go before St. Charles.

Maybe not appropriate under the circumstances, but Jonathan chuckled, internally, at the originality of the float design and the costumes of the riders. Each rider wore a red, white, and blue pullover smock with "ARES" emblazoned diagonally on the front. They wore wide-brimmed, camouflaged "boonie" hats. But it was their masks—or, more accurately, their non-masks that struck Jonathan as the most unique. Each rider had painted their face—either in a standard flat black, leaf green, and mud brown military camouflage "woodland" pattern or in a similar pattern using purple, green, and gold face paint. Wrap-around "operator" sunglasses—like they were Navy SEALS or Army Green Berets—and, voila, no need for a cardboard, make-you-sweat, standard Mardi Gras mask. What a perfect combination of anonymity and comfort.

"Who's your Float Lieutenant?" Jonathan displayed his badge and spoke to one of the riders on The Helmet stationed on the street—right—side near the rear of the float.

"Major Allen. Neutral Ground—left—side. First Position. Lower deck," the rider replied.

"Thanks." Jonathan hastened behind the float and up to the front. He displayed his badge. "Major Allen?"

"Yes, sir."

"We have a medical situation. We need to pull your float out of the parade and proceed to a safe place up Napoleon for quarantine."

"Understood." Allen's face crinkled, showing his apparent puzzlement. "But a quarantine? Can you—"

"No time for details, Major. Please keep your riders calm...and on board. They can sit, but need to stay in position. Under no circumstances can anyone disembark the float."

Jonathan sprinted forward and climbed onto the running board of the tractor, pulling The Helmet. Prytania Street. Just two blocks before St. Charles. That should be enough time. He showed his badge to the driver and instructed him to keep going straight when they reached St. Charles. Ahead, NOPD had already cleared a corridor across St. Charles. Several police vehicles waited on the other side, apparently ready to escort them to the park.

They'd averted the potential crisis of having an explosives-laden float traveling mile after mile along the narrow confines of St. Charles Avenue, just an arm's length from thousands of innocent civilians. But now came the hard part.

Chapter Sixty: Defusing the Sweeper

Flanked by NOPD cruisers, the no doubt overwhelmed tractor driver guided The Helmet right, onto South Saratoga Street. Police had performed yeoman's work, with no advance notice, in forming a protective cordon around the small park at Samuel Square. The tractor angled left and pulled the float onto a concrete basketball court. Jonathan, standing next to Betsy Sprance and Sergeant Willa Delacroix, commander of the NOPD Explosive Ordnance Disposal unit, made a slashing motion across his neck, and the driver cut the tractor's engine.

Jonathan spoke into a bullhorn. "I'm Jonathan Gray, Coroner of Orleans Parish."

No panic among the individuals on the float—at least not yet. Probably good luck that the riders were current or former military personnel. Kudos to Major Allen for maintaining discipline.

"Apologies for the secrecy. And thank you for your cooperation."

"What's the meaning of this intrusion?" The voice came from the VIP platform—Lieutenant General Javius Norsworthy. "You owe these fine patriots an explanation. I demand you—"

"General," Jonathan again spoke into the bullhorn. "I need you to remain silent and listen to my instructions."

"Well, I never. Do you know who I am?"

"Yes, General. I'm well aware of who you are. And I need you to sit down and shut up. The more you speak, the longer you delay resolution of this situation."

The riders, collectively, stared at General Norsworthy, then turned back toward Jonathan.

Jonathan continued. "We've received intelligence that your float has been boobytrapped with explosive charges."

Despite some panicked looks and murmurs, the riders stayed calm.

"Earlier, trained police dogs alerted on your float, indicating the likely accuracy of that intelligence." He inhaled deeply, then continued. "We believe that the charges are set to explode based on weight distribution. So, we need you to stay in position while Sergeant Delacroix and her EOD personnel inspect the float to confirm the particulars."

Delacroix motioned to a group of police officers standing behind her. Four of them, each in heavily padded protective clothing moved forward. Two of them crawled under the decorative cloth skirt surrounding the base of the float. The other pair used binoculars and similar magnifying apparatus to inspect the visible areas of the double-decked float. Once done, the four inspectors returned to Delacroix and Jonathan.

Jonathan spoke into the bullhorn. He needed to make sure no one shifted positions so they could hear him better. "Please remain calm." That was one hell of an ask under the circumstances. "EOD confirms presence of explosive charges attached to the springs and shock mechanism of the float." Now was the time to demonstrate that he had things under control. Everything would be fine if they just followed instructions. "Several of the devices are associated with flash-bang grenades. Large amounts of C4 are attached to the VIP platform." He lowered the bullhorn and angled his head slightly upward toward the VIP platform. "Sorry, General, but that means you're probably the target of whoever set the charges." He again spoke into the bullhorn. "And for everyone, any shift in the weight distribution will set off the charges. Again, we need you to stay in place to keep that from happening."

"What are you going to do to keep these heroes safe?" General Norsworthy asked. "They shouldn't be put in danger because of me."

"General." Jonathan didn't rely on the bullhorn. "Would you shut the hell up?" Jonathan again spoke into the bullhorn. "NOPD has arranged for trucks carrying stone barriers and concrete fragments. As we add ballast to the float, we can remove riders without any issues. The trucks are on the way and should be here within three minutes."

"Screw this." The words came from a female rider on the lower level, in the float's mid-section. "I'm not dying for some asshole General."

The woman pulled a small item from her backpack. A smoke grenade. She dropped it on the ground near the float and jumped over the side. Other riders followed her, the air now filling with acrid white smoke, curse words, and screams. As more individuals exited the float, the flash-bang grenades ignited. Not enough to cause substantial physical damage, but the light, noise, and additional smoke added to the confusion.

A rifle shot echoed. General Norsworthy toppled off the platform and pitched onto the ground. The resulting explosion rocked the scene, sending shards of wood and papier mâché flying through the air. The blast knocked Jonathan, Betsy, and others nearby to the ground.

Jonathan rolled over onto his stomach. Sergeant Delacroix lay several feet away with a large piece of wood protruding from her upper arm, near her left shoulder. Only a small amount of blood flowed from the wound. Jonathan turned toward Betsy, who appeared dazed and bruised but otherwise uninjured.

"I'm fine," Betsy yelled. "Check on the General."

Jonathan pulled himself forward, still on his stomach, using his arms and elbows to drag the rest of his body along. Jesus, he hadn't executed a combat crawl since "knife-and-fork school" in Newport when they tried to teach doctors, lawyers, and nurses to be Naval officers. He hadn't had to use the skill in all the years since. But thank God he remembered how.

General Norsworthy lay on his back. Face and arms showed contusions and abrasions. A bone protruded from his left calf—a compound fracture. A bullet appeared to have struck his left shoulder. Blood oozed from the wound. Most immediate injury needing attention was a large wood splinter in his right thigh. A pool of blood spilled from the gash. Jonathan placed his hand on Norsworthy's neck. Damn. A barely noticeable pulse. "Call an ambulance. We have a bleeder."

The blast had apparently been strong enough to pull Norsworthy's parade harness and the grommet connecting it to the float out of the wall. Good, the harness would make a perfect tourniquet under the circumstances. Jonathan loosened the strap and looped it around Norsworthy's upper thigh. A small piece of metal rod nearby would have to serve as a windlass. He twisted the rod several times, drawing the harness tighter and tighter. Sirens in the distance signaled that an ambulance was on the way. The makeshift device would do, for now. Better than nothing, but not by much.

No other gunshots since the one that struck the General. Likely, the shooter was long gone in the confusion. Jonathan rose to a squatting position, surveyed the area, then stood and hastened toward Betsy.

"Did you see where the shots came from?"

Betsy pointed toward a line of trees near the edge of the Square. Over there, I think."

"Did you see the shot?"

"No," Betsy said. "But I think I know who the shooter is."

"What?" Jonathan asked. "How"

"Remember that casino employee I thought I recognized when I was taking photographs?"

"Sure."

"That might have been the woman who jumped off the float." Betsy shrugged. "Can't be sure because of the camo face paint."

"The one who threw the smoke bomb?"

"Maybe she had a takedown rifle in her backpack."

"Wouldn't take much time to reassemble, depending on the model."

"Bingo."

Jonathan looked at the ground. "Goddammit."

"What's that, Doc?"

"Dan Rossignol telegraphed it."

"Telegraphed what?"

"Loyola basketball. Women in the Army."

"Soup to nuts, Doc. What now?"

"Got an address?"

"On the phone right now." Betsy returned to her phone conversation. "Affirmative." Betsy ended the call and turned to Jonathan. "The RV Park off North Claiborne. Unit Twenty-Seven."

"That's near St. Louis Cemetery Number One."

"And Lafitte Greenway," Betsy said. "Just over three miles from here. Probably fifteen minutes by car."

"At least the shooter's on foot. Assuming that's where she's headed."

"Well." Betsy shook her head. "About that." Betsy pointed toward South Saratoga Street. "Looks like the utility vehicle's gone."

"All right. Call it in. Have them lock down the RV Park. No one in or out. And put out a description of the utility vehicle and the shooter."

"Will do."

"She got a name?"

"Yeah." Betsy placed her phone to her ear. "Stryker. Janet Stryker, First Sergeant, U.S. Army, Retired."

Chapter Sixty-One: Casting the Net

Saturday, February 7, 2015 – 5:47 p.m.

With Jonathan riding shotgun, Betsy jammed the gas pedal to the floorboard of the NOPD SUV she had commandeered. Impending darkness as sunset descended would make their hunt for retired Army Sergeant Janet Stryker—apparently masking herself as the so-called Mardi Gras Sweeper—more difficult.

"Two minutes out," Jonathan said.

The radio crackled. "All units. Be on the lookout for a Red 2013 Honda CR-V. Texas license plate, numeral 1, letters SGT dash USA. Last seen exiting Tremé RV Park off North Claiborne. Female driver, possible ID: Janet Elaine Stryker, considered armed and dangerous. Request air assets assist."

Betsy and Jonathan pulled up to Unit Twenty-Seven in the RV Park—what looked to be a thirty-five-foot-long Class C motorhome. Medium-sized, but apparently large enough to tow a Honda CR-V. They could figure out the exact size and class later. The stolen police utility vehicle sat catty-cornered to the front of the motorhome.

"Must have just missed her," Jonathan said. "Thank God responding officers issued a *Be-on-the-Lookout*."

Betsy lowered her window. "What have we got, Officer Vu?"

"You best come take a look for yourself."

Inside—in plain view for anyone to see—the motorhome seemed more like a command post for a special military operation than a place to live.

A small cabinet, both doors apparently left open by Stryker, revealed multiple newspaper articles, photographs, and maps pinned to a corkboard. Subject matter covered by the contents included Lieutenant General Javius Norsworthy, Carnival, the New Orleans Axeman, and the Mardi Gras Sweeper. A small shelf contained several books, including copies of *The Anarchist Cookbook*, *Explosives: The Five Cs*, and a U.S. Marine Corps technical publication, *Deconstructing IEDs*.

"Jesus." Jonathan shook his head. "She's like a bounty hunter tracking her prey."

"No telling what else we'll find once we get a search warrant," Betsy said.

"Officer Vu," Jonathan said, "how long ago did you arrive?"

"Ten…maybe fifteen…minutes. Door wide open. Facility manager said we barely missed the suspect. After we cleared the RV for potential victims, we secured it, waiting for backup."

"And called in the BOLO?" Jonathan asked.

"Affirmative. Seemed like the logical thing to do under the circumstances."

"Heads up work, Vu," Betsy said. "Keep the area secure. We'll need to get the necessary warrants for a more detailed search."

"Roger that, Lieutenant."

"She's got a fifteen-minute head start. Maybe more," Jonathan said. "Betsy, let's hit the road. I have a hunch."

"Okay, where to?"

"The Crescent City Connection. I'll explain on the way." He turned toward Officer Vu. "Have authorities block the bridge from the West Bank. Hopefully, we're not too late."

Betsy guided the SUV onto Interstate 10 and headed toward the iconic twin bridges spanning the Mississippi between New Orleans—the East Bank—and Algiers—the West Bank. She engaged the blue lights in the grille and on the roof.

"No blue lights," Jonathan said. "She's probably driving on secondary streets to throw us off the trail. We don't want her to panic if she thinks we figured out where she's going."

"Got it." Betsy turned the lights off. "Why the bridge? You think Stryker's going to jump off—like the last time? Doesn't seem to make sense."

"Possibly," Jonathan. "If she's so steeped in Sweeper-lore, the symbolic pull has to be great."

"I guess she's done enough damage that she might as well off herself."

"Maybe. But Stryker's proven pretty crafty to this point. I suspect she hasn't given up."

"So why the West Bank? If she heads out of town any other way, there's more directions she can go."

"Your thought makes the most sense," Jonathan said. "And she'll bet we'll be thinking that way. It's the most logical."

"So?"

"If she makes it across to the West Bank, it'll be easier to get into bayou country. Plenty of places to hide there."

"Especially if she gets access to a boat." Betsy pumped the brakes as traffic slowed. "Must be the roadblock."

"That's quick," Jonathan said. "Thank God for Officer Vu."

The radio sprang to life. "This is Air One. Stationary, upriver side of the Connection. Red CR-V spotted stuck in traffic westbound. Far right travel lane."

"Bingo, Doc. Way to trust your gut." Betsy turned on the flashing blue lights in the grille and eased around traffic. "Got her now."

She picked up the radio handset. "This is Coroner One. On scene. Will advise when we locate suspect."

"Roger Coroner One. Air One, standing by. Will maintain spotlight on target. Increasing altitude above bridge structure for a better view."

"Look," Jonathan pointed. "There's the CR-V. A hundred yards ahead." He opened his door. "I'm going after her."

Apparently spooked by the helicopter's floodlight, Stryker exited her CR-V and angled toward the downriver side of the bridge—away from the chopper. And she was hard to miss. Red, white, and blue Warriors of Ares costume smock and face decked out in full camouflage colors. She must have known that authorities were hot on her tail if she didn't take time to change or remove her face paint.

Stryker appeared to have something—a length of rope, maybe—coiled over her left shoulder. If she intended to jump—or repel—from the bridge, she had three more lanes of stopped traffic to cross.

The floodlight followed Stryker as she dodged around vehicles. The chopper was now directly overhead. She ducked behind a large tractor-trailer, then emerged with her handgun pointed toward the helicopter. Sparks flew as her first shot ricocheted off the bridge's steel superstructure. A second shot met a similar fate. Stryker shifted her position slightly, dropped the bundle—definitely rope—from her shoulder, and fired a third time. Bingo. Scratch one spotlight. The chopper gained altitude and pulled back out of range.

Stryker picked up the coil of rope and slung it over her shoulder. Between the bridge's superstructure and so many civilians around, a kill-shot from the aerial unit seemed unlikely. It would take several minutes for police manning the roadblock on the West Bank side to cover the distance to Stryker's location on foot. Stryker again moved toward the downriver side of the bridge. She maneuvered through the obstacle course of vehicles. If they were going to stop Stryker from escaping, it would be up to Jonathan and Betsy.

A shot echoed. Something, must be a bullet, whizzed past Jonathan. He turned around as he ducked. Betsy, approximately seventy-five feet behind him, grabbed her shoulder and fell. No time to check on her now. Damn it. Jonathan climbed onto the hood of a car and jumped to another one. Just one lane behind Stryker now. He'd catch up to her in just a few seconds.

He didn't hear the sound of a weapon firing. The slug clipped his pants about midway down his right calf and struck the passenger side of the car windshield just behind him. The driver's side door opened, and the driver tumbled out of the vehicle. She crawled toward the back of the car. Most people seemed to be sheltering in place, but several had exited their vehicles and were crawling away from the shooting.

Thank God no one had decided to take matters into their own hands. New Orleans had plenty of legally armed citizens to make quite a formidable posse. No use adding to the number of potential victims, though.

Jonathan, now crouching, duck-walked toward the side of the bridge. He reached the final travel lane—the one adjacent to the downriver side of the bridge. He rose slowly, his sidearm in low-ready position. Stryker was nowhere to be seen. The rope she'd been carrying had been tied around one of the bridge's steel support beams. The end of the rope was out of view—somewhere over the side. The noise of the helicopter above, its remaining spotlight cutting through the darkness, added a surreal touch.

"Goddammit." Jonathan holstered his sidearm. As he hastened toward the concrete barrier wall, Betsy appeared in his peripheral vision. He stopped. "You okay?"

"Not again." Betsy slammed her fist on a car's roof. Blood oozed from her left arm near her shoulder. "Fuck me to tears. Not again."

"You okay?"

"I'll live." She winced. "Flesh wound."

Jonathan shone a flashlight over the side of the bridge. The end of the rope swayed in the breeze, approximately ten feet above the surface of the river. Too dark and too far away to get a clear picture of what had happened. Perhaps Stryker had dropped into the water and was swimming—most likely underwater—toward shore. Or maybe the ripples in the water resulted from the wind and natural flow of the river.

"Where the hell could she have gone?" Betsy holstered her pistol. "Goddamn Houdini bitch. I'm not going to lose another one to the Mississippi."

Jonathan guided his flashlight along the side of the bridge to his right. Nothing. He followed the beam down the side of the bridge to his left. "Betsy. Over there."

About a hundred feet away, a pair of hands inched along the side barrier of the bridge.

"Now she's a Goddammed acrobat," Betsy said.

As if she sensed that she had been discovered, Stryker pulled herself up on a section of chain-link fencing and clambered over the barrier, back onto the bridge. She sprinted away, pulling something from her jacket as she ran.

"Halt or I'll shoot." Jonathan raised his handgun into firing position.

Stryker was probably too far away for an effective handgun shot, but he at least needed to try.

Without turning, Stryker fired twice. Jonathan and Betsy ducked between a car and the side of the bridge and crawled toward Stryker. The bullets ricocheted off a couple of vehicles and the bridge girders. Stryker shot at a lock on the door covering the cage of a maintenance ladder. She put her weapon in her jacket pocket and squeezed into the cage.

"She's heading for the catwalk," Jonathan said. "Let's move. She's trying to escape."

"Over my dead body." Betsy winced and grabbed her shoulder.

"You stay here." Jonathan removed his tactical vest. "Let the chopper know what's happening."

"But—"

"Give me your cuffs."

"Here."

Jonathan maneuvered himself into the small circular cage surrounding the ladder up the rungs. He definitely wouldn't have fit if he was still in the vest. As he moved up to the second rung on the ladder, his foot slipped. He latched onto the ladder with all his strength. His teeth throbbed as if his heartbeat had moved into his jaw. "I'm too Goddamn old for this crap." He inhaled a deep breath, then exhaled. "Where the hell is that chopper?" He continued his climb.

As he emerged on the catwalk—a two-foot wide strip of steel plating with small handrails on each side—he swayed in the wind. He grabbed the handrails and eased himself into a kneeling position. Best to establish his footing before moving forward.

Stryker stood on a wider section of the walk perhaps seventy-five-feet away, adjacent to another ladder. If she made it down the ladder, that would put her back on the bridge surface. She'd be close to the end of the bridge. Hopefully, Betsy would be there to greet her. Otherwise, Stryker could easily make it to the East Bank. She'd be able to lose herself in the maze of streets in downtown New Orleans. Betsy might not be in position or too injured to intercept Stryker. It was now or never.

"Halt or I'll shoot." Jonathan, still kneeling, raised his handgun into firing position.

Stryker turned toward him. She unholstered her handgun. Jonathan's shot hit about midway up her right calf. She went down, face first, like she'd had a rug pulled out from under her. The shot must have hit bone. Her sidearm tumbled from her hands and crashed onto the roof of one of the cars below.

Jonathan holstered his weapon and stood. His hands shook. Firing a gun—and wounding someone—wasn't as easy as movies made it out to be. Especially for someone trained to heal, not take a life. As Betsy said, 'First do no harm.'"

He was so focused on his target that the wind and sounds of standing on top of one of the country's most recognized bridges didn't register. He made his way along the catwalk—holding firmly to the handrails with both hands—to where Stryker lay wincing in pain. Protocol was to keep your firearm in low-ready position as you approached a downed suspect. But a breach of protocol was better than falling off a narrow piece of metal because you lost your balance. And at this point, Stryker sure as hell wasn't going anywhere.

He pulled the handcuffs out of his pocket and knelt down next to Stryker. Blood oozed from her calf. A flesh wound. No major blood vessels involved. Just enough, thank God, to bring her down.

Stryker's eyes reflected resignation and defeat—and a bit of relief, as if she realized that this was the end. It was over. She breathed in short bursts. "Why the hell…didn't you…kill me?"

"There's been enough killing." Jonathan snapped the cuffs closed. "Time for the wheels of justice to grind."

Air One finally appeared overhead, shining its spotlight on Jonathan and Stryker.

Jonathan waved, then made a thumbs-up sign. He turned to Stryker. "As soon as we figure out how to get you down the ladder, Lieutenant Sprance will remind you of your right to remain silent. I suggest you take it."

Chapter Sixty-Two: Throw Me Somethin'

Sunday, February 8, 2015 – 4:17 p.m.

"Throw me somethin' mister!"

Jonathan stood in his position on the first level, neutral ground side, of the *Monty Python and the Holy Grail*-themed float rolling as part of the Krewe of the Roundtable parade. After starting its journey nearly three hours ago, the float was now well along St. Charles Avenue, a few blocks past Lee Circle. He pointed at the source of the request.

Yeah, me." A boy, maybe ten years old, jumped up and down and waved his arms.

Jonathan tossed a glitter-covered fedora to the young reveler.

"Thanks, mister."

The kid put the hat on, then turned toward another krewe member on the float. "Throw me somethin', mister!"

"Jesus, Fen." Jonathan threw a string of purple beads to an elderly woman holding her arms in the air. "I'd forgotten how much fun this is."

A father, with a toddler wearing pigtails adorned with pink barrettes sitting on his shoulder, approached the float. Jonathan handed a yellow light-up rubber chicken to the girl. She flashed a toothy grin.

"Thanks, man," the father said.

Jonathan returned the girl's smile. Thank goodness his mask didn't cover his entire face.

"Didn't think you'd make it," Emma said.

"I guess we did cut it kind of close." He removed a string of medium-sized red beads from a hook on the wall behind him. He made eye contact with a woman, probably in her seventies. The woman smiled and raised her thumb after catching the beads. Jonathan returned her smile and waved. The genius of Mardi Gras. Not a care in the world—at least for a few hours.

But what a week it had been. So many twists and turns on their path to stopping—once and for all—the Mardi Gras Sweeper, albeit an imitator. And the depth of planning and calculation that went into Stryker's plan. Stalking Norsworthy for years. Living in a motorhome, working as a blackjack dealer in casinos across the country. What a great cover story. It allowed her to be near Norsworthy without raising suspicion as she planned how best to bring him down. And finally executing her plan when everything came together must have been satisfying. Perhaps with a little more luck, Stryker would have escaped, and the Sweeper legend would have remained intact.

Maybe they should have figured it out before they did. A murder in Washington Square Park reminiscent of the Mardi Gras Sweeper—the so-called Two-by-Four Killer. But the contents of the notes—the Sweeper's Manifesto—once deciphered, were modeled after the message allegedly penned by another serial killer—the New Orleans Axeman—who had graced the city in 1918 and 1919. And like the current round of the Sweeper, there had been several grizzly killings and a letter to the public offering them "a little proposition." Be listening to jazz—at a local club or in their homes just after midnight on a designated night and the Axeman would leave them alone. As mysteriously as he had appeared, the Axeman vanished, never identified, crimes remaining unsolved to this day.

Two legendary serial killers for the price of one. With the additional curveball of using sailors' rigging knives and their connection to several murders in different locations. Too good to be true. And the other clues—coming in bits and pieces—were there. Betsy's mention of transient workers when Jonathan asked her to join the team. Dan Rossignol's cryptic conversation about Loyola basketball and women in the Army. Several of the incidents within easy walking distance or a streetcar ride from the Tremé RV Park. Hindsight was twenty-twenty.

He turned to Emma. "And I'm glad we're one of the first floats—just behind Royalty." He tossed a string of multi-colored glass beads to a woman balancing a young child on her hip.

Had Stryker's violence only been visited on Norsworthy, a jury might decline to convict her—jury nullification. In many ways, he deserved whatever punishment she inflicted on him. But a jury of her peers would likely understand the circumstances that made Stryker snap. Her descent into a dark world that blotted out everything but visiting horror on the object of her obsession.

But vigilante justice wasn't true justice. Stryker chose to be judge, jury, and executioner for two other humans beyond Norsworthy. And only by the Grace of God—and intervention from NOPD—had she avoided adding a third to her tally. Three imperfect humans—a rapist, a whoremonger, and a drug dealer—but humans, nevertheless. Now it was time for another imperfect human—Janice Stryker—to be judged and, if appropriate, executed after full due process of law. Certainly more due process than she'd offered her victims.

Her victims—not just the ones murdered or maimed. Others had been changed forever as well. Arguably, some for the better, like Janelle Harrison. Stryker had prevented her assault from becoming something worse than it was. And Jonathan. Maybe he'd changed for the better, too. More confident. More determined than ever to root out injustice. And now he could get back to his longstanding goal of improving the Louisiana Coroner system. Rededicate himself to being a good husband to Emma and father to...

Jonathan flexed his knees and grabbed the side rail as the float jerked to a stop. "What the hell?"

"Gallier Hall," Emma said. "Krewe Captain's stopping to toast the Mayor."

"I'd forgotten how far along the route we are. Looks like we'll get an up close and personal view of Mayor Assho...Mayor Jamerson...doing his thing."

Ahead on the left—across from Lafayette Square—the Master of Ceremonies stood at a podium overlooking the "official" viewing stand constructed on the steps of the original New Orleans city hall. His voice reverberated through the public address system. "Mr. Mayor, I have the honor to present the Royal Krewe of The Roundtable."

Max Jamerson raised a champagne flute. "The City of New Orleans and her mayor salute the Royal Krewe of the Roundtable." Max sipped champagne, then again raised his glass. "Happy Mardi Gras. *Laissez le bon temps rouler.*"

The crowd cheered, and the parade again moved forward. Jonathan glowered at the mayor as his float passed the reviewing stand. By now, Max was probably enough sheets to the wind that he wasn't really paying attention. And, no doubt, he had no idea that Jonathan was in the Krewe of the Roundtable, much less on a float passing by, throwing imaginary daggers at him. Thank goodness the mask provided a level of anonymity.

But Max would soon hear from him. Jonathan still had another week to complete his package to register as a candidate for Coroner in the special election Max demanded. Then, thirty days to campaign. Thirty days to prove why he was worthy of the job and more qualified than Cass Melançon. Thirty days to figure out whether to use the information provided by Ranger Sprance. Thirty days to…

"Mister. Hey, mister."

Jonathan snapped out of his funk at the youthful voice coming from his left.

"Throw me somethin', mister!"

Acknowledgments

Penning the Acknowledgments section is, and ought to be, one of an author's greatest pleasures. Your manuscript's in the final stages of the publication process. An exciting cover reveal is just around the corner. And the release date is in sight. It's an opportunity to sit back, relax, and take a victory lap before returning to your next work-in-progress. Time to say thanks to all those who helped *Shadows of Frenchmen* along the way.

Yet, the previous sentence underscores an author's fear in this otherwise joyous moment—"all those who helped." What if I omit an individual or group providing support, input, or encouragement? Maybe I should simply say, "Thanks to everyone, everywhere, all at once." No. That won't do. So, with apologies in advance for anyone I leave out, here goes.

In my view, "all writing," like "all politics," is local. Of course, authors want their work to gain a national (or even international) audience. But that effort starts "at home." If your manuscript doesn't "play in Peoria," you won't stand a chance once you send your novel into the world of discerning—and demanding—readers. So, thanks to the Virginia Beach Writers, a dedicated and supportive group of creatives, for your patience, comments, and encouragement. Our weekly meetings and your critiques, whether on Zoom or in-person, were invaluable as I wrote, and re-wrote, *Shadows of Frenchmen*. Although, I will say that I got (and continue to get) more enjoyment out of our bi-weekly in-person sessions because of the post-meeting group lunches we attended.

And thanks to the members of Mystery by the Sea, the southeastern Virginia chapter of Sisters in Crime. I can't say enough about the chapter's support, especially in arranging for book-selling events. And many of the pointers I learned during our monthly meetings and other activities found their way into the finished novel.

As with my debut novel, *Voices of the Elysian Fields*, I owe a debt of gratitude to Howard M. Rigg, III, M.D. for advice on the medical aspects of *Shadows of Frenchmen*, especially the innerworkings of the Louisiana Coroner System. Thanks for looking out for me, big brother. Add your fee to my tab.

Beta Readers Ginger Davis McSween and Robert Ausura each provided a critical review, along with insightful comments and recommendations. Their influence and guidance are evident throughout the finished novel. Ginger, let's plan on a "staff meeting" at the Carousel Bar in the Hotel Monteleone next time we're both in New Orleans. And Robert, I owe you a cup of your favorite beverage—coffee. Pick out your preferred blend— except for that really pricey stuff involving exotic animals' digestive tracts. This one's on me.

Kudos to Outliers Writing University and its co-founders DP Lyle and Kathleen Antrim. You've developed an exceptional writing program. Thanks to you both for your professionalism, personal example of excellence, and encouragement to a new (notice that I didn't say "young") writer. I profited from the many lessons learned from your cadre of instructors. Each Outliers session made my manuscript stronger. I wish I had discovered your courses earlier in my writing career.

When I started my writing journey, I didn't know where it would lead and what—or who—I might encounter along the way. During my one-minute in the spotlight at the Debut Author Breakfast during the 2025 Thriller Fest, I expressed this sentiment in a short verse inspired by "Oh, the Places You'll Go!" by Dr. Seuss. Perhaps corny, but certainly heartfelt. And among the individuals mentioned were three with a New Orleans connection, Heather Graham, Connie Perry, and Ellen Byron. Heather and Connie, many thanks for your continued support and encouragement during Thriller Fest and Bouchercon, and throughout my journey.

And Ellen, my Mardi Gras krewe-mate. I can't tell you how much I appreciate you introducing us during the Krewe of Cork pre-parade luncheon as "mystery writers." For a "newbie" to be included along with a distinguished author of multiple books as a fellow mystery writer! It doesn't get any better than that.

To the team at Level Best Books, especially Shawn Reilly Simmons and Deb Well, I appreciate your continued trust and support. Being a "Bestie" means a lot to me. I pray that I don't let you down.

The antagonist in *Shadows of Frenchmen* is a serial killer who strikes during Carnival. To my many friends in Krewe of ALLA, Krewe of Cork, and Krewe of King Arthur, I hope I captured the mechanics, elan, and spirit of New Orleans and Mardi Gras. Little did I know that when I first participated in parades in 2018 "for research," that I'd become hooked.

Finally, to my family, and especially my spouse and life partner, Martha. I could write pages about the importance of your love, support, and encouragement. But I'll stop with this brief mention. You are why I do what I do. My appreciation of you is in inverse proportion to the brevity of this tribute to you.

Laissez le bon temps rouler!
Michael Rigg
Virginia Beach, Virginia

About the Author

Michael Rigg, a lawyer for more than four decades, writes mysteries and thrillers set in two very different locations: Virginia Beach (where he lives) and New Orleans (which he visits as often as possible "for research," including participation in three Mardi Gras Krewes). He is a retired Navy Judge Advocate and a retired civilian government attorney, formerly working for the Department of the Navy Office of the General Counsel. He is a member of International Thriller Writers, Mystery Writers of America, and both the Sisters in Crime national organization and its Southeastern Virginia Chapter—Mystery by the Sea.

AUTHOR WEBSITE:

Retired Navy Officer: Short Stories & Novels | Michael Rigg, Author (https://www.michaelrigg.com)

SOCIAL MEDIA HANDLES:

Facebook: Facebook (https://www.facebook.com/michael.rigg.author)

Twitter/X: Michael Rigg (@MDR102030) / X

Instagram: (2) Instagram (https://www.instagram.com/michael.rigg716/)

LinkedIn: Michael Rigg | LinkedIn (www.linkedin.com/in/michael-rigg-4567b591)

Pinterest: (116) Pinterest (https://www.pinterst.com/michaelrigg716/)

Also by Michael Rigg

Novels:

Voices of the Elysian Fields (Level Best Books)

Novelettes:

Ghosts of the French Market – A Novelette (Witchduck Press)

Short Stories (in anthologies):

"In a Faubourg Far, Far Away" - *Mardi Gras Mysteries* (Mystery and Horror, LLC);

"The Courier" - *Coastal Crimes: Mysteries by the Sea* (Wildside Press);

"Ghosts of Sandbridge" - *Virginia is for Mysteries, Volume III* (Koehler Books); and

"Grandma Connie's Strawberry Pie" – Coastal Crimes 2 (Wildside Press).